Sweeping from fabulous country estates and hunting lodges to the opulent ballrooms and salons of Russian nobility, two lovers embark on a journey of tempestuous romance and treacherous power plays.

NIKKI

a dashing Russian prince, is rich, spoiled and utterly charming.

ALISA

innocent and beautiful, knows nothing of romantic passion until Nikki cold-bloodedly seduces her.

They are destined to love from the moment they meet, but fate and fierce emotion stand blocking the way.

Seized by Love

Susan M. Johnson

PLAYBOY PRESS
PAPERBACKS

SEIZED BY LOVE

Copyright © 1978 by Susan M. Johnson.

Cover illustration by Jordi Penalva: Copyright © 1978 by Playboy.

All rights reserved. No part of this book may be reproduced, stored in a retrieval system or transmitted in any form by an electronic, mechanical, photocopying, recording means or otherwise without prior written permission of the author.

Published simultaneously in the United States and Canada by Playboy Press, Chicago, Illinois. Printed in the United States of America. Library of Congress Catalog Card Number: 78-62016. First edition.

Books are available at quantity discounts for promotional and industrial use. For further information, write our sales-promotion agency: Ventura Associates, 40 East 49th Street, New York, New York 10017.

ISBN: 0-872-16503-5

First printing, February 1979

Then talk not of inconstancy,
False hearts and broken vows;
If I, by miracle, can be
This live long minute true to thee,
'Tis all that Heav'n allows.

JOHN WILMOT,
SECOND EARL OF ROCHESTER
CIRCA 1670

XV. THE VOLTE-FACE.

CHAPTERS

I.	THE WAGER	9
II.	THE SEDUCTION	41
III.	THE UNBIDDEN SPECTATORS	69
IV.	THE RECONCILIATION	79
V.	THE BLISSFUL INTERLUDE	85
VI.	THE DENOUEMENT	97
VII.	THE NECESSARY OPTION	103
VIII.	THE RECALCITRANT MISTRESS	123
IX.	THE BEGUILING BELLE	193
X.	THE ANGRY LOVER	201
XI.	THE STALEMATE	237
XII.	THE CHASE	263
XIII.	THE HALCYON DAYS	269
XIV.	THE RELUCTANT BRIDEGROOM	275
XV.	THE VOLTE-FACE	311

I
THE WAGER

Karelia Province
Grand Duchy of Finland
April 1874

The last goblet had, long ago, been flung aside in toast and joined the brilliant display of broken crystal gracing the stone hearth. There, the litter of crystalline shards reflected and transformed the firelight into a dazzling, fluttering phosphorescence. A few surviving candles guttered low in their branches while the shattered stumps of others bore mute evidence of Prince Nikolai's capricious fancy for a contest of marksmanship several hours earlier.

Now, on a low stage at one end of the large room, a weary group of musicians continued playing wild, haunting gypsy music, while nervously watching the brooding face of their master, the young prince. They hoped to successfully anticipate or assuage Prince Kuzan's mercurial moods and thus avoid, at least this night, any more dangerous whims.

At times like these when the tedium of the world was too much with him, the Prince retired to his hunting lodge to brood upon the melancholy inequities.

Nikki's hunting lodge was a timber and stone villa constructed by local artisans in the early years of the seventeenth century. A Swedish noble had this retreat built for himself, situating it prettily on a

9

rocky rise in a pine forest. The terraced gardens, in
the Italian manner, were added by a later heir after a
tour of Italy. With the advent of the romantic English garden, yet another descendant landscaped
acres and acres of forest, transforming the wilderness
with an extravagant hand and the toil of hundreds
of laborers over ten years into charming green
alleys, wide vistas of rolling terrain, crowning the
elaborate scheme dramatically with a Greek temple
perched on a distant grassy knoll. The local stone-
masons had erected a reasonable facsimile in rough-
hewn granite; a rustic, but altogether lovely
interpretation symptomatic of the then fashionable
rage devoted to whimsical follies.

Although the high Renaissance had already come
and gone when the main structure had been built,
none of the lighter attributes characteristic of Renaissance architecture had filtered up north. The villa
itself retained an overwhelming medieval character;
stone turrets crowned with peaked tile roofs punctuated the walls, bottle mullioned windows caught and
reflected the northern sun, enormous stonework on
the ground floor supported the heavy timber walls of
the second story. In a lavish display of his wealth,
the Swedish aristocrat had the walls pierced wherever possible with windows, lighting the interior with
dazzling color through the multicolored panes.

Tonight Prince Nikolai Mikhailovich Kuzan had
been entertaining a small party of fellow officers
from his Guards Regiment. After participating in the
April sixth fete-day of the Chevaliers Gardes with its
day-long riding exhibition and religious celebrations,
they had felt the need for a holiday and Nikki had
invited them to his lodge for a fortnight of hunting.

However, in the eight days elapsed, the quarry had been confined exclusively to the two-legged female variety, since Nikolai had thoughtfully imported a bevy of gypsy wenches to provide diversion.

Now, as morning approached, men and women lay entwined in each other's arms about the room, some on pillows scattered on the Tabriz carpet, others on the colorful divans. One couple, in what to a less dissipated audience would be a tasteless lack of decorum, was busy on top of the dining table; all were in diverse states of drunken abandon and deshabille.

Tanya, a beautiful young gypsy girl, was swaying in a provocative, sensual dance before Nikki's sprawled form. One of his hands lightly held a small flask of brandy on his powerful chest. The other hand, lying carelessly on the chair arm, would occasionally move listlessly to the nearby table and turn over another card in the game of solitaire he was indifferently and infrequently pursuing while regarding Tanya, who skillfully undulated to the wild, frenzied tempo. Through narrowed, tawny eyes Nikki watched her tantalize him. Her graceful young body, half-revealed in a scanty blouse and silken skirt, twirled close, then retreated, displaying a wanton invitation from brilliant, dark eyes. The firelight caught the coruscation of golden highlights from the heavy hoops in her ears and from the multitude of sparkling necklaces twined round her slender neck and swaying against her trembling half-naked breasts.

Behind the curtain leading to the kitchen corridor the youngest footman whispered to an old retainer familiar with the idiosyncrasies of his new employer. "Is the Prince always so surly and moody?"

Igor admitted that the Prince was not in the best of spirits. "The Kuzans have a devilish temperament, sometimes little better than savages," the old servant explained without malice, having happily served the household for decades. "They like fast horses, bad women and good wine. Between father and son they have developed one of the finest studs in the Empire, crossing English mares with bloodstock from the Orlov-Rostopchin and the Provalsky stud. They also breed Stryelet stock which are even more rare. Their horses are world-renowned. The young Prince doesn't do so badly in the breeding department either." The old man chuckled. "Like father, like son, they say," he added softly, remembering the reckless pace the old Prince Mikhail had set in his youth before marriage to a young gypsy girl had tamed his ways.

"More brandy!" The roar from the hall beyond echoed as Prince Kuzan impatiently banged on the table. The old man lifted his eyebrows and shrugged in cheerful resignation. Both servants hurried to obey the command.

Tanya's hips still moved to the hypnotic tempo. Her dance was intended to arouse, to primitively and seductively provoke the animal mating instinct.

It did and he was.

With a casual wave of his lace-covered hand, Nikolai abruptly dismissed the musicians and picked up his fresh bottle of brandy. Then he lunged to his feet and slapped Tanya, who now stood quietly before him. As the music slowed to a stop, he lifted her and disappeared into a curtained alcove.

The musicians discreetly stepped over the drunken bodies, avoiding, when possible, the broken glassware and china littering the floor. As they edged cautiously through the elaborately carved double doors, never certain of their safe departure from the eccentric young Prince and his raucous group of intimates until well out of sight and sound, their exit was hastened by a wine bottle thrown violently against the door jamb, crashing into a thousand fragments and narrowly missing the last violinist. Some drunken music lover, no doubt, annoyed at the termination of the pleasant background accompaniment to his love-making.

Scurrying through the narrow, dimly lit hallway and foyer, out into the relative security and peace of the deep porch of the hunting lodge, the musicians exhaled a collective sigh of relief.

"Heaven help the servants in the morning who have to attend young Prince Kuzan. There is going to be hell to pay for his pounding head and thick tongue. Praise God, we won't see him again until evening when the worst of his headache is gone." The leader of the musicians sighed.

"Maybe the pain of a throbbing head might make him more docile or at least more silent. I have never seen Nikolai so sullen as tonight. He must be tiring of his newest gypsy bed-warmer. Did you see him smarten her up with a slap on the face when she insisted he go to bed? She should know better; he has never been one to cater to the wishes of a mistress," the second violinist said wearily.

"Well, thank sweet Jesus, we'll be out of his range at least until tonight. Maybe Tanya will be able to soothe the dark mood he is in. Let's go to sleep, although the night is practically over," the youngest member of the troupe suggested.

In the alcove, Nikki casually dumped the girl on-to the couch, thus freeing his hand to tip the brandy bottle to his mouth. The liquor flowed warmly down his throat. Thank God for brandy, he thought. It made life more bearable as it blurred the morbid edges of reality.

Sinking down heavily next to the recumbent girl, Nikki set the brandy bottle carefully on the floor and began to pull off his hunting boots. Tanya soft-ly crept up into one corner of the large pillow-strewn couch and leaned back against the tapestry-hung wall, watching him with her dark eyes.

"I'm not in the mood," she said, pouting.

Nikki barely glanced at the sultry woman nestled against the wall, and continued without a pause to divest himself of his garments.

"You'd better get in the mood," he growled.

A thrill coursed through the black-haired beauty and passion blazed into her dark eyes. Tanya, al-though only seventeen, had long ago learned to accommodate men's varying tastes in bed, but she preferred violence with passion; hostility intoxicated her.

"I won't. I'm tired," her petulant tone persisted as she swung her long, shapely legs over the edge of the bed and began to rise.

The prince's bare, powerfully muscled arm shot out and grabbed a handful of her satiny black curls, yanking her back onto the bed, pulling her down until she looked up into his golden eyes snapping with irritation.

"Bitch!" he whispered furiously, well aware of

Tanya's sexual preferences by now. But, having watched her enticing dances all evening, he was not in a temper to be toyed with.

"You're always playing games. However, tonight, my sweet little whore, you find me in a suitably black humor to accommodate your preferences. If it's rape you want, I shall be obliging."

Tanya's hand lashed out, long nails poised to rake Nikki's face. He caught her hand in mid-air, his reflexes still relatively sure despite the large amount of alcohol consumed. He crushed her wrist in a savage grip and she winced in pain—or was it pleasure? He couldn't tell.

As he held her, Tanya's little pink tongue appeared and ran provocatively over her full red lower lip, her dark eyes began to moisten, her breathing became ragged.

"Ah, my dear, you *do like* pain. I should introduce you to Prince Gorcheviv. He has a penchant for whips."

The gypsy girl's half-closed lids lifted and she moaned sensuously.

"Damn!" Nikki whispered savagely into her hair, "How can I rape a woman as aroused as you? There is no pain great enough to make you cry before I stop in disgust."

Roughly he pushed her down into the pillows, spreading her legs with his knees, pulling her nipples up and away from her necklaces into hard points of desire. Her body writhed beneath his force and her teeth bit into her full lower lip to keep from crying out in joy. She held her arms out wide, reaching for something to cling to as he pushed her skirt above her waist. Then forcing her wider he fiercely drove into her melting body, each violent thrust releasing a part of his frustration, each powerful surge a mindless hope for temporary oblivion. She began whimpering as he moved faster into her, more savagely pulled away, then back again. He didn't notice his back was running with blood where Tanya had run her sharp nails over the hard muscles which now moved rhythmically above her.

Much later, Nikolai abruptly woke from his sleep. The slightest sound was enough to instantly arouse him after many campaigns on the eastern frontiers, where the merest noise could be warning of danger from a stealthy Kirgiz intent on dealing a slashing *hallal*. Without moving, he slowly opened his eyes and through heavy black lashes swept a glance about the alcove. Tanya was searching through his clothes, which lay discarded on the floor. Looking for roubles, no doubt, he thought, dropping back to sleep. Prince Kuzan was extremely charitable to his light o'loves, showering them with gifts, jewelry, furs, as well as money, with a careless generosity. Greedy little bitch, he later reflected sleepily, but not unkindly, for, after all, Tanya had to think of her future; her youthful charms would quickly fade.

By mid-afternoon, Nikolai's fractious, irascible temper and pounding head were somewhat subdued; his two cohorts in arms, Major Cernov and Captain Illyich, and his young cousin Aleksei relaxed in the solace of a small clearing in the birchwoods. There they lay warmed by the April sun, calmed by the peacefulness of their surroundings, free from the chattering, volatile young gypsy girls who had been discourteously dispatched and told to remain out of sight until called for.

Nikki lay sprawled at ease on the soft, green grass, casually attired in superbly fitted cavalry boots, buckskins and an embroidered moujik shirt open at the throat. His hands were clasped behind his neck as he squinted slightly into the bright sun of a gentle spring day—a poetic, storybook day redolent of bursting buds, fresh turned earth and fertility.

Nikolai Mikhailovich Kuzan was a giant of a man. His mother's long-ago heritage from the Caucasus highlands was proclaimed in his swarthy complexion, heavy dark hair, prominent cheekbones and aquiline profile. From his father's White Russian roots he had inherited not only his tremendous physique but also his enchanting tawny, liquid eyes, the pupils so large and dark as to appear black; magnificent, beautiful eyes, brooding beneath heavy brows. The same kind of eyes that gazed out from opulent, exotically gorgeous, Byzantine icons for 800 years; arrestingly splendid eyes that could be piercingly alert, indolently shuttered or benignly calm. His harsh-featured face was softened by those redeeming eyes and by a sensitive mouth, now pursed in discontent.

Nikki tensed, stretched his lean frame like a great cat, then relaxed once again; the quiet sounds of the forest washed over him—new young birch leaves rustling in the breeze, a soft whisper from the bubbling stream lapping at the shore near the boundary of the clearing, the unceasing chatter of the birds overhead. The tranquillity of the woodland eased his tired body but failed to more than superficially alleviate the restless dissatisfaction of his spirit. Nikki was bored. Boredom—that constant and irksome companion that trailed him with a dogged persistence. Nikki had been leading the arduous and difficult life of leisure now for many years. Chronic leisure with its deadly, restless tedium was inexorably closing in on him.

He propped himself up on one elbow and from under slack lids surveyed his companions lounging carelessly around the remains of the repast the servants had brought out from the lodge. The ice had almost melted in the silver wine cooler and the half-empty bottles were sweating in the heat of the spring sun. The remains of the sumptuous *déjeuner sur l'herbe* lay scattered across the damask cloth and two wolfhounds were diligently eating them. Cernov and Illyich were carelessly tossing dice on a silver tray on the grass between them while Aleksei was engrossed in a novel by Turgenev.

Nikki listened with his usual tolerant aloofness to the friendly bickering going on during the dicing.

"Tonight I want Cecelia; you had her the last two nights and I think it's my turn," Cernov said in a faintly bearish tone.

"Can I help it if she prefers me?" Illyich smiled complacently.

"I don't care. It's my turn tonight," Cernov insisted.

"What can possibly be the difference?" Nikki inquired in a low, husky drawl. "The wenches are all agreeable in every way if one does not mind being bored in short order."

"Oh, no. I fancy Cecelia's long legs and slender grace to those more voluptuous charms of Olga,"

Cernov responded ardently, recalling Cecelia's dancing performance the previous night.

"Come now, Gregor," Prince Kuzan remarked with the disenchantment of his 33 years, "one woman is as good as another." Then he lay back in the warm sun and shut his eyes.

"Speak for yourself, Nikki. I find Cecelia much more attractive and I intend to have my turn," Cernov stated with a slightly aggressive emphasis.

Nikki's golden eyes fixed a look of mild contempt on the good-natured, but now thoroughly heated, Cernov.

"As you wish, of course, Gregor," Nikki replied soothingly, "Illyich, you understand, as host, I must attempt to placate all my guests. Perhaps tonight, I could persuade you to take Tanya instead of Cecelia," he suggested politely, as though he were offering courteously the less blemished of two pears to a dinner guest.

"With pleasure!" Astrakan Illyich responded avidly. Tanya had been Nikki's mistress for three months now and no one dared approach her, but if Nikki were graciously relinquishing the girl, Illyich would be a fool to refuse the offer.

Nikki calmly continued, "It is my firmest conviction that in order to survive it is necessary to be amused; that one of the requisites in life is to stave off as long as possible the unpardonable sin— monotony. Tanya has become monotonous so she's yours if you wish, Astrakan," he finished with finality.

Nikki tolerated a certain amount of boredom, but he had his limits and Tanya had become tedious. He would give her a suitable parting gift after they returned to Petersburg. Nikki was known to be benevolent to his mistresses and she would find a new protector soon enough if Illyich didn't wish to keep her, he assured himself.

Prince Kuzan was one of those aristocrats who filled their leisure with a dilettante's interest in literature, art and even science. He spent the required time in social intercourse, gambling, clubbing, and country sports, but, above all, practiced an adroit venal gallantry, as he dallied with the most exquisite of time-killers, amour.

He deliberately flaunted those principles which supposedly assured the continuance of the patrician order of society and publicly repudiated the cult of Victorian temperance and earnestness which was gripping even the volatile Russian mentality in the 70's.

In the creme de la creme, the genteel and refined upper reaches of Petersburg society, Nikki had been the despair of all the hopeful and enterprising mamas these fifteen years past and now at 33 had been reluctantly abandoned by all but the most tenacious and optimistic matchmakers. The only child of a rich and powerful Prince, young Prince Nikolai was himself rich beyond avarice, too handsome by half, a master of charm if the occasion warranted it and his fickle temperament acquiesced, well-liked and generous to a fault with his friends, doted on by his parents, and consequently marked by the complete absence of moral prejudices. He looked out on the world with the serenity which birth and wealth made possible; a spoiled child of fortune who accurately assessed the world as his pleasure garden, for nothing had yet occurred to disturb this comfortable and perfectly orthodox belief.

"Nikki! You can't simply give Tanya away! We no longer have serfs!" young Aleksei responded with the youthful, passionate chivalry of his 19 years.

"Don't fear, Sasha, I don't intend to brutally turn her out in the cold. Tanya shall be well taken care of," Nikki said softly to soothe his young cousin.

Perhaps Aleksei was too young to be exposed to this licentious, whoring life he led, Nikki reflected uncomfortably. Maybe I should send him home. Aleksei's mother, indulgent in all things to her youngest son, had hesitated at Aleksei's pleas for an extended holiday with his favorite cousin Nikki. Perhaps she was right. He himself had been thoroughly schooled in the notorious depravities of life before he was nineteen, but maybe this new generation was different. The rumblings of discontent and revolution, the promise of the industrial age were beginning to be felt more insistently throughout the land. Maybe this seriousness of purpose was typical of Aleksei's generation. Although the revolutions of '48, which had toppled thrones and melted governments away overnight had barely touched Russia, and where they had, in outlying provinces, been ruthlessly suppressed, even the autocratic Russian monarchy had found it reasonable and prudent to free the serfs in '61.

Nikki had been indulgently raised in an aristocratic society without purpose. Had society changed that much in 15 years or was Aleksei by nature, simple less quixotic, less reckless? he wondered.

"Ah, chivalrous youth," Nikki teased Aleksei, "so quick to come to the defense of some poor damsel in distress, so ready to jump to the obvious generalizations and conclusions, always striving for the whole truth, as your present author so clearly points out."

"You've read Turgenev?" Aleksei asked incredulously holding up the book, having never seen his older cousin so much as page through a magazine in his presence.

"Yes, I have, young sprout. I *can* read, you know." Nikki's leisure offered considerable free time. After all, one can only spend so many hours of the day and night in gambling and copulating, he thought, laughing to himself.

"It doesn't hurt to search for the truth," Aleksei protested. "It's better than just drinking, gambling and whoring, which is all you ever do." He stopped abruptly, afraid he had overstepped the bonds of friendship between the two disparate individuals, and his adoration of his older cousin was remarkably close to hero worship.

Nikki didn't take offense, ever ready to indulge his young cousin's moods, but said softly and thoughtfully, "You young people crave primary colors, crave certainty, must have absolute answers to the 'accursed questions.' When you're older, you'll discover absolutes are often so elusive they defy the most optimistic determination. Don't worry about Tanya, though, I'll not let harm come to her."

Nikki sighed to himself and marveled at the fresh vitality and naivete of Aleksei's youth. Had he indeed ever been that young? He knew the sobering answer to that question and tried to shrug off the depression which always accompanied the contemplation of his past seventeen idle, world-weary years.

Nikki had never been able to deal in absolutes, right or wrong. He had, from a very early age, been plagued by doubts. He saw human beings in the glaring nakedness of their frailty.

The excellence of his education could be blamed, at least partially, for this slough of harsh reality. The diverse succession of scholars lured to 'Le Repose' to instill in the only child and heir the fruits of their learned disciplines had found ready and fertile soil in the mind of the alert, vital, precocious young Prince. The monumental amount of knowledge of past civilizations he had absorbed early on had re-enforced his pernicious inclination to see each generation's touted achievements as puny human efforts in the ongoing scheme of things.

This lack of illusion left Nikki at times feeling helpless, if not, in fact, cynically melancholy. He often chose to dispel these bouts of depression by engaging in drunken, mindless orgies of pleasure. These week-long escapes into inebriated madness would for the brief interval anesthetize the worm of discontent. But his discontent was never sorted out, only assuaged or suppressed by the frenzied activity, the bottle of wine, a woman's touch.

Illyich broke into this morbid reverie with his usual jovial bonhomie.

"Aleksei, rest easy. I'll take excellent care of the beautiful Tanya," he assured the young boy.

"If she doesn't take care of you first," Nikki observed sardonically, raising one mocking eyebrow. "I hope you can afford to mount her. Like all women she is never satisfied, although, in contrast to the rapacious Countess Amalienborg, the price for Tanya's pleasure is cheap," remarked Nikki, remembering Sophie's insatiable demands for jewelry and furs.

"Have you no romance in that black soul of yours, Nikki?" Cernov inquired.

"Very little." Nikki replied drily. His was a cynicism born of disenchantment, born of a constant struggle to keep a deepening melancholy at bay. "Most of the women in my reprehensible and chequered experience are ultimately vastly more interested in my considerable fortune than my romantic inclinations. And rich or poor, young or old, they are all willing—too willing. I've been whoring up and down this country for years and done my share of tasting the debauchery Europe has to offer as well, and I have yet to discover a woman who is any different. They are all yielding, all willing, all delightful, but inevitably all boring." To Nikki there was a deadly sameness to the affairs that all began so promisingly and then became so monotonous.

"Daily living is becoming so damnably dull, I'm beginning to consider the life of an ascetic as an alternative to this routine," Nikki complained.

Cernov clucked his tongue sympathetically and laughed. "My heart really bleeds for people like you, Nikki. If you do, you'll leave many unhappy and unfulfilled women behind in Petersburg. There have been allusions to your giving the Duc du Richelieu's reputation a run for the money in the boudoirs, as well as pressing the Elector of Saxony's record in the nursery.[1] Maybe Illyich and I could attempt to console those languishing doves in your absence."

"If we waited a fortnight or so the ladies would be extremely anxious for our—ah—solicitous ministrations, I should think," Illyich concluded playfully.

"Do you care about anything at all, Nikki?" Astrakan asked, half jesting, half seriously.

"Not a damn thing to care about, seems to me." The Prince yawned.

"Not even women?" Cernov asked.

"Least of all women, Gregor," the lazy drawl avowed. "On a scale of one to ten, I would be forced to reply—Is there a number lower than zero?"

"Admit it, Nikki," Illyich continued more earnestly, "you'd be more bored after a week without women than you are this way. At least, there is a variety to the boredom."

"You're right, of course," Nikki agreed reluctantly. "If only they weren't all so yielding; it takes away the piquancy of the chase. There's simply no challenge anymore. I can have any woman I please." The Prince closed his eyes.

"Oh ho! Such illusions, such a lack of modesty." Cernov laughed.

"Three to one you can't," Illyich interjected quickly, the obsessive gambler in his nature unable to pass up an opportunity for a wager. He would quite happily lay odds even on his mother's demise.

"Can't what?" Nikki asked, not altogether sure what Illyich was betting against, but always ready to gamble too. His eyes sparkled with interest.

"Can't have any woman you want."

The Prince sat up. "You're on. But kindly soul that I am, I'll give you even odds. And let's say 50,000 roubles just to make it amusing."

"Done!" Illyich laughed with pleasure. "A limit on the time allowed, say three days. That should be enough time and I choose the woman, of course."

"Of course." Nikki replied affably. A small flutter

of anticipation coursed through him, and a glint of amusement lit up his eyes as thoughts of the chase ran through his mind. Anything—any brief bagatelle, to release him from this glazed lassitude. Yes, a seduction would be more interesting than hunting four-legged game. And in the case of a woman, the chase was not everything; one was always assured of additional delights upon completion of the hunt.

One can excuse Nikki, perhaps, for his lack of scruples, his indifference to others' feelings, his selfishness, when one considers that in the society in which he lived, his opportunities for observing noble thoughts and deeds were scarce in comparison with his opportunities for observing the utterly selfish ruthlessness with which pleasure was pursued.

"You're sure it matters not who my choice is?" Illyich inquired. He thought for a few moments, then a faint smile warmed his cheerful countenance as his eyes strayed across the river, over a picturesque but small meadow to a figure of a woman sitting near a grove of birch trees engrossed in her sketch book and watercolors.

"It makes absolutely no difference," Nikki replied arrogantly. Then he hesitated. "You wouldn't be thinking of some old dowager, would you?" I categorically draw the line at age fifty," he said suspiciously, scrutinizing Illyich.

"No, no," Illyich assured him. "Have no fear, she is suitably ripe."

Nikki sighed, his momentary pang of dismay dispelled.

"Ripe, you say. I look forward to the game," he said as he stretched supine once more on the green grass, conscious for the first time in weeks of a tangible excitement in his loins. With Illyich's money riding on the wager, it wasn't going to be child's play. Illyich bet to win, but Nikki was equally confident of success. He believed in his ability to overcome any woman's reservations, and Illyich's choice of a difficult, wary victim would make the predator's reward that much sweeter.

"Feel free to begin anytime," Illyich remarked as he smirked at Cernov and indicated the object of the wager with a nod of his head in the direction of the river.

Nikki's reverie was interrupted by these words. What did Illyich mean? Surely there was no one in these secluded acres except gypsy or peasant girls, and neither of those would present him more than a second's hesitation before rolling in the hay. Was Illyich drunk this early in the afternoon?

As he slowly rose from his position of comfort under a flowering wild plum bush, Nikki stretched his long arms and flexed the muscles of his powerful shoulders to shake off some of the torpor of the lazy afternoon. His muscles rippled under the fine linen of his embroidered peasant shirt as he lifted both hands to run his fingers through his long black hair. He wore no beard, as per regulations for the Imperial Guard requiring a clean chin, nor chose to cultivate a mustache; his only concession to the hirsute fashionableness of the day was the growth of sideburns which extended several inches down his jawline.

Nikki strolled leisurely over to where Illyich and Cernov still rolled their dice. "Surely you jest. There can't be a likely female within ten miles of this spot," he said with mild incredulity.

"Beg to differ with you, my fine stud, but do direct your bloodshot eyes across the river and over yon grassy meadow. I believe you will take notice of a blaze of coppery hair with a delectable young body underneath the glorious coif." Illyich couldn't control his mirth any longer and sputtered and guffawed rollickingly as he looked up into Nikki's horrified face.

"Good God! You can't mean the old merchant's wife. Come now, Illyich, that's even too bad for you. I recognize your necessity to make the assignment formidable and I didn't anticipate an easy or willing quarry, but let's keep this somewhat within the bounds of propriety."

"Sweet Jesus. You and propriety don't even have a nodding acquaintance," Illyich retorted, still chuckling, immensely pleased with his choice.

"Look," Nikki pleaded, in an effort to persuade Illyich of the folly of that particular woman, "why not choose a married Petersburg 'lady' who has already produced the necessary heir but has not hitherto strayed from the path of virtue, perhaps, an untried peasant or gypsy girl who also values her innocence, even some bourgeois wife conscious of the earnestness of marital duty. Any of these would be difficult enough, but my God, Valdemar Forseus' wife! She's totally outside the pale, rarely out of his sight, as closely guarded as a harem houri. And in addition, from the few times I've caught a glimpse of her in the Viipuri market square at her husband's side, she looks as cold as an ice maiden.

"Excluding those 'slight' problems," Nikki's eyebrows emphasized the euphemism, "my father would horsewhip me or have one of his apoplexies if he

caught wind of such an escapade. Forseus' land
marches with ours along the entire river and father
insists on friendly relations with the locals, so he is
forever lecturing me that one must govern with mild-
ness and justice. He is absolutely adamant about not
misusing one's power and influence in autocratic
actions. Why do you think I always import my females? It's safer than wenching all around the coun-
tryside and leaving by-blows so close to home. Father
says the winds of change are bringing a new era, in
which noble, bourgeois and peasant will dwell together in a vast social mutation of some kind. You
know he is perpetually concerned with the produc-
tivity of his estates, the conditions of his peasants,
maintaining the dignity of the working class and
establishing a rapport with the hoi polloi. God, the
whole idea is unmentionable!

"Besides, have you ever met Forseus? He is not
entirely rational, I suspect; his eyes burn with a
fever that is unnatural. I shall, with your gracious
consent, beg off this particular female, if you don't
mind, Illyich."

"Nikki, I don't mind one whit. Au contraire, an
easy profit, I say. That's 50,000 sweet roubles and I
frankly admit, I don't mind taking it from you,
Nikki dear, since you can so readily afford it."

"Damn!" Nikki exploded sullenly, "I didn't renege
on the wager. I just think you should choose another woman."

"Sorry, Nikki, you said it was my choice and
there is my choice," Illyich said and pointed theatri-
cally toward the small figure on the opposite bank,
completely oblivious of the attention she was at-

tracting, unaware that her virtue was a subject of interest and debate among complete strangers.

When Nikki recognized that argument was pointless, with his characteristic charm, he graciously conceded Illyich's point.

"Dare say, I might as well be off to commence the chase. There's no time like the present, et cetera, et cetera." He smiled, already half-amused and anticipating the flirtation. For Nikki obstacles existed only to be swept aside. He brushed away impediments that would bring lesser men to their knees and more sensible and prudent men to a cautious stand-still.

"Nikki, reconsider," his young cousin Aleksei interjected uneasily, "it's not right. Your father, depend on it, would find it totally unacceptable. Suppose he does catch wind of it."

"With any luck, father won't find out," Nikki responded calmly to his cousin's objections. "The lady scarcely would be inclined to bandy the news about, and we all are capable of holding our tongues."

Once Nikki's mind was made up, he could be unusually obstinate to change and, after all, he did have 50,000 roubles riding on the outcome. Even though he didn't personally need the money, it would indulge his pet project of embellishing his cavalry troop. The magnificence of his troop outshone all others, and outfitting the men and horses in such extravagant adornments gave him a great deal of pride, but the personal expense was astronomical. He contemplated the new tack that could be purchased with the 50,000 roubles. Some dark blue leather bridles ornamented with silver had caught his eye just a week or so ago at Neimeyers. Besides, after a few moments Nikki had convinced himself that the confrontation was not so insuperable as first imagined. His growing excitement over the unique and piquant diversion was enough to allay any slight misgivings he might still harbor.

Once a decision was made, Nikki faced all prospects undaunted. He looked on the world as available for his pleasure alone, and therefore his inclinations, however extraordinary, must be satisfied.

Nikki stood gazing across the small river with a cold, calculating look. Half musing, half aloud, he quietly murmured, "Now this calls for a nice judgment, this art of seduction. You must be plain but not too plain, be adept at murmuring fulsomely expressed endearments with a delicate sincerity, and you must smile politely as you pretend to take what is, in fact, willingly given. It goes without saying that one cannot be overhampered by scruples."

"That may all be very fine in the society in which you move, Nikki," Cernov retorted, "where everyone knows the rules of amorous jousting and seldom departs from the proscribed formula, but in the case of Forseus' wife, I think you'll be dealing with a female unfamiliar with those 'niceties.' "

"I am credibly informed," Illyich stated with cheerful maliciousness, "that she is untainted by scandal."

"So *far,* she has been untainted by scandal," Nikki remarked humorlessly, and with a careless gesture of farewell, walked toward the river.

Thus these elegant, bored, restless young blades became involved in this peccadillo to breathe some freshness and vitality into their boredom. The nascent industrial energy of the age had doubled their already princely revenues without efforts of their own. They were, in the words of a contemporary chronicler, "dulled by luxury, enervated by ease, staled by amusement."

As for the object of this chase, the pursued, the diversion to the restless young birds of paradise, Alisa, the young wife of the old merchant Forseus, was an innocent. She was not an innocent to deliberate cruelty or coldness of a man (no one who had lived with Valdemar Forseus for 6 years was unacquainted with evil) but unschooled and innocent in receiving kindly overtures from a man playing the game of seduction. An education from books, however exceptional, lacks the necessary information that real-life experience teaches. In the gilded circles of Petersburg society, amatory dalliance and flirtation had attained the status and perfection of a fine art, and over the years, Nikki had refined and polished his practical and aesthetic skill to a virtuoso proficiency.

So here we have the age-old confrontation.

The unsophisticated and untutored young girl encountering the master technician with an artist's touch.

Nikki's career in dalliance had, in fact, begun in earnest when he was barely seventeen and that first episode had disastrously left its mark.

One afternoon sixteen long years ago, while squiring maman to one of her numerous visits in the manner of a dutiful son, he had caught the practiced eye of one of his mother's friends; in fact had almost heard the audible click in Countess Plentikov's beautiful head when she had, for the first time, seriously noticed that the moody, sulky, darkly romantic boy had turned into a man.

Even at seventeen and not grown to his full height, Nikki was formidable, inches over six feet, lean, with raw-boned powerful shoulders tapering to a narrow waist and slim hips. The sulky coltishness, restless under the conflicting urges of his adolescence, had suddenly intrigued the Countess. With the eye of a confirmed connoisseur of male flesh, Soronina's glance had appraised the splendid young body, as if he were standing at stud.

Countess Soronina had known Nikki from the cradle and at thirty-six she had two marriageable daughters of her own. She was, however, still an exquisitely beautiful woman, slim, petite, golden-haired; her figure carefully maintained, the soft, pale complexion still perfect although its beauty took increasing time to care for.

Like most patricians of their class, the Count and Countess Plentikov had many years before acquired the habit of being unfaithful to each other, but out of tacit agreement and courtesy had overlooked each other's numerous infidelities. Count Plentikov spent more time in the country or on the Continent than he did in Petersburg and this arrangement was mutually satisfying. Soronina's silver and white boudoir had been the scene of many tumultuous encounters as a succession of men had paid amorous homage to one of the reigning beauties of the day.

Nikki absently listened to the ridiculous flow of trivial remarks and pleasantries that fell from Soronina's full red lips that first warm summer afternoon. He gave the obligatory answers in a desultory fashion, but he preferred to let his eyes play over her bounteous curves while mentally visualizing that soft body under his.

Nikki at seventeen was by no means the consummate lover, but not altogether unskilled either, and Soronina was definitely offering him more than sherry and madeleines as they sat in one corner of the huge drawing room conversing. His mother would occasionally glance toward them during the course of the visit, knowing full well what Soronina was up to, but resigning herself to the inevitable. For half a lifetime, Soronina had been aware of the seductive power of her beauty and had never failed to exert its influence successfully. In this case Nikki was more than willing to be agreeable.

And so began a long summer of sweet delirium for them both. The sweetness overtoppled mind and sense; they had something unique, something to be cherished. She taught him much about women and love and she drew from him bittersweet memories of what raw, uncontrolled youthful passion could be. He was to her simultaneously both anguish and ecstasy. Anguish for her youth forever beyond recall, and the ecstasy of blossoming under Nikki's ardent naked desire. There was no permanent cure for the dreaded fears of approaching middle age that plagued Soronina, only temporary relief in the arms of the young Nikki who made her forget for the moment the threat of the future without her beauty.

Nikki's parents returned to Le Repose after a month but he stayed behind. He had come into an inheritance from his grandfather on his 16th birthday which allowed him to further indulge his propensity for independence. Nikki's mother attempted to persuade her son to return with them. She felt he was being drawn in too deeply, after having seen Soronina's overt, frankly loving gaze envelop her boy one evening at a ball. It was so unlike the frivolous, shallow Soronina and terrifying in its possible consequences. Much as Princess Kaisa-leena adored Soronina as a friend, one did not care to contemplate her as a daughter-in-law. Prince Mikhail kept his peace and forbore issuing any unwanted words of fatherly advice, hoping that his reckless son would tire of the affair in due course. If not, time enough then to intercede.

That summer, the affair swiftly reached notoriety, as Nikki, with blazing indiscretion, escorted Countess Plentikov everywhere. He arranged his life to please her because it pleased him also. When they went out he was at her side, masterful, proprietary.

However, on the rare occasions when he would decide to leave town for a few days, no amount of coaxing, either amorous or petulant, would change his mind. Regardless of their easy intimacy, Soronina lacked her usual control. Nikki simply went when he wanted to go. He never stayed long and when he returned she would look into those tawny brooding eyes and a shiver of pleasure would run through her.

By the end of August, Prince Mikhail stepped in. The gossip and rumors were becoming serious. Never one to pander to discretion, Nikki had practically installed himself in Count Plentikov's town palace during that nobleman's absence. Dangerous rumors were making the rounds of the clubs to the effect that the cuckolded husband was about to ask for satisfaction from the young pup warming his wife's bed. Because Count Plentikov's reputation as a superb sportsman was nonpareil, Prince Mikhail didn't wish to contemplate a duel between such unmatched parties. Nikki didn't have the experience to survive an encounter regardless of his skill with rapier and pistol. His youth was quite dramatically a disadvantage on the dueling field in contrast to its obvious advantage in the bedchamber.

One morning Nikki was bodily removed from Countess Plentikov's city palace by four of Prince Mikhail's body servants, as he strolled down the marble stairway toward the breakfast room to join Soronina. All that day Nikki raged and stormed and threatened his father as Prince Mikhail attempted to explain the seriousness of the dilemma. Unfortunately neither party was open to reason.

Late that night, Nikki managed to elude his jailers and immediately returned to the Countess who was distraught over the possible repercussions of this scandal. Having long adhered to the aristocratic principles of unlimited dalliance, so long as no hint of it reared its ugly head, she was beside herself now with terrified misgivings. What had come over her this summer to so wildly throw away all restraint and discretion? Nikki's impetuous temperament had overcome her sensible prudence. Dreadful forebodings of being cut from polite society plagued her.

Pacing her bedroom chamber, Nikki pleaded with Soronina to marry him, but she shuddered to think of a May-December marriage between a youth and a woman old enough to be his mother. She could not tolerate the ridicule. Then he begged her on his

knees to go to the Continent with him. He had
plenty of money, they would have a glorious life
together, they would be happy. Again she shuddered—to be a kept woman was beyond her comprehension. Nikki insisted he would then kill her
husband in a duel. Again she was appalled at the
raw, passionate nature of her young lover. Tears
came to her eyes and spilled over onto the entwined
hands.

Above all, their love must not be lost, he said. No
hazard was too great. He wildly promised her anything she wanted. He waited for her answer.

But it was not to be. All her life Soronina had
unquestioningly accepted the dictates, the refined
etiquette and protocol of exclusive Petersburg society
and would no more consider ostracizing herself from
the comfortable confines of that world than she
would consider becoming a circus performer. She
tried to explain to him that one must do what's expected of one's class, understand the necessity for
society's conventions, serve as an example.

Even at that young age, Nikki was sufficiently
his father's son to curl a well-bred lip. When he broke
in contemptuously, standing erect and spat coldly at
her to spare him any more of those inconsequential
platitudes, Soronina was grief-stricken and the young
boy's heart reached out and longed to give her comfort, but he couldn't give her what she wanted:
security, safe, comfortable, snug, luxurious security.
She cried harder when the door burst open and
Nikki's father and servants once more dragged young
Prince Kuzan away. She wept bitterly and whispered,
"I'll never be the same."

The young prince was never the same either.

What shreds of romantic illusion and idealism and naive belief in happiness he had managed to retain in the brittle society in which he lived were swept away that night and eventually obliterated during the next two years he spent in Europe.

Prince Mikhail had not taken any chances of losing his only child to some dueling pistol held in the hands of an irate husband. He had kidnapped Nikki to save him. And after his confrontation with Soronina Nikki was unhappy, disillusioned and consequently could be persuaded to sojourn away from Petersburg.

"You will forget her, my son," his father had said and he was partially right. Once in Europe nothing was too rash to attempt. Morality, never of great concern, was gone from his mind. Unfettered, feverish activity prevailed and before long the pursuit of this wildly dissipated life served to dislodge most of his old romantic memories, but not without its price of self-torture.

Two years later a much wiser, more cynical young man came back to Petersburg, cool, restrained, elegant, guarded. He took his place in society and never again was persuaded to turn from a confrontation. He was, in fact, extremely quick to take offense, indeed, provocative to an unnerving degree, soon bordering on the notorious after his fifth duel in the same number of years. Nikki could even manage to meet Countess Plentikov in public and blandly pass the time with her as if their tempestuous amour had never been. It took an effort, for one never quite forgets the sweetness of first love, but he had grown up and civility demanded that much from him. One must set an example, he would mirthlessly remind himself.

But the unhappy affair set the direction of his future liaisons. Never again did he expose his heart, swearing that the ignominy of offering his heart and soul only to find them refused would never be repeated. Women became merely an amusement, a convenient receptacle for his passions when the need came over him or else a frivolous pursuit to idle away the measured tedium.

II
THE SEDUCTION

Lightly jumping across the gurgling expanse of water, Nikki silently walked up behind Alisa. She was seated with her back to the water, a sketchbook on her lap, rapidly capturing the woodland scene in vivid watercolors.

"Nikolai Mikhailovich Kuzan at your service, my lady." he said softly (and unthinkingly in the habitual French spoken by the Russian aristocracy; it was not the language of this area of the duchy).

Alisa jumped up, wildly scattering her sketchbook, paints and brushes in the process.

"How do you do, sir," she stammered, replying in the same language, but totally flustered by the unexpected, handsome stranger looking down at her. She flushed uneasily under his close inspection.

Nikki lifted one eybrow quizzically, smiled slightly and calmly waited for her to introduce herself. The silence lengthened.

Nikki prompted her.

"I believe I've seen you on occasion in Viipuri, but unfortunately, always at a distance," he said smoothly; "I fear I don't know your——"

"Of course," Alisa blurted out, embarrassed at her lapse in manners, but shaken by meeting the piercing scrutiny of those pale golden eyes. "I'm sorry, forgive me, Monsieur. Mrs. Valdemar Forseus,

41

at your service, sir," she responded rapidly and bobbed a quick curtsey.

I certainly hope so, Nikki said to himself. His eyes swiftly swept her bowed figure as she gracefully executed the curtsey.

Nikki's former glimpses of Mrs. Forseus hadn't done her justice. She wasn't simply another wholesome country lass, merely pretty and vivacious. She was breathtakingly beautiful. Her hair at a distance seemed to be copper. It was in fact a scintillatingly luxuriant golden-red; her eyes were large, dark violet, seductively lashed; her lips inviting (still slightly parted in surprise); her creamy complexion was flawless; her figure full bosomed and slender hipped. She was a lovely sight and Nikki viewed her with a slow smile of sheer aesthetic appreciation. On second thought, alas, only partly aesthetic, for she had an opulent, ripe lushness about her which generated a surge of pure lust in Nikki's libertine soul.

Her long-lashed eyes lifted, bright with a startled vivacity, and meeting Nikki's gaze, she encountered a hungry look which made her creamy skin glow again for an instant with rose.

For a man of his experience and jaded appetites, Nikki felt, ridiculously, a crazy, youthful elation as he contemplated the beautiful upturned face; a stirring in his vitals that comes on one at the sight and scent of a perfect masterpiece of female flesh. This little seduction should prove to be tantalizing, he speculated pleasantly to himself.

"You must be related to the Prince Kuzan who owns the hunting lodge," Alisa remarked a little unsteadily, feeling she must say something to break the spell of those magnetic, unnerving, tawny eyes.

"One and the same, Madame," he carelessly retorted in a deep, husky voice. "Allow me to retrieve your sketching materials which I so heedlessly forced you to scatter," Nikki continued agreeably as he dropped to one knee and began gathering her supplies.

"Oh, no, Monsieur, that's not at all necessary," Alisa quickly responded in supreme embarrassment, "I can do it myself," and she too knelt down and frantically began picking up the pencils, brushes and paint containers.

The Prince Kuzan here! It was horrifying! It quite shattered her composure. Rumors and gossip of his eminence and escapades had penetrated even her confined, retired world. She would simple die of mortification if she stammered one more time; she must certainly appear as the most gauche, discomfited girl he had ever met.

At one point, their hands accidentally brushed as both reached for the same object. Nikki was amused to see her drop her eyes self-consciously and snatch her hand back as if burned. A true innocent? Nikki reflected. Impossible! She was married to that old misanthrope Forseus. No doubt she was merely an accomplished coquette who could very effectively blush on cue. Whatever the case, he thought, innocent or actress, he would know the answer before three days were past.

All the artistic paraphernalia properly replaced in Alisa's small basket, Nikki disposed his lean form comfortably on the grass, remarking politely as he scrutinized her landscape sketch, "You're a most accomplished artist, Mrs. Forseus. Are you self-taught or have you studied with someone?"

Alisa did not answer.

"Please sit down," he requested cordially and patted the grass as she remained kneeling. "It's such a pleasant spring day I impulsively decided to taste the pleasures of nature, and upon seeing you painting, intruded on your privacy. Do forgive my impertinence." And he grinned warmly to disperse the lie.

With consummate skill he continued to try to put her at ease. What could she say unless she wished to be rudely uncivil?

"Of course, Prince Kuzan, there's no need to apologize. You're right," she said as she settled less stiffly on the grass, but keeping her distance from him, which did not escape Nikki's notice, "the weather is altogether remarkable for this early in the spring."

"*Have* you studied somewhere?" he repeated politely.

"Oh, no, I've never been beyond Helsinki, but my parents studied in Paris; in fact they first met while sketching at the Louvre. Both served as my teachers, although father viewed his painting as a hobby and was rather more interested in gathering information on the historic roots of the Kalevala. He quite devoted his life to the enterprise and had collated 34 stanzas of the epic before he and mother died——"

An unmistakable expression of pain passed over her lovely face and her sentence trailed off.

She was from the gentry. That accounted for her delicate beauty and fluent French, he thought.

"My condolences, Madame, the memory must be painful."

Alisa nodded, unable to speak. Recalling her

parents' death could still paralyze and stupefy her even after all this time. With a palpable effort she returned to the present and quickly brushed off Prince Kuzan's sympathy and her self-pity. "It all occurred six long years ago; I am quite reconciled to my loss."

Nikki, however, could see she was not, and he experienced an uncharacteristic pang of compassion for the obviously distraught young woman. She at least wasn't acting when it came to her bereavement over the loss of her parents.

"With your training, you no doubt are interested in the new exhibits of the Wanderers," he conversationally stated, hoping to distract and cast aside her painful thoughts. "I saw an extraordinary reception of their work last winter in Petersburg."

The diversion was more successful than he had anticipated. Mrs. Forseus' eyes, her expression, immediately, patently brightened.

"The Wanderers!" she exclaimed. "Have you *really* seen their work?"

"Yes, I have several catalogues of their exhibitions and a small landscape of Shishkin's."

The violet eyes widened in fascinated excitement. "You do?" she breathed in wonder, her face overcome with a child-like awe.

Nikki refrained from revealing to her that he was relatively uninterested in the Wanderers or any other painters for that matter. He had been cajoled against his will into attending the exhibitions because his mistress, Countess Amalienborg had seductively insisted, and he was in a receptive enough humor to yield to her extremely pleasurable methods of entreaty. And as for his purchase of the Shishkin landscape, the only reason he had bought it was to annoy that pompous ass, Count Borcheff, who was bent on having the painting. Nikki had derived inordinate satisfaction from carelessly raising each one of Borcheff's bids until the bombastic Count had been forced to drop out and lose the painting. His personal secretary, Ivan Dolorosky, conscientiously bought the exhibition catalogues, as well as every other new book, pamphlet and article published and added them to Nikki's extensive library. Ivan had been given carte blanche to purchase for the library since the pursuit was so gratifying to the young man. Nikki vaguely recollected Ivan speaking rapturously of the newest Wanderer catalogue; thank heaven, he had attended, however superficially, to Ivan's enthusiastic monologue.

Alisa conversed freely, after Nikki's fortuitous attempt at diverting her morose memories, explaining her admiration for these new painters, who with a technical skill, *par excellence,* portrayed socially significant subjects, historical scenes, landscapes from life, that were poignantly effective as well as exquisitely rendered.

Alisa glowed with fervor when she spoke of the courage it took for Kramskoy and a group of fellow students to resign from the Academy in a dispute over subject matter. How the "Mutiny of 13" had become the "Peredvizhniki" or "Wanderers," basing their approach on N. Chernyshevski's revolutionary book "Aesthetic Relations of Art and Reality," which stressed the superiority of reality over its representation in art.

"You see, my parents, too, painted from nature; painted outside and not exclusively in the studio. It was revolutionary in their generation, but they were acquainted with many French painters who vacationed at Barbizon and worked directly out of doors."

"Ah, yes, the vanguard of the—what are they calling those young painters in Paris?—the Impressionists?"

"Yes, that's exactly right!" Alisa replied in delight. Since the death of her parents she had not had a single opportunity to discuss art with anyone. "And Repin . . ." she breathed ecstatically, "such subject matter; it brings tears to one's eyes."

"His new painting 'Volga Boatmen' was just finished last year after three years of preparation. Marvelously stunning when I viewed it," Nikki said.

"Oh!" another gasp of excitement and Alisa chatted away volubly, free from restraint. Nikki had only to murmur appropriate responses intermittently and he was not, after all, completely untutored in the new movements in art. Having lived in Paris for two years, he toured Europe often and extensively, and when lured to the new art exhibits by Countess Amalienborg's desire to be seen at the avant-garde displays, he was not altogether unseeing. Behind Nikki's normal posture of indifference was a keen mind and a perspicuity beyond the common. He observed much without appearing to. As a matter of fact, on the occasion of his purchase of the Shishkin landscape, he had also impulsively bought an extremely small Savrassov still life which he had sent to his mother and until the present moment completely forgotten.

"I have some of the catalogues in the library at the hunting lodge and also the Shishkin landscape," he lied. "Perhaps you would like to come over for tea some afternoon and see them," he casually suggested. He would send a message to Ivan this evening in Petersburg and have the catalogues and painting delivered to him post haste, wherever they were.

"No! No!" Alisa exclaimed in highly nervous agitation, "I couldn't—I'm sorry, I'd love to, but . . ." she stopped in a near state of panic.

Were his intentions that transparent? Nikki wondered uncomfortably, and decided not to press the suggestion. He quickly changed the subject, exerting his charm to calm the unusual display of alarm his invitation had occasioned.

Nikki could not have known that fear of her husband's actions rather than Nikki's had prompted her inordinate manifestation of fear. Valdemar Forseus had on two recent instances beaten Alisa, not grievously, but enough to frighten her. After years of almost total indifference, since the birth of their daughter Forseus had once again begun, infrequently, to press her with bizarre and unwelcome demands. Alisa was dreadfully terrified, and more sure every day that soon she would have to take her daughter and leave her husband regardless of the consequences. The last few months had become so increasingly intolerable, she now wondered daily how much longer she could last.

Nikki restricted himself to polite and innocuous inanities for the next fifteen minutes, ultimately succeeding in restoring Alisa's lively spirits and bringing the delightfully ingenuous smile to her lips. Feeling it best to depart now that her cheerful disposition was re-established, Nikki rose from his relaxed sprawl and, towering magnificently above her, remarked equably, "Perhaps if you're sketching here tomorrow I could bring my catalogues to show you."

"I don't know. I can't, I mean . . . I don't think so," she stammered falteringly.

"It does not signify if you're otherwise engaged," he reassured her. "I'm rather at loose ends at the moment and if you're not here, the stroll over will, at least, be a pleasant occupation of my time." He smiled faintly. "Charmed to make your acquaintance, Mrs. Forseus. Good day."

"Good day to you, Monsieur," she quietly replied.

And bowing courteously he strode slowly away.

Alisa was left with multitudinous and conflicting emotions waging war in her mind, a sweet confusion holding sway. He was so handsome, faintly foreign and exotic looking. Alisa could not drag her memory from the strikingly attractive maleness he exuded. Prince Kuzan was also enchanting company (of course, since Nikki was out to ingratiate himself), so kind to her and wholly conversant in the new art movements, a topic of infinite delight to one who could only keep abreast of the new currents by irregular periodicals which might find their way to Viipuri. Alisa didn't allow herself to dwell on his handsome attractiveness. In the six years since she had been forced into marriage with the 61-year-old Forseus, no man had ever treated her gently. The entire encounter that afternoon was bewildering and left her unusually agitated. She could not concentrate on her painting anymore. All thought of color and form had left her mind. She knew she wanted to meet Prince Kuzan tomorrow. But dared she follow her own warm feelings of pleasure he engendered within her this afternoon? If her husband had been home she would have had no choice. But he was not and these few days of freedom from his tyranny had brought a prince into her life.

Alisa gathered her supplies and walked home slowly, lost in tumultuous thought, hugging each enchanting memory of the Prince to herself. Arriving home, she devoted herself to her five-year-old daughter, Katelina, who had just awakened from her usual afternoon nap, and in entertaining her child endeavored to push aside the distracting, disturbing thoughts of Prince Kuzan.

When Nikki returned to the lodge, he was greeted with rapid-fire, coarse and teasing questions from the importunately inquisitive, now slightly drunken Cernov and Illyich.

"Well, how is the bull of Petersburg doing with Forseus' ice maiden?" Illyich laughed uproariously, more amused than ever at his choice of prey. He felt quite certain of collecting his winnings.

Cernov slyly added, "I see your clothes are as unruffled and immaculate as ever. Didn't get to her this afternoon, eh, Nikki? Losing your touch?"

Nikki good-naturedly accepted the crude jesting interspersed with much helpful and extremely graphic advice. He was eminently familiar with barracks humor and also entirely satisfied with the course of the afternoon's efforts. He looked forward eagerly to a leisurely, unhurried seduction; the victory would be sweet.

"My friends," Nikki explained with a patient forbearance, "Mrs. Forseus is not a common slut. She is surprisingly, in spite of having married that peasant-merchant Forseus, of gentle birth and upbringing. She's a lovely, skitterish young filly, unused to the bridle, and I must gentle her slowly before she'll be tame enough to ride. Today was not entirely unsuccessful so don't count your winnings yet, Illyich."

Nikki had been unprepared to find Alisa so well-bred. Her French was fluent and without accent. She wasn't a peasant after all, although Nikki had no scruples or class distinctions when it came to taking his pleasure. His sexual diversions were international, inter-denominational, non-ideological, entered into with a true and open spirit of brotherhood.

That evening, Nikki remained aloof from the ordinary orgy of drinking, dancing and whoring. With barely tolerant amusement and ultimately total indifference, he watched the drunken antics of his friends. Finally, to the astonishment of the servants, for the first time in years he retired alone to bed at the relatively early hour of one o'clock. He was even sober. Now they were worried. Was the master ill?

For all his drunken wildness and eccentric behavior, Nikki had an old-fashioned regard for his responsibilities to his peasants and was, in turn, adored by them. He was generous to his servants, a quirk denoted by most as softness or eccentricity. He was genuinely interested in their problems, laughed and joked with them, would partake in their amusements, had learned to ride, hunt and ski from his father's Finnish Lukashee (trackers).[2] In fact, Nikki's ardor for hunting interfered considerably with his regimental duties, but his superiors favored him and intervened more than once to save him the consequences of overstaying his leave or being absent without consent.

Nikki, oblivious to the servants' whispered solicitude for his health, slept deeply and peacefully throughout the night.

Alisa, for her part, was not so imperturbable. She tossed and turned, in long stretches of wakefulness restlessly wondering if she should meet Prince Kuzan the next day. Still distraught with indecision, she finally fell into an exhausted sleep at four in the morning.

Nikki had dispatched a trooper to Petersburg 100 versts away (66 miles) the evening before, with a message for Ivan instructing him to gather all the current art catalogues from the library and send them back by return messenger. Ivan was also to ascertain the provenance of the landscape by Shishkin and have that delivered as well to the hunting lodge.

By mid-morning of the second day of the wager, the catalogues were in Nikki's hands and a note from Ivan explained that the painting was being sent by carriage since its size made it impossible to be carried on horseback. Nikki selected four of the newest catalogues he felt would be of most interest to Mrs. Forseus.

Dressing leisurely, he left without waking his friends who were still sleeping off their fuddled heads, although the day was well advanced beyond noon. He wore the buckskins and peasant shirt he preferred as country dress. Books tucked under his arm, Nikki strolled without haste to the small meadow on the opposite side of the shallow river. There, he lay down in the warm sun, arms hooked behind his neck, and waited for Alisa. He had deliberately arrived very early in order to precede the woman to the assignation. Alisa's quavering trepidation had been extremely evident yesterday and Nikki was afraid she might quickly reconsider and bolt if he was not there first to greet her.

Nikki entertained himself as he waited, by mentally cataloguing the various and delightful attributes of the beautiful Mrs. Forseus. This pleasant exercise was eventually disturbed by the arrival of the subject of his musings.

The hunt was on once more. The luscious quarry was full in sight. She was even more delicious in the flesh, he noted as Alisa walked toward him with a long, graceful stride, her slender hips swaying beneath the sheer dimity of her apple green dress. Nikki closed his eyes briefly and controlled his rising passion. To have that fair creation of womanhood alone in the forest and refrain from making love to her was going to require superhuman discipline.

"Good afternoon, Mrs. Forseus," Nikki greeted her courteously, rising politely from the ground and sweeping her a formal bow. He could see her hesitancy and uncertainty and hoped by remaining coolly formal to allay any misgivings she might have about having come here to meet him. One more day and they would be experiencing the ultimate familiarity, he thought, so he was willing to bide his time today. He didn't want her to flee in panic, sorry that she'd come. That wasn't out of the question, he realized as she stood trembling before him, holding tightly to her basket of art supplies. Her demeanor reminded him of a very young girl, an unsure adolescent on the threshold of first love.

"Good afternoon, Prince Kuzan," Alisa softly replied in greeting.

"Come, Mrs. Forseus, please call me Nikolai and may I address you by your Christian name? All this rigid etiquette seems out of place in the natural arena. I brought the catalogues," he quickly added when he noted the alarm with which she viewed him.

However, the lure of her favorite topic was enough to overcome her apprehensions, and the lovely young woman visibly relaxed as Nikki held the booklets out to her.

"My name is Alisa," she said demurely without lifting her eyes to Nikki's face. She held out her hand for the books, touching them as if they were a precious metal. Then she gracefully seated herself on the ground a safe, respectable distance away.

Nikki didn't make any sudden moves, because Alisa exhibited the unmistakable nervousness of a frightened doe. Soon, however, her natural vivacity surfaced as she oohed and aahed over the colored lithographs in the catalogues. Nikki contentedly watched her and ventured a comment or two on some of the artists or explained occasionally just how a certain painting appeared in its large format. He talked to her of his meetings with Kramskoy, Repin, Shishkin and Savrassov and Alisa's interest was itself intoxicating; her eyes shone in wonder, her cheeks flushed with fervor. After hearing Nikki had actually been in their company, she was full of eager questions and did not notice or appear unduly alarmed when he moved closer to point out some special quality or detail in one or two of the catalogue plates.

The afternoon passed thus pleasantly in this discourse on art; she, animated, high-spirited, inquiring; he, politely courteous and ever-restrained while answering her myriad questions.

Apparently by accident, since the maneuver was performed with such discretion, Nikki would occasionally touch Alisa's hand while pointing out a particular object of interest in an illustration, or brush her arm as he leaned across to turn a page; these stratagems were carried off with an unqualified innocence for all their contrived planning.

Alisa vividly responded to Nikki's casual touch; a rosy blush, a start, down-cast eyes. He was pleased to see that she was aware of his presence, and it wasn't coquetry, he decided; she was indeed virtuous. But a virtue that was assailable, it appeared, from her agitated reaction to the unexpected contact. If Alisa was susceptible to slight brushes of his fingers, it presaged well for her response to his more ardent and practiced caresses. This was no ice maiden after all.

Alisa herself was overwhelmed by her strange feelings. She had lain awake the greater part of the night and hadn't been able to stay away today, although she had consciously made the attempt. These tremulous sensations within her were new and unfamiliar. The warm flush running through her body was terrifying in its pleasure, a driving physical longing astonishing in its intensity. Surely she must leave. This would never do! She *must* leave! But she couldn't.

It was Nikki who decided he would either have to leave now, or he would be recklessly and perhaps disastrously seducing a still uncertain (bewildered, wavering, but still uncertain) woman. With a tremendous effort of will, Nikki suggested that Alisa should be departing for home since the air was beginning to cool as the sun dropped toward the horizon.

"Yes, of course." Alisa jumped up breathlessly, eagerly grasping the opportunity to escape from an encounter that left her filled with flurries and pulsations, while at the same time, and quite improperly, she chided herself, curiously reluctant to leave. "You're kind to notice. Thank you so much for showing me your catalogues. I haven't had such an interesting conversation in years," she said and dazzled him with an ingenuous smile.

Nikki rose, and standing quite close to her, was warmed by the unpretentious sincerity of that smile.

"If I might suggest, Alisa," he said, skillfully choosing his words, not wishing to disturb the delicate balance of her desires against the obvious perils she envisioned, "if you would care to stroll in this direction tomorrow afternoon, I could have one of my servants carry over the Shishkin landscape for you to see, since you feel you cannot take tea at my lodge."

Alisa hesitated only briefly. She eagerly wanted to see the painting, and she also wanted to see Prince Kuzan, and he did say his servant would be present. Nikki's reference to the servant gave Alisa, already susceptible, the needed sop of respectability to arrest her qualms.

"I'd like that immensely. Until tomorrow." Alisa waved gaily and ran off through the delicate birches.

Thank heaven, my husband is in Helsinki on business, Alisa breathed gratefully. Her husband normally kept a very careful watch on her activities, but his son, who was supposed to take over the vigil in his father's absence, was rather less concerned than the jealous Mr. Forseus. And Alisa *was* given considerably more freedom *within* the estate. The acres were so extensive and isolated that Valdemar Forseus felt his prize possession relatively safe from strange eyes.

The following morning dawned overcast and drizzly.

Alisa was strangely upset upon awakening to find her maid pulling back the heavy curtains on a gray cloudy day. She wanted to see Prince Kuzan again, but she didn't know why, and the weather might not permit her to go out. She sat by her window most of the morning, reading to her daughter and trying not to think of his disquieting effect on her.

Nikki, too, woke to strong feelings. "Merde," he swore. A seduction in the rain would be troublesome even if she did come out in spite of the wetness. And this was his third and last day to win the wager.

Why was he so anxious to make love to Mrs. Forseus? Nikki pondered. He who had just recently decried the monotony of women. It wasn't the money from the wager; he hardly needed it and to win or lose the bet didn't signify; on the rare occasions when Nikki lost, he lost as graciously as he won. But he was feeling some strange and remarkable attraction to the chit, an attraction removed from his usual lust. Alisa is virtuous, he reflected; a previously unassailable virtue about to be conquered. That was what was giving him such delicious pleasure.

At noon the sun came out in blazing glory.

Nikki called for his valet de chambre, Yukko, and

had him fetch the painting. The luncheon basket he
had ordered was sent for and the two men set off
toward the rendezvous. Yukko, a friend as well as
a servant, having been Nikki's companion since
childhood, was better company than nine-tenths of
his betters. And the best knife-thrower he had ever
seen. Nikki good-naturedly accepted the teasing
directed toward him.

"Don't worry, Yukko. I'll be careful. Just do as I
ask. After Mrs. Forseus has had an opportunity to
satisfactorily inspect the painting, I'll give you a
discreet nod and you take the painting back to the
lodge and leave us alone. Urho informed me yesterday when he was saddling my horse that the old
merchant is in Helsinki and isn't expected back for
two weeks; Urho's sister is a parlor maid at Forseus'.
So you see, I anticipate no angry husbands," Nikki
said as he grinned into Yukko's widely smiling face.

"In that case, I won't have to stand guard with
my pukko to stave off intruders."

"No, Yukko, no need this time. Just go back to
the lodge when I nod and try a bottle of my new
brandy. Ask Aleksei to find you one; he knows
where it is."

Intentionally arriving early once again, Nikki
watched as Yukko propped the large canvas against
some birch trees, then both men sprawled in the
grass waiting for Mrs. Forseus.

She appeared shortly, slightly breathless, having
run the last quarter verst fearing she might be too
late. In an effort to dissuade herself from meeting
Nikolai, she had postponed her departure until long
after Katelina was asleep and then impetuously
decided to go regardless of her fears.

Yukko's presence was reassuring and the three sat
on the grass admiring the delicate depiction of a
birch grove, like the one surrounding them. Shishkin's skill at capturing the atmosphere of early morning, his rendering of lacy ferns, the dawn stillness
so powerfully evoked on the canvas were very im-
pressive. Alisa exclaimed in delight, Nikki was
courteously agreeable, and Yukko, after a summary
glance at the landscape, ignored the painting and
chose instead to observe the protagonists in this
elaborate courtship dance.

After a reasonable interval, Yukko discreetly rose
and left with the painting. Immediately stepping into
the breach, with the military precision of a trained
field officer (to hesitate is to be lost), Nikki smiled
warmly and said, "Could I interest you in some of
my chef's concoctions for a *dejeuner sur l'herbe?*"
handing Alisa the hamper as he lifted the lid. Any
woman would be awed by the sumptuous display
arranged in the large basket.

Nikki spread out a damask cloth, crystal, silver
and china while Alisa enthusiastically marveled over
the exquisite cold collation; a spiced Cornish hen
stuffed with truffles and herbs, pickled artichoke
hearts, asparagus vinaigrette, smoked salmon and
caviar twirled into delicate pink lily shapes, pâté
fluted into a petal-shaped mold, fresh strawberries
sprinkled with sugar in a scalloped silver bowl, and
pale, golden madeleines artfully arranged in a silver
lattice work basket. While Alisa set the food before
them, Nikki poured champagne into two fine-
stemmed goblets.

He handed a glass to Alisa, remarking lightly,
"Shall we first drink a toast to the Emperor since

we're drinking his favorite brand of champagne—
Clicquot?" [3]

Alisa nodded, wide-eyed.

"To the Emperor," Nikki toasted and drained his
glass.

"To the Emperor," Alisa repeated with a timid
smile and took a sip of her champagne.

Le picque nicque proceeded gaily, Nikki exerting
his considerable charm, with the help of the food,
champagne and ideal weather, easily enchanting
Alisa; reminding her of all the attractions of the
luxurious, entertaining life she had been removed
from for six years.

They chatted cheerfully, laughed at trivialities; he
talked to her lightly, fascinating her, hypnotizing
her. She listened and responded, heedless of this
breach against propriety. She had been a virtual
prisoner of an old and depraved husband for six
years and she was still very young.

And now the joy she had not allowed herself to
hope for came back to her. Alisa delighted in Nikki
without reservation, in his burning eyes which held
hers, in the caressing compliments he offered her,
for the blithe joyous world he exemplified and which
was lost to her forever.

The silly banter stopped abruptly.

A tremulous silence hung between them. Nikki
was seated very close to Alisa. He caught her
frightened glance and held it. He could see that she
was near yielding.

"No, no," she whispered in fright and began to
get up. He ignored her words. Reaching out, he
caught her shoulders and pulled her towards him.
He knew she would now either freeze in his arms or

respond to him. She half-opened her mouth and bent her head back, her breath came unevenly, her body trembled under the pressure of his hands. He kissed her lips tenderly, her arms lifted around his shoulders, her fingertips brushed the soft hair on his neck, lightly, tentatively; she was quivering like a frightened animal.

Almost immediately the enormity of her acquiescence washed over her and she attempted to break away.

"Loose me," she whispered pleadingly, "Loose me, please," she cried softly, struggling weakly against his chest, unable to still the wakening desires in her own body.

"No, love," he murmured thickly, kissing her. His hand slipped under her knees and he lifted her into his arms. Ignoring her timid protests, he carried her under the trees and there on the soft, green moss laid her down and began deftly undressing her, all the while murmuring endearments, kissing her lips, stilling her fears with soft caresses. She closed her eyes and lay still.

Skillful in the intricacies of hooks, buttons and laces, he opened her dress and pushing it off her shoulders, untied the straps of her chemise and kissed her shoulders, tasting the rich perfume of her scent. The smell of a woman always roused him; he loved their fresh sweetness. He was wild with desire yet restrained himself. After removing her voluminous petticoats, pulling off her dainty kid slippers, garters and silk stockings, he opened the tapes of her lace trimmed drawers. Slipping them down her slender hips and well-shaped legs, he pulled them free and tossed them aside. A flood of crimson swept over

Alisa's face as she lay gleaming white before him, while his devouring gaze ranged the length of her splendid, opulent beauty.

Nikki bent and kissed her softly, opening her mouth under the pressure of his lips. Then he gently stroked and caressed her, his fingers sliding over her bare thighs toward the very source of pleasure, with gentle fingers gained the opening and toyed delightfully with her until she quivered and trembled beneath his touch. He could feel her quickening under his titillation. Her flesh was delicious to the touch, smooth and soft and warm. Alisa drew a long breath and opened her eyes. Seeing that she did not intend to resist him, Nikki kissed her more demandingly. She turned her face fully toward him and of her own accord returned his kiss, opened her soft lips to the pressure of his probing tongue and fierce burning kisses.

He had tamed her, but it was merely the beginning.

Nikki quickly stripped off his clothes and lay beside her, gathering her warm body in his arms. A shiver ran through Alisa at the contact with his naked skin. Her hands moved down his shoulders, closed around his back, as though she would press herself into him forever.

The tender caresses, his long, lean, manipulating fingers, the lingering kisses, the sweet murmured endearments had all served their purpose. Nikki gently lifted her legs, without resistance mounted her, and with a few merciless thrusts buried himself inside her incredible warmth. Alisa cried out softly. He was momentarily shocked as he penetrated her, for although obviously aroused, she was tight as a virgin. She would take some patient gentle stretch-

ing, for the vigorous lovemaking he was used to.
Could all the ribald jests and rumors be true? Was
her husband, indeed, too old?

"I'm sorry." Nikki whispered into her tangled
hair, "Did I hurt you?" Eyelids fluttering, lips parted,
Alisa murmured "No," as she clung to him, her arms
laced round his powerful body, her legs twined
round his.

Enveloped in her warm, throbbing flesh, he carefully, gently explored its luscious interior as she
stirred restlessly beneath him. With a slow, delicate
rhythm he moved in her, adeptly controlling his passion, slowing his exertions to savor the tide of
pleasure, intent on further rousing Alisa's senses,
deliberately compelling her to need him, compelling
her to respond to the exquisite sensual pleasure he
was intensifying with each deep, plunging stroke. He
was in no hurry now, wisely delaying the climax,
enjoying each wave of delight.

Soon the last vestiges of Alisa's guilt and fear were
swept away before the fury of the untrammeled passion Nikki had adroitly provoked in her newly
awakened body, and with a deep, drawn sigh she
clasped him tighter.

Nikki continued his slow rhythm, caressing her
tenderly, listening to the murmurs wrung from her
parted lips by the strange rapture she was experiencing for the first time and which she accepted with
a growing passion by arching instinctively to meet
each forceful stroke.

"Come, sweet princess, come with me," he murmured softly and touched her neck gently with his
warm lips as he breathed sensuous endearments to
rouse her further.

Nikki had discovered while still a mere youth that whispered phrases, passionate sentiments of affection, a few lustful words can do more to take a woman over the edge than twenty minutes of the most ardent physical stimulation.

The flush on Alisa's cheeks was rising, a warm blush of color was spreading down her soft, white, heaving breasts.

"Follow me, sweet angel." he murmured tenderly.

She was almost there.

Nikki held her crushed to him, his arms wrapped tightly around her slender back, holding her impaled on his rigid engorged stiffness. His breathing was harsh and rapid, his warm whispers brushed her ear, his masculine scent touched her nostrils, tendrils of damp dark curls clung to his forehead. Now he was fully roused, desperate for relief, as if he hadn't had a woman for a long time. As if Tanya no longer existed. Finally he allowed himself release, succumbing to his mounting passion, riding the crest of his desire as if it had no end. Alisa, too, with guiltless wonder and a long dormant sensuality abandoned herself to the full glory of their desire. She returned Nikki's kisses wantonly, crushed her mouth feverishly against his, ran her hands over his magnificent body, revelled in the pressure of his firm, muscular frame, hard and demanding against her tender flesh, voluptuously joined him in the selfish, sensual dance of love. Finally she gave herself to him, willingly opened her body for his pleasure, sobbed with a passion too long deferred, keening a quiet, soft cry of rapture as he brought her to an ecstasy she had never known, as he pressed against the mouth of her womb and poured his warmth into her.

Now she knew this was what she had wanted from the first time she had seen him and caught that hungry look in those golden eyes; his strength, his wildness, the feel of his powerful body on hers.

Her violet eyes opened slowly and lifted to his, eyelids heavy with a sweet, languorous memory and he realized as he gazed down upon her beautiful, flushed face, how men could feel the torturous self-doubts of jealousy. That drowsy, voluptuous, yielding look, the curve of her full, red lips, the heightened color, the gentle smile of surfeit—she was a sated woman remembering her lover's caresses. To picture another man plundering the soft riches of her luscious body evoked in him an unfamiliar blaze of jealousy.

Alisa had seen lust in a man's eyes; the fanatic, burning, frankly covetous eyes of her husband when he stripped her or beat her, the surreptitious, carefully concealed lust in the eyes of strangers. At this moment, however, Nikki's golden eyes shone not only with a sensual desire, but also with a tenderness as he marveled at the magnificent beauty of the creature before him. He must have her. He would gently teach her the pleasures of her senses, with deliberation rouse her, delicately caress the graceful form and make her his. This beauty *must* be his. . . .

For Alisa, who had only been used, her body torn apart and abused by a selfish, brutal, bestial lust, Nikki's glance of passionate tenderness drew her like a beacon of warmth in a cold, black night.

Nikki kissed her lips lightly and murmured as he moved off and lay beside her propped up on one elbow. "Thank you love. Do you feel content?"

He ran a light finger down her belly.

Alisa smiled with a winsome satisfaction, then nodded, with a delightful almost childish openness, putting up her lips to be kissed again.

"Sweet nymph, we make a fine pair, Alisa," Nikki whispered as he kissed her. She was everything and more than he had imagined. She was a nymph, a bacchante, with a natural wantonness that stirred his ardor.

Nikki rose to his knees and looked at her lying quietly with her thighs still slightly parted. The seductive lure of Alisa's beauty, her compliant, provocative posture brought his manhood standing proud.

"Look at me, Alisa," Nikki said softly.

She looked at him, embarrassment, shyness, desire all there in confusion, but kept her eyes averted from his obviously aroused masculinity.

"Look at me," Nikki insisted quietly, but she again resisted.

After a moment, Nikki continued teasingly.

"Look what you do to me, you siren." He was laughing and relaxed. Alisa blushed but still avoided looking at him.

"Come, now, dearest Alisa. Do as I ask."

Alisa shivered, then reluctantly obeyed him. Hesitantly and trembling slightly, she raised her eyes to his stiff erection.

"Touch me, Alisa," he continued quietly, drawing her unwilling hand to him. "Here, I'll show you how I like you to touch me. Hold me thus," and he gripped her hand tightly in his, showing her how to rouse his prick for her satisfaction.

With his free hand he slowly stroked her warm body, rubbing her nipples softly between his fingers till they stood taut and hard, caressing the silky inner flesh of her thighs, probing her soft warmth now wet from his lovemaking. She began stirring under his practiced fingers, breathing irregularly, quivering with the pleasurable sensation mounting within her.

He released her hand and whispered, "Now just lie quietly and enjoy yourself." He eased himself into her until he could penetrate no further and began to warm her with slow steady thrusts, exercising all his constraint in order that Alisa would have every opportunity to satisfy her newly roused sexual appetite; so she could fully taste the rapture her senses craved. He continued the steady rocking, turning lightly from side to side, moving inside her with practiced skill, watching her blushing, upturned face and reading from her fluttering eyes how she was feeling, then he set to work in earnest and drew her to new heights of pleasure, finally pleasing himself as he pleased her.

III
THE UNBIDDEN SPECTATORS

Alisa was lying quietly now, enclosed within Nikki's strong arms, the trembling of her body having ceased.

Into this wonderland of pleasure, this paradise for the senses, drawled a lazy voice.

"It looks as though you win the bet, Nikki. I should have known better since your skill in these matters is widely renowned. Must say, I envy you the ride."

Nikki swore and rolled onto his back, his eyes glaring contemptuously at the mocking, derisive smile of Illyich. Cernov was at his side, blandly surveying the delicious display of Alisa's body. He gave the faintest flick of a wink at Nikki.

Alisa lay there, eyes still closed, caressed almost into insensibility. Nikki quickly drew his shirt over her nakedness.

He watched her floating slowly back into awareness from the nirvana of sexuality where she had so wondrously expired. She opened her torpid eyes, deliciously languorous, still remote, unfocusing.

"You bastards!" Nikki snarled, turning to the two men.

"Now, now Nikki, don't be vulgar. You know perfectly well I escaped illegitimacy by ten days." Cernov imperturbably retorted.

"Damn voyeurs!" Nikki spat, a frustrated, blazing anger igniting his mind.

Alisa's lovely eyes opened with a startled look, at last fully conscious of the scene and its spectators.

"Nikki!" she whispered frantically. She was appalled, lying almost naked before two strangers.

"I'll give you two seconds to get out of here or I'll kill you both!" Nikki said in a voice that was solid ice.

Sensible of the reputation Nikki enjoyed as a brawler, the two officers judiciously turned on their heels and left. Cernov, grinning, calmly blew a kiss in Alisa's direction as he wheeled around.

"Who the hell would think Nikki would get angry over some little piece and a frolic in the woods?" Cernov exhaled softly in amazement. "I've never seen him regard a woman as anything more than a serviceable convenience."

"God only knows, but when Nikki's in that murderous a mood, I'm not going to wait around to find out why," Illyich responded with a prudent expediency that had served him well in the past. Together they returned to the lodge to satisfy the desires that Alisa's lush body had stirred within them. Nikki listened to their hasty retreat through the underbrush then turned to the dismayed woman.

"Forgive me, Alisa, for the crude stupidity of my friends." he apologized softly.

Alisa, feeling quite numb, could not utter a word. As Nikki watched her silent face, he saw a tear well out of one corner of her eye and trace a course down her rosy cheek.

SEIZED BY LOVE 71

Damn them, damn them to hell, he muttered to himself, of all the abominable luck.

"I'm sorry," Nikki said aloud and moved toward Alisa as if to offer what comfort he could.

Nikki had had vague misgivings and qualifications about this seduction from the beginning and even more so after their second encounter, but he had brushed them aside. For Nikki had lived a life unhampered by restrictions, ungoverned by rationale, totally unconcerned with consequences. Now he found himself uncomfortably conscious of being the cause of Alisa's painful and humiliating position. He felt guilty and this guilt upset him because it was foreign to his nature.

In addition to the guilt, he was smolderingly furious at those wretched friends of his. If he had been honest with himself, he could have understood their puzzled reaction to his rage. For years, the men had participated in many "shared" experiences with women. How were Cernov and Illyich to know that in this rare instance, they were not supposed to join the fun?

Alisa cringed from Nikki's sympathetic gesture. He hastily stayed his hand in mid-air.

"Please go," she whispered.

"Alisa, let me explain," Nikki began, forcibly struck by the pain in her tear-filled eyes.

"Please," she remonstrated in a barely audible voice. "Just go, you've had your amusement." Her body involuntarily shuddered. "Just go!" she cried hysterically.

"Very well," Nikki said stiffly. Again, this scene was new to him. He dressed swiftly, apologizing formally when he withdrew his shirt from her naked form and replaced it with one of her petticoats.

"Please accept my deepest apologies, Madame," he said in a clipped, cool voice as he bowed briefly to her recumbent form, her eyes staring, unseeing, averted from his. Then he walked quickly away, flushed with frustration and anger.

Quite suddenly, all the light went out of Alisa's day. She wept and wept, hugging her petticoat to her as though to keep herself from breaking apart from the great wracking sobs of humiliation. She wasn't ashamed of the men seeing her unclothed, she could survive that; she was ashamed for wanting Nikki so, for willingly giving her body to him; he hadn't had to force her, she had wanted him. She wept for her capitulation, she who was strong and willful, resolute enough to withstand an intolerable man and marriage for six years; determined enough to patiently plan and wait for escape from a husband she despised. Now, brought low by an unfathomable desire for a man with a reputation for treating women casually and at this very moment, no doubt, considering her simply another pleasant diversion.

Alisa's life had not been happy since the death of her parents; everything she had loved and cherished had been swept away in a few days when influenza had claimed both her parents within hours of each other. The raging fever which had held them in its tenacious, deadly grip had never broken. Her lovely, gay mother and quiet, scholarly father had eased into a coma from which they had never wakened. Alisa had often wished in the years following that she, too, could have died, but her young, strong body had defeated the disease.

Then so shortly after, indeed quite improperly so, the incredulous demand of her hand in marriage by old Mr. Forseus, that had actually been arranged by her father. Unthinkable, but apparently true since her father's signature was on the document.

If she had not had Katelina to love after that first year, a child to bring joy to her, she would not have had the strength or courage to continue her existence. Katelina, her darling Katelina, her only solace, had given her reason to live.

Now, the one time she ignored reason, negated logic, passionately made a daring, bold grasp for momentary happiness, she had been utterly shamed and humiliated. Maybe there truly was no hope for joy or pleasure in her life, Alisa thought sorrowfully. But she had been happy, deliriously happy with Nikki. That she couldn't deny.

Alisa cried afresh at her wounded heart and pride. She cried for all her sorrows and all her misery these many years and sobbed all the sobs that had been so long suppressed. When she had finally drained all the pent-up tears, she took herself to task with the indomitable spirit that had sustained her always.

Be sensible, you'll survive this mortification. She still had Katelina and before long, perhaps they would be able to leave Forseus and make their way in the world. Arni, her father's old groom, Maria, her old nanny and Rakeli, Katelina's nanny, were devotedly loyal and always ready to assist her should that hope become reality.

Washing herself hastily at the river then dressing carefully, Alisa adjusted her clothes into a semblance of order, her face in a spurious repose, and walked home.

Nikki partially assuaged his black rage and frustration by summarily driving Cernov and Illyich out of his lodge, spurring their departure with a string of vivid obscenities. With a considerably more polite choice of words, Nikki convinced his young cousin Aleksei to repair to the town house in Petersburg for a few days until Nikki joined him. The gypsy girls were promptly ousted, as well; piled into a carriage in which they contentedly counted their money all the way back to the city.

Nikki immediately shut himself into the music room with two bottles of brandy and a brooding anger which turned into a brooding melancholy by the bottom of the second bottle.

He roared for his musicians and commanded they play sorrowful, quiet Finnish love songs, the old familiar songs of Nikki's childhood. His mother's Tzigane ancestors had settled north of Lake Ladoga over one hundred years ago when a grateful noble had deeded them a large tract of land and citizenship in return for having preserved an only son's life from a runaway horse. Nikki's paternal grandfather had begun construction of Le Repose, northeast of Viipuri in 1810; the country estate was to become the favorite seat of the Kuzan family. Nikki had been reared there and grew up in an atmosphere of Karelian tradition.

Play "Kalliolle Kukulalle," he would sullenly mutter every second song, and the musicians would lapse again into the sad, minor key and play the single melody Nikki wanted to hear.

*Kalliolle kukulalle
Rakenan minä majani
Sine hajan oman ystávān
Asuman minuu ransani.*

The poignant lyrics spoke of a lover bringing his sweetheart to a secluded forest cabin and plunged Nikki still deeper into an agonizing, gloomy depression. He couldn't dislodge visions of Alisa from his mind. They had shared a sexual response that had struck even the surfeited, world-weary Prince as rare and unique. She was a beauty, unutterably so, artless, dazzling, sensual. He *must* see her again!

At one o'clock in the morning, Nikki's glazed, drunken eyes lit with a brilliant flash of an idea. He impatiently waved the musicians away and called for his steward. After sending four riders out with a message for his father's gardener, Nikki, eminently satisfied with his resourcefulness, fell into a drunken sleep, having left adamant orders to be wakened when the messengers returned.

Fifty versts (33 miles) away in the sunny breakfast room of Le Repose, Prince Mikhail Petrovich Kuzan's principal seat and model estate of 172,000 dessiatins (484,400 acres), Nikki's parents were enjoying the early morning companionship of a breakfast à deux.

"What in the world is Nikki up to?" his mother curiously inquired; she was a petit, dark-haired Tzigane woman, still lovely and slim at fifty.

"Need you ask?" his father replied drily. "When Nikki strips our greenhouses of ten dozen orchids and twenty baskets of strawberries, I would hazard a guess your dear boy has found some woman who adores orchids and has a passion for strawberries. Let us at least hope this sudden passion for strawberries does not signify yet another enceinte mistress. He has populated the world quite adequately already with his bastards."

"Now, dear, don't be too harsh on Nikki." Princess Kuzan remonstrated gently. "He is supporting them all quite satisfactorily, even lavishly, and need I remind you that you quite put him in the shade by your reckless escapades until I tamed you into the joys of domesticity. The rumor mills put his streak of wildness at your door, Misha, my dear, for as you well know, the Kuzan blood lines have long possessed a reputation for vice," she finished sweetly.

Nikki could do no wrong in the eyes of his loving mother. He could be wild and a hellion, but her love was unconditional and she served as a conciliatory influence on the occasions when father and son's obdurate temperaments clashed.

"I could perhaps argue about who tamed whom, and from whence the taint of wickedness came, but I politely defer to you as a gentleman should," old Prince Kuzan graciously replied, smiling at his wife. Even after thirty-four years, she continued to delight him. The wild, Tzigane heritage of the ripe sixteen-year-old gypsy he had married had never been submerged. That wildness had been but thinly veiled with the veneer of sophistication necessary to move in Prince Mikhail's aristocratic circles on the rare occasions it suited him to remove himself from the comfortable, elegant seclusion of Le Repose.

"I wish someday Nikki could find a love like ours, Misha," Princess Kaisa-leena Kuzan wistfully murmured.

"We had rare luck, love. It does not happen often in this world," the Prince replied with obvious feeling, recalling their first tumultuous meeting thirty-four brief years ago.

IV
THE RECONCILIATION

Early the next morning Alisa was shaken awake by Maria whispering frantically, "Mistress Alisa, Mistress Alisa, you must get up!"

Alisa brought herself up out of a deep dream of Nikki, and reacted immediately when she saw the terrified fear in Maria's eyes.

"What's the matter. Is Katelina ill?" Alisa asked anxiously, sitting up.

"No, my lady," Maria said, wringing her hands.

Alisa visibly relaxed, settling back to her soft pillow.

"It's much worse," Maria moaned nervously.

Alarm again sparked in Alisa's violet eyes.

"Mr. Forseus has returned." She began looking wildly around the room as if to flee.

"No, my lady."

"What is it then, for heaven's sake? Speak up Maria," Alisa insisted.

"A carriage of orchids, my lady," Maria whispered quaveringly.

"A carriage of orchids? What in the world are you talking about?" Alisa asked incredulously as she jumped out of bed and rapidly stripped off her nightgown.

"Well, my lady, you know I always go to the chicken house very early in the morning to gather fresh eggs for your and Katelina's breakfast. As I was slipping out the side door, I saw a strange carriage coming up the driveway and ran out to see who it was. The driver said he was Prince Kuzan's coachman and he had orders to deliver the orchids, and Mistress Alisa," she continued aghast, "there are also baskets and baskets of strawberries he has instructions to deliver to Mrs. Forseus, as well, and," she paused to catch her breath, "and also this letter for you. I told him to wait behind the bend in the driveway so he wouldn't be visible from the house, but my lady, you must hurry, the servants will soon be up."

Alisa had already snatched the heavy envelope embossed with the golden seal of Kuzan from Maria's hand before the old servant was finished with her explanation.

She tore open the envelope and pulled out the single sheet of paper. Swiftly her eyes scanned the heavy, careless scrawl.

"If you don't meet me at the meadow in forty minutes, I shall ride over to see you."

The note was simply signed "N."

Oh, Mon Dieu! It must have taken the coachman twenty minutes to drive over here on the circuitous roads. This left her a bare twenty minutes to dress, talk to the driver and cover the distance to the meadow or else Nikki would be at her door.

"Maria, quickly find a dress for me. After I've gone, if any servants question you, tell them I went to bring blankets and clothes for Mrs. Niemi's new baby. Put those baby clothes you made in a basket and I'll stop at the Niemis' cottage on my way back. Hurry, quickly now, I don't have much time!"

Within five minutes, Alisa was dressed and dashing down the main stairway. The door closed quietly behind her just as the household servants began stirring.

Alisa ran down the driveway to the bend where, thankfully, the carriage and coachman were still waiting. Gasping for breath, she addressed the man severely, "You must return to Prince Kuzan."

"I can't ma'am. I have my orders. I'm supposed to deliver these to Mrs. Forseus."

Alisa looked in wonder at the glistening, open landau, the Kuzan signet initialed on the door, the highly polished green lacquerwork and green velvet upholstery an ideal foil for the stunning display of enormous, resplendent yellow and lavender orchids, orchids in baskets, orchids spilling out of shallow basins, orchids carpeting the floor, interspersed with a prodigious number of wicker baskets containing perfect, red, hot-house strawberries.

"*I* am Mrs. Forseus and am on my way to see Prince Kuzan now. If you don't return to his lodge immediately, I promise you he'll be angry."

"I don't know, ma'am. Prince Kuzan was quite explicit about my instructions," the man uncomfortably equivocated.

"I'm sure I'll be able to change his mind. Please, please, go back!" Alisa implored frantically.

You might at that, the coachman reflected admiringly as he looked at the beautiful, breathless young woman before him. He knew Prince Kuzan's susceptibility to beautiful women and had spent many a nocturnal vigil wrapped in fur robes in carriage or troika, waiting for the Prince to re-appear from some lady's boudoir.

"Very well, ma'am," he agreed, but added carefully, "if you promise to explain to Prince Kuzan."

"Oh, I will, I will!" Alisa finished in a rush of grateful relief, "Thank you." She waved and disappeared into the forest.

With a quiet cluck of his teeth and a pull on the reins, he turned the landau around and retraced its journey.

Alisa ran through the woods, afraid she would be too late; would he really come to the house to find her? Horror! Please, please, make him wait, she prayed silently.

Her heart gave a leap of pure happiness. She would see Nikki again!

If you had an ounce of pride, she told herself. Well, she didn't when it came to Nikki. She wanted to see him with all her heart.

Alisa broke from the shelter of the birches into the meadow, the dew lacy and sparkling on the grass, the early morning sun casting long shadows across the glistening meadow. Suddenly she saw the tall figure of Nikki leaning against a tree, restless, impatient, fitfully slapping gloves to thigh as he moodily contemplated the toes of his boots. Alisa stopped abruptly, confused emotions coursing through her.

Looking up at a slight sound, Nikki beheld Alisa hesitantly arrested at the edge of the grove, her gold-red hair tousled, loose tendrils falling around rosy, flushed cheeks, her breasts heaving with the exertion of the headlong rush through the woods, her yellow, flower-printed linen dress damply clinging at the hemline from the dew's wetness.

Their glances met.

In his eyes she saw some strange emotion. Was it

relief? The transient expression vanished in an instant. Nikki smiled and started forward, opening his arms wide in welcome. Alisa hesitated then dropped her basket and ran flying into his open arms. Nikki enfolded her in a crushing embrace.

"Thank you for coming," he murmured against her hair in an odd voice. "Forgive me," he quietly added as he clasped her tightly, burying his face in her hair, taking in the smell of her, the scent and feel of clean, silken hair and sweet, young flesh, the exquisite sensation of her body against his.

As Alisa clung to him, tears of joy ran freely down her cheeks. She was lost to the world in his arms, oblivious to right or wrong, or duty or conscience. Only aware of a thrilling happiness.

For them the world held promise once again.

"I can't stay long," Alisa whispered nervously.

"I know. May I see you this afternoon?" Nikki asked with a husky urgency.

"Yes," she answered, surrendering heedlessly, renouncing with a giddy delirium any thought of propriety.

"At one then, I'll meet you here. Hours to wait. That will be hell," he groaned softly against her ear.

"I must go!" she fearfully murmured.

"I'll walk you back," he insisted quietly, still not releasing her from his strong arms, not wanting her to leave.

"No! You mustn't. Please! If someone should see you," she pleaded, lifting imploring eyes to gaze into Nikki's warm, golden eyes, already kindling with an insistent passion. "I'll be here at one," she promised.

Raising on tiptoe, Alisa brushed Nikki's mouth

softly with trembling lips, turned, pulled free from his grasp, and fled, picking up the basket which had been abandoned at the edge of the meadow. She still had her errand to complete.

V
THE BLISSFUL INTERLUDE

Nikki was waiting long before 1:00, thinking only of holding Alisa again, of feeling the warmth of her body against his. My God, he wanted her.

When she came and saw him, her face lit up as he knew it would; no coquetry, no pretensions, just a guileless, naive happiness; her marvelous violet eyes shining with pleasure, her gaze disconcertingly direct.

Nikki took both her hands in his and, surveying the smiling face, bent his head and tenderly kissed the tip of her nose.

"What do you want to do today?" he asked gaily. "This is our first day together. Come to my lodge. I've sent everyone away but the servants. My home, my servants, my estate and I are at your disposal." His warm smile caressed her. "Anything you want you shall have, anything you want to do, I will do," he offered with a joyous expansiveness.

Alisa looked up into his handsome face and shamefully blushed.

"Well, if you insist, we shall do that first," he teased.

The music room, Nikki's favorite, immediately caught Alisa's fancy. Alcoves strewn with embroidered pillows fronted each large gothic framed win-

dow; the walls and vaulted ceiling were entirely
mosaiced in glittering lapis lazuli, gold and ultramarine green tiles, portraying sinuous, entwined
vines, flowers and birds. The effect was breathtaking.

When they walked into Nikki's sitting room, a
large portrait gazed down on them; his mother
painted by Winterhalter. She was small, dark, beautiful, seated in a gilded chair with Nikki at eight
years, sturdily erect, angelic, childishly handsome at
her side, his toys scattered on the rug before them.
A great tenderness flooded through Alisa when
viewing the child that he had once been.

"Your mother is very lovely," Alisa said as she
looked at the young woman depicted many years
ago.

"Yes, she is," Nikki agreed. "You must meet her
sometime soon," he continued with a marvelous,
open assurance.

"Oh, no! I couldn't," Alisa protested in embarrassment.

"Nonsense. Maman is a Tzigane and has a very
realistic outlook on life. She'll adore you, just as I
do. Come here now," he said impatiently, "enough
talking and sightseeing. Let me hold you." He pulled
her through the doorway into his bedroom, transformed since the return of the landau into a bower
of orchids.

Thus began the first day of a week of afternoons
they were able to spend together; a carpe diem existence, two mutually obsessed creatures making love
through the warm springtime hours, both avoiding
thoughts of the future. Particularly for Alisa, this

decision to disregard the future was absolutely essential to her present happiness. Nothing must spoil these few days with Nikki.

For them there was only the wonderful, passionate, extravagant present. Young lovers lost to the world, only conscious of each other's presence. They drew every sensation from every transient hour, from every exquisite touch, look, caress. Their sexual pleasures were of the simplest, old-fashioned, natural, a unique bond of affection enhancing the rapture as they satisfied their lusts in a simple variety.

As an accomplished aficionado of Eros, Nikki had long ago learned the pleasure of afternoon amours. One was refreshed from having but recently risen from one's night's sleep and eaten a light lunch. The mind and body were fresh, vital, vigorous, not staled by hours of drinking or gaming as was the case with a midnight rendezvous. Not that he was adverse to late night assignations, but he knew that he performed more ardently, more zealously, more resiliently in the gentle hours of afternoon.

The second afternoon Alisa timidly inquired as she lay in Nikki's tender embrace, "Do you think perhaps—that is to say—do you think you should use some precautions?"

Nikki opened his eyes, lifted his head a scant inch off the pillow and said drowsily, "French letters? Condoms? They spoil the pleasure; I never use them." He reached out to touch her hair. "They would not feel good to you, my love." His eyelids fell and he dozed off, still holding her tightly to his rugged form.

Alisa knew she should force the issue for her own

safety and protection, but she didn't want to spoil their little remaining time together.

Nikki hugged her closer and they both slept.

Instinct told Nikki, when he was alone and away from Alisa's tempestuous excitement, that he was getting in too deep this time, that this was not another light flirtation or trivial affair, but regardless of this premonition, he plunged boldly in. He hadn't enjoyed himself so much for months—more—years. It was a time of deepest content.

Alisa, too, lived in the bewitching, sensual present, grasping at the opportunity to postpone the end of these halcyon days. If time could just stand still.

She resolutely refused to consider the future. She wouldn't, she wouldn't, yet she cried inwardly when conscience raised its unwanted head above her repression. She deserved some gaiety, some brief taste of love, she told herself. For the most part, Alisa was blissfully happy. Since living in "durance vile" for six years, who could blame her for ignoring the admonitions of her conscience, the call of duty?— when gay, charming, handsome Nikki was bathing her senses in rapture and extravagantly indulging her caprices.

No such irresolution or discordant meditation preyed on Nikki's mind, for he had long eschewed regrets as both useless and fatiguing. He had quite simply decided that he would bring Alisa back to Petersburg when he returned and install her in a comfortable house on the Quai des Anglais. If the neighborhood was good enough for the Emperor's mistress, it was good enough for his.[4]

Nikki never pondered over or curbed his selfish wishes. He had never had to. Alisa was delightful, lovely, vivacious, intelligent (the latter quality hitherto avoided in Nikki's amorous adventures). But her overwhelming quality, the major attraction, the most fascinating enticement in this week of tumultuous pleasure was purely sensual. This woman roused him, teased him, fired his jaded senses to new exquisite limits. Her spontaneous response as he instructed her in the delights of the flesh, her first tentative, then more assured forays into the game of love, her guilelessly greedy appetite for pleasure, stimulated and whetted Nikki's weary spirit. Alisa had all the sensual abandon of the primordial female without the repugnant vulgarity of the harlot.

Surely he would be a fool to walk away from the pleasures Alisa offered him. She was the fetching, enchanting antidote to the ennui that had threatened to engulf him.

Over the years, Nikki had, with caution and scepticism, scrupulously avoided any permanence in his relationships with women, preferring married women of his class, already lawfully tied, or else expensive tarts and actresses easily satisfied with lavish gifts and generous purses of gold. He avoided the obligation to provide an establishment for any one woman for even the transitory duration implied in those arrangements. Nikki's fierce independence had survived all attempts to ensnare and clinging women had always been anathema to him. He turned quite cold and remote when pressed by the importunities of an ardent female. But now Nikki was quite willing to make the necessary adjustments to his normal, selfish regimen. To have Alisa comfortably settled convenient to his town palace would offer him the most pleasant recreation.

One afternoon as Alisa lay nestled snugly in Nikki's arms, drifting back from the idyllic depths of pleasure, he quietly said, "Today must be our last day at the lodge. I received a message this morning which necessitates my attendance with the Chevaliers Gardes at the Emperor's review Sunday. You must come with me. Pack what you need tonight; I'll send my carriage round for you in the morning."

Alisa wished she had misunderstood, but knew she hadn't. Nikki had simply said, "Come with me," as if it were the most natural thing in the world, nothing more, no promises, no assurances; she was to him merely another woman of a certain class.

Happiness that he wanted her was overlaid with shock and dismay. But the thing that shocked her most—the daughter of landed gentry, well-bred and gently reared, was that she wished with all her heart she could disregard her conscience, her parents' ideals, and answer simply—I will come.

If she hadn't a daughter who must have opportunity for a normal life, she might have been even more tempted to say "I will."

Sighing unhappily, Alisa reminded herself that she had known this all must end when Mr. Forseus returned home. This "pleasant interlude" (what a deceptively benign term for these tumultuous stirrings of her heart) had merely ended a few days earlier than expected.

"I can't," Alisa softly replied.

Nikki's complacency was abruptly shattered.

"Why not?" he questioned in faint irritation, unused to negative replies.

"I have a daughter to consider," was her straightforward answer.

Nikki hesitated momentarily. Of course, he should have remembered—What was the child's name? It escaped him. A girl, she had said. After a short pause Nikki replied decisively, "Bring her along."

"No, I can't," Alisa repeated.

Now fully awake, Nikki asked with a sort of baffled impatience, "Why ever not? You shall have as large a house as you wish. I'll hire a niania and a governess—an English one, everyone seems to prefer English ones. There, that's taken care of," he said with satisfaction.

God, why couldn't she just say—Yes. Nikki was so good to her and God knows she deserved some happiness after all those miserable years. Why *couldn't* she say, "yes"? Even when Nikki tired of her, Alisa knew his generosity wouldn't allow her to become destitute. With all her heart, she wanted him. The precepts of a lifetime held firm, however.

"No, Nikki. It wouldn't do," Alisa retorted with a quiet sadness.

Nikki's irascible temper was rising. Was she like all the rest, after all? Holding out for a larger prize, for more remuneration, jewelry, perhaps, maybe a more sumptuous house, the right kind of horses and carriage? Had he been deceived by the artless sincerity and air of innocence? He thought not, but apparently he had.

He'd pay her price if it wasn't too high. He wanted her and, Hell, he gambled vast fortunes at a single throw. Certainly he could afford whatever her asking price was.

"Tell me what more you want then," he drawled coolly, determined to outbid her demands.

"I don't want anything from you, Nikki," Alisa's unhappy voice replied. "You have given me one week of blissful happiness and I knew it would have to end when Mr. Forseus returned from Helsinki. I'm sorry. I must think of my daughter."

"You told me yourself you won't stay much longer with that sadistic lecher." Nikki spoke accusingly, for Alisa had in the course of the last week, to her own immense surprise, confided to Nikki the whole wretched story of her marriage, when he had questioned the vestiges of many bruises on her tender flesh. (That first afternoon in the meadow, events had moved too rapidly for him to be certain, but the following encounter, the next afternoon, in his bedroom at the lodge, when time and the lack of spectators permitted a leisurely appraisal of Alisa's beautiful body, the faint discolorations were apparent.) Alisa had, at first reluctantly and then more volubly, as the pressure of six years' enforced silence were lifted, described her coerced marriage at fifteen, Forseus' bizarre aberrations and cravings for a nubile young girl-woman to rekindle his flagging desires, his abrupt rejection of her for several years after the birth of their daughter, and his renewed sadistic demands which he had forced on her twice lately.

Alisa's ungainly body during pregnancy had repulsed Forseus and after Katelina's birth, he had fearfully shunned the baby as an incarnation of the devil's child. Forseus' religious fanaticism (so often mutually complementary to sexual deviation) had convinced him that a birthmark on Katelina's leg was the devil's sign. He had been appalled by the pale pink birthmark in the shape of a half-moon and from the day of her birth had refused to have any contact with the child.

Nikki was enraged at her story. That old man was the man who possessed Alisa, owned her, slept with her, touched her, caressed her, abused her. God, how could she, he thought angrily. And, damn him, Forseus was a savage monster even by the none too exacting standards of humanity afforded contemporary husbands.

"I know I said I would leave him someday, but I must first find some employment," Alisa explained patiently.

"Damnation!" Nikki was furious now. He wasn't having his way. "Work?" he incredulously inquired, his face blank for a moment with disbelief. Immediately denying the staggering heresy, he demanded, "Why work when I will take care of you?"

He really didn't understand, Alisa thought with a feeling of despair. For Nikki, a woman's dignity, her pride, were at best, nebulous, and more aptly much overrated. In his experience women almost universally opted for security rather than independence. Rich or poor, highborn or low, they were all the same to him. But Alisa was not cut from the same mold. She, too, had a stubborn inclination and an inordinately determined will of her own. How else had she survived Forseus?

"You wouldn't understand, Nikki. There's such a thing as a woman's dignity and pride. I am not a whore to be acquired for the price of a house and a governess and a nanny."

"Damn right I don't understand!" he said through clenched teeth, trying to control his rage while groping vaguely for some reason for Alisa's violent affront, the entire issue of a woman's dignity and pride beyond his comprehension. Woman's pride? Sweet Jesus! Their pride was between their legs!

"You won't come then?" he continued hotly, furious at having his wishes thwarted, irritated at Alisa's monumental naiveté which presumed that there was a whore in the world he would have offered the luxurious, privileged existence he had offered her. By God, he had even consented to allow her damn brat to tag along.

"No," she replied stiffly.

"Very well," his voice was steely, "allow me to thank you for a pleasant week." Nikki rolled over and pulled open a drawer on the bedside table. Taking out a purse of roubles, he tossed them on Alisa's naked belly.

"It's been amusing," he said coldly, one sardonic eyebrow raised.

Alisa lifted the purse from her stomach, gently set it on the floor, rose from the bed and dressed as rapidly as her numerous petticoats permitted.

Nikki watched sullenly, not uttering a word. He let her go and then laughed scornfully at himself for allowing passion, once again after all these years, to overcome his usual cool reserve. Stupid fool! he chastised himself.

Seconds after the door closed behind Alisa, Nikki reached for the bell pull and when the servant arrived, requested in a dangerous voice, "Three bottles of brandy, *immediately*."

As the afternoon shadows turned to evening dusk, even the three bottles of brandy failed to dislodge or dull the cold fury of his thoughts.

Damn inconsiderate slut! He had offered her a pampered, luxurious life, the considerable influence of his protection and a damn sight less sadistic treatment than that peasant she was married to. I am not a whore, she had said. Insufferable arrogance—Why oh why would none of them ever admit to being what they were?

VI
THE DENOUEMENT

"Where the devil is she? I told you to keep watch over her!" Valdemar Forseus shouted wrathfully at his large, lumbering son.

"She couldn't have gone far without a horse or carriage," the middle-aged son calmly replied to his father, who was quite livid with rage, having already harangued his son for several minutes. Forseus' sparse gray hair was standing wildly about his bald pate, his small sunken eyes flashed with anger, his carefully manicured, blunt, peasant hands clenched and unclenched on his riding quirt.

"We weren't expecting you for six more days," the son continued, with the puzzled simplicity of a dull intellect.

"That's obvious!" Forseus thundered. "Is that devil's brat with her?" Forseus asked suspiciously.

"No, I saw Katelina out in the orchard with Rakeli."

"Very well, get out of my sight!" Forseus spat irritably. "I should have known better than to expect any competence from you. You take after your mother, you lout!"

Far from being disconcerted by this tirade, the simple, ponderous son merely turned on his heel and walked slowly back to the stables where he was most happy and content, brushing, feeding and talking to the horses. After years of listening to his father's fulminations, they scarcely made an impression on him.

Forseus stalked into the house, threw his coat, hat and quirt on the hall table and bellowed for his butler.

"Bring me some kvass into the study," he instructed grimly. "Leave the door open," he ordered as the butler set the pitcher of kvass before his master and retreated from the room.

For perhaps forty-five minutes Forseus sat sunk deeply in his leather chair, drinking steadily, his scowling, beady eyes trained on the hallway.

The object of this vigil finally opened the front door and walked into the hall. Alisa's eyes widened with alarm immediately she spied the coat and hat on the table in the center of the foyer. A startled catch of breath froze in her throat as an ominously calm voice spoke from the study.

"Out for a stroll in the spring air, Mrs. Forseus?" her husband inquired smoothly as his eyes flicked shrewdly over Alisa's figure, observantly taking in every detail of her ensemble. He hadn't amassed a fortune as a merchant because of a lack of perspicuity and at once noticed the rumpled skirt of the dress and the damp hem and slippers.

"Down by the river, my dear?" he questioned suspiciously. "Rather a long way from the house, isn't it?"

Alisa stood frozen in her tracks. The unexpected arrival was quite out of character for the punctilious, meticulous Mr. Forseus. Her mind rushed through a hundred excuses, none suitable, which might allay the sinister direction of her husband's inquiries.

"Yes," she flushed helplessly, unable to present a calm facade with the rising terror in her soul.

"Yes?" he repeated softly, his anger flaring higher as fanatic jealousy displaced reason. Forseus had wanted Alisa as a collector might want a fine painting, in order to possess it. She was a showpiece, another possession to be flaunted and displayed as further indication of his wealth, but not valued more highly than any other representation of his fortune, no more than his blooded stallion or his antique carpets or his gun collection.

He had also wanted her, to demonstrate to the world that by virtue of his fortune, he was now august enough to marry into the gentry. He had also coveted the young girl because his flagging sex drive at sixty-one had required more and more stimulation, and young virgins were an obsession with him. After the novelty of the first few months of marriage had worn off, however, even Alisa's young, tender body was no longer enough to rouse his ardor.

Mr. Forseus had left her alone at that point, finding stimulation in the brothels catering to deviates who sought young girls. But even those had failed to satisfy him of late. Quite by accident, in a drunken rage, three weeks ago, he had struck out in anger at Alisa and was astonished to discover that beating her had stimulated him sexually. Not sufficiently to consummate the act, but it become satisfaction in itself.

"Perhaps, Mrs. Forseus," her husband suggested smoothly, raising his obese bulk from the deep chair with some difficulty, "you would accompany me on a stroll, since you seem to enjoy the out-of-doors so much."

He walked up to Alisa, still frozen in her tracks, gripped her arm below the elbow in an iron grasp and steered the frightened Alisa out into the waning afternoon sunlight.

He forced her in the direction of the barnyard, relentlessly keeping up a trivial chatter that grated on Alisa's raw nerves and tremulous fears. Opening the door of a shed with a key he kept on a chain at his waist, Forseus pushed her inside the empty granary and shut the heavy door.

"Now, then, Mrs. Forseus," he breathed with a fanatic gleam in his eyes as he stripped off his coat and rolled up his sleeves, "we might discuss where you were this afternoon."

Reaching out to a hook on the wall, he took down a length of rope, tied a knot slowly and carefully on one end, let the knot drop to the floor, and wrapped the excess length around his hand.

"Now, my dear, we begin. Where were you?" He swung the rope sharply and caught Alisa on her shoulder. She shuddered from the pain, but spoke not a word, nor would she look at him.

"Come, dear, lost your tongue?" he sneered coldly, lashing out again and striking Alisa viciously across her breasts. The strength of the blow dropped Alisa to her knees. God help me, she prayed silently, for she didn't dare tell him the truth. He would certainly kill her then. If she could just tolerate the torture, steel herself to keep from screaming in agony, perhaps, merciful God, perhaps, after a time, she would be lucky enough to faint.

Ten minutes later, Forseus was breathing hard and just about to cease, when Alisa lost consciousness and sank gratefully to the floor and the beckoning solace of a black oblivion.

After rolling down his sleeves, wiping his perspiring face with a silk handkerchief and carefully adjusting his suit coat on his shoulders, Forseus quietly walked out of the shed and locked the door behind him.

Much later that evening after explaining to a suspicious and distrustful Maria that Alisa had gone to Viipuri shortly before sunset, he ordered a tray of food and a glass of wine brought to him in his study.

When the house had quieted sufficiently and it appeared all occupants were sleeping, Valdemar Forseus carefully maneuvered his way through the moonlit shadows of the barnyard, unlocked the shed door and deposited the tray on the floor beside his still unconscious wife.

Before departing, he drew a small vial from his waistcoat pocket and poured half the contents into the glass of wine.

VII
THE NECESSARY OPTION

Alisa woke in the early hours of morning and lay for a moment with her eyes still closed, flooded with a hopeless, bottomless despair; overwhelming—she could almost taste it. Her eyelids blinked open; she saw the knotted rope hanging back again on its hook on the wall and instantly renewed terror gripped her mind, tightened her stomach. Her one brief chance for happiness was gone. Sent away by her own words. Any future offered only terror and abject misery. She felt completely empty of hope.

She felt extremely weak and when she moved her head a sharp pain began to throb in her temple. Seeing the tray before her, Alisa bent to soothe her parched, dry throat with the contents of the wine glass, but the food remained untouched.

Almost immediately a vast drowsiness overcame her, but Alisa thought this the natural result of her battered and fatigued body requiring needed rest. The violet eyes dropped shut and her breathing slowed into the labored cadence of a heavily drugged repose.

Maria hadn't believed Forseus' lies for one minute and had solicited Arni's assistance in trying to find Alisa. Rakeli would not be able to long allay the growing fears of Katelina.

Early next morning, returning surreptitiously up

the servants' back stairway, Arni informed Maria of his findings. He had seen Forseus as he emerged from the house at dawn and watched him go directly to the shed, enter the building and remain inside briefly. On re-emerging, Forseus had carefully re-locked the door, bidden a stable boy saddle his horse and left for Viipuri. Arni had discovered the destination upon questioning the lad.

Peering through one of the cracks in the log structure of the shed, Arni distinguished the body of Alisa lying on the floor apparently asleep. When Maria was informed, her alarm mounted.

"What are we to do? He's beaten her again, you can be sure." Nothing went unseen or undetected by a personal maid who was also a loyal friend.

"We must get her out. Mistress Alisa has been wanting to leave. We can't wait any longer. Dare we steal some of Forseus' horses and make our escape while he is in Viipuri?"

"I don't know," Arni replied cautiously, "Forseus' arm is long and his money can buy much. I think we should appeal to Prince Kuzan. He is much more powerful than Forseus. He could protect Alisa where our poor credit could not."

Maria, Arni, and Rakeli, Alisa's old servants from her parents' home, had protected and aided Alisa as best they could in the years since she had been forced to marry Forseus; carefully concealing their loyalties for fear of Forseus dismissing them, they had been able to smooth some of the sorrow of her existence.

They were all very aware of her relationship with Prince Kuzan since Maria had insisted Arni follow Alisa that morning when the carriage had come from

Prince Kuzan, to insure their mistress was in no danger. After viewing the tender reconciliation in the meadow, Arni assured Maria that the Prince was not a dangerous villain intent on harming Alisa. On the contrary, he had brought an obvious ecstatic happiness to their young mistress, and her faithful servants were silently pleased to see Alisa singing again after years of quiet, hopeless despair.

If the question of morals were to be raised, the inhuman marriage forced on the young fifteen-year-old girl they loved was the most immoral of acts in their minds. That union was a travesty of the bonds of marriage, obscene and repulsive.

"You're right, Arni!" Maria exclaimed with renewed hope. "Go quickly and tell Prince Kuzan. He won't let our Alisa be hurt!"

Racing down the back stairs and out to the stables, Arni saddled one of Forseus' swiftest horses and was galloping down the long driveway in less than five minutes.

That same morning, Prince Kuzan was being dressed for his return to the city. He was still in a black fury, kicking furniture about, cursing loud and long in three languages, with a fluency that amazed even Yukko, abusing his steward and any other servant who was unfortunate enough to come within his line of vision.

Nikki's troopers who had accompanied him out to his hunting lodge approximately three weeks ago were mounted in the courtyard, nervously eyeing each other and hoping Prince Kuzan's rage did not descend on their heads.

For the last twenty minutes as their horses restive-

ly sidled and figeted beneath them, a steady stream
of explosive invective had been issuing from the open
windows of the lodge. Initially, the series of vitupera-
tive sounds made themselves heard from the second
floor, and presently the main floor rang with violent,
verbal denunciations as Nikki descended to spread
his wrath democratically on breakfast, butler, cook
and steward. The coffee was too hot, the eggs were
too cold, the butler didn't pour the brandy rapidly
enough—the arrangement of luggage in the front
hall grossly offended him, so the poor steward was
frantically having footmen dispatching the offending
luggage out of sight of their master. It was quickly
loaded into the waiting wagon and sent out of view
around the corner of the building.

Ten minutes more and three healthy bumpers of
brandy later, Nikki emerged from the front entrance
and critically surveyed his troop now drawn up in
parade-ground precision. Even the careful scrutiny
found nothing to criticize. The Prince threw himself
into the saddle and swept one more glance round his
familiar environs. Each vista only served to further
remind him of Alisa. We walked there. We sat down
there. Alisa admired those flower beds. I showered
her in rose petals from that climbing rambler. The
sun was warm on their bodies that day. Damn her
voluptuous memory! Well, that's what it was—a
memory now, nothing more! he irritably reminded
himself.

The black bulk of his favorite horse, Koli, was
comfortingly familiar beneath the saddle. Nikki
made a soft clicking noise with his tongue and Koli
swung his ears back, anticipating his master's command. Nikki's grip relaxed on the reins and he

moved his horse forward at a slow walk. There was no shouted command. A slight sigh was heard, a passing zephyr as the troopers took a breath of relief. They were on their way at last! Saddles groaned as men gripped harder with their knees.

Nikki could hear the harnesses of his men's mounts jingle behind him and the pad of hooves on the soft dirt of the road. The troop traveled slowly in the warm air of the spring morning, following the road that curved languidly over pine and birch-clad hills and valleys, traversing the vast Kuzan estate.

Nikki's thoughts were on Alisa. After three bottles of brandy, after a restless, tormented night of little sleep, after relentlessly reminding himself that he was a fool—after all that—he wanted her still and that insistent feeling could not be dismissed.

Within twenty minutes the southern border of his hunting reserve was crossed. He must force thoughts of Alisa from his mind. Too much mental recrimination was debilitating. The past was gone. Their brief affair was over. Nikki gently spurred his horse to a trot. With the trot, the sound of metal harness jingling intensified and softly resounded in the quiet morning air. As Nikki nudged Koli gently with his knees, they increased to a canter. Seconds later, feeling only the lightest of pressure from Nikki's legs, the black stallion snorted, changed his pace with that faint encouragement from his rider, and the troop was in full gallop. Nikki surveyed the road ahead. He began to visibly relax as the comfortable rhythm of a familiar horse, the warm spring air and the exhilaration and pleasure a full-out gallop always evoked, now soothed his churlish temper. In seven hours of hard riding they would be in Petersburg.

Arni had ridden cross country to the hunting lodge only to discover that the Prince had left for Petersburg thirty minutes before. Lashing his horse, Arni continued in frantic pursuit of the Prince. He couldn't hope to overtake Prince Kuzan with that great a head start unless he cut over the fields and through the forests. With luck, perhaps he could do it. Arni dug his spurs into Forseus' bay mare. The horse leapt the first fence and charged across the ploughed field.

As Nikki's troop was riding in correct position, following the Prince's blooded stallion, a rider became visible, galloping diagonally across their line of vision from east to west. They all granted he must be a fine rider to be forcing his mount that recklessly across that uneven field. Soon, he could be heard shouting something, wildly waving his arms, but the message was lost in the morning breeze. As the man galloped hell-for-leather directly toward them, Nikki drew to a halt. Arni thundered up, sawed his horse to a rearing stop before Nikki who was firmly keeping his skitterish animal in check before the flailing hoofs of the rearing horse, and gasped out his message, "Alisa's in danger! Forseus has beaten her and locked her in the shed! She appears unconscious and—"

Arni's sentence was left hanging in the air as Nikki savagely swung his horse around and charged back past the halted ranks of his troopers. He waved his sergeant to give orders to follow.

There was no time for speculation; little enough time for thought. Alisa was in danger, and no doubt because of him.

Within seconds the troop was once again in full gallop. Nikki forced the huge black hard, pressing him furiously.

Damn sadistic misogynist! He'd break Forseus' neck with his bare hands! Beaten her again, had he? It would be the last beating that old reprobate would ever administer! He'd see him burn in Hell!

Arni had kept pace with Nikki. Nikki kneed Koli alongside the groom and shouted, "How long ago did you leave her?"

"About forty minutes ago!" Arni yelled in reply.

Nikki prayed he wasn't too late. All his frustrated fury of the morning had a new outlet—Valdemar Forseus!

Koli was tired by the time Forseus' driveway was in sight, his mouth foaming, his flanks running with sweat. Nikki kept him at a gallop up the long driveway. Nearing the main house, Nikki snatched the pistol from his saddle holster and twenty troopers followed suit. He spun Koli sideways, reining hard to ease around the east wall of the house and rode headlong into the stable yard, glanced briefly around the outbuildings, spied the shed and hauled his stallion to a stop in front of the building.

Jumping down, he tossed his pistol aside and flung his huge frame against the locked door and both hinges shattered at the violent impact. Two of his men who had dashed to his assistance lifted the door away.

In the dim light of the empty room Nikki saw Alisa's figure lying motionless, her tattered clothing scarcely covering her bruised and torn flesh. Rapidly divesting himself of his braided tunic, he wrapped

Alisa gently in the garment and gathered her from the dirty floor into his arms.

She was so still! My God! had Forseus killed her this time? He carefully scanned the pale face so close to his and was relieved to see faint color on her cheeks. Walking outside, he carefully laid her on the ground on a blanket hastily retrieved from a haversack, covered her lightly with another blanket and began snapping orders.

"Find Forseus for me! I want that foul monster dragged out from wherever he is. Fetch some brandy for the lady! I want some lint and warm water! Immediately!"

Everyone scattered to obey his commands.

Arni was kneeling at his mistress's side, tears of rage in his eyes. Then he peered at her more closely, "I believe she's been drugged, Prince," he cried.

Nikki leaned over the slight, almost still form and felt for a pulse. Slowly he pulled her eyelids back to reveal red vacant eyes. Carefully closing the lids once more he nodded agreement. "You're right. We must have her away from that fiend. You were right to come for me."

"What can we do?" Arni asked, terrified.

"Find her daughter and her maidservants." Nikki was aware of Alisa's affection for her old servants. And certainly Arni's loyalty must be rewarded with safety from Forseus' wrath. "Do you wish to accompany your mistress?"

"I go where Miss Alisa goes," Arni said gravely. "I promised her father."

"Very well, assemble those servants who wish to come with us, her daughter and a change of clothing for Alisa. Take nothing more from this barbarous pig Forseus. After I've dealt with him we'll leave."

Maria came to Alisa within minutes with warm water to bathe her face, but the drugged woman did not respond and could accept no brandy.

The troopers' careful searching turned up no master of the house. Frightened servants explained that he and the son had ridden into Viipuri early that morning.

"As well," Nikki muttered grimly. His father would not have appreciated Nikki murdering a neighbor.

Alisa was placed in Nikki's arms once he mounted, and the cavalcade slowly retraced the route of its headlong chase. Arni held Katelina, while Maria and Rakeli rode behind two sergeants. Returning within the hour to the Petersburg road, the troop continued to the first post stop where Nikki's luggage wagon and carriage had been left instructions to wait. The servants, Katelina and Alisa were placed into Nikki's beautifully sprung landau and continued the journey south.

Aleksei greeted the strange group of guests late that afternoon when they and Nikki entered the town palace of pink Finnish and Siberian marble, situated just east of the Hermitage on Millionnaya, the most genteel street of old Petersburg. The serene classical palace facing the Neva was built between 1768 and 1785 as a present from the Empress Catherine II to her favorite Platon Kuzan.

A doctor was immediately called to Alisa's bedside and pronounced her out of danger. The dose of laudanum had been powerful but not fatal. For two days and nights Nikki kept servants round the clock at Alisa's bedside to monitor her needs as she drifted between sleeping and waking. On the morning of the third day when he checked in to see what her condition was, Alisa was reclining comfortably against numerous lace-trimmed pillows, totally awake.

"You're looking much better this morning." Nikki smiled warmly in greeting. "For the past few days it's been like having the sleeping beauty in our midst."

"I must thank you for rescuing me in such a fairy tale fashion," Alisa smiled gravely in return. "Maria told me everything. I'd despaired of surviving Mr. Forseus' last tantrum." Tears came to her eyes. Nikki knelt by her bedside and brushed them away.

To Nikki's insistent questioning Alisa related the proceedings after she had arrived home to find Mr. Forseus there. Nikki paced the room as she told him of her beating, of finally becoming unconscious. Murderous thoughts again sprang to his mind. Would he ever be able to take revenge on the bastard?

"He'll never again dare to touch you, by God," Nikki said grimly as Alisa finished her story. Then once more he went to her and took her hand. "You're safe here, with me."

"Oh, but I can't accept your hospitality for long. Surely, your parents won't like strangers in their home."

Not wishing to enter into that argument again, Nikki temporized placatingly, "You're not quite yourself, yet, so please accept my hospitality, at least temporarily, and as for my mother and father, they haven't entered this threshold in over three years, much preferring the air of the country. So rest assured, you'll not be disturbed.

"Now please, ask for anything you require and I hope your health soon returns, although you're looking remarkably fit this morning," he added with a languid smile. "Perhaps you could join me for dinner this evening. Now, I must be off briefly for regimental duties. Au revoir."

"Au revoir, and thank you again. I hope I'll be able to repay you someday."

"You shall, dear, you shall," Nikki reflected as he strode down the hall resplendent in full regimentals, the silver braid brilliant against the white superfine tunic, his dark hair still damp from his bath and curling at the nape of his neck over the stiff silver-embellished collar. With an uncharacteristic flash of romantic sympathy, he had not only refrained from touching the beautiful, warm, sleeping woman, so inviting in her helpless vulnerability, but had, more remarkably, eschewed other women in the last three days. No gypsies on the Islands, no Countess, no ballet dancers. With a curious whimsy, the Prince rather fancied waiting for the sleeping lady. He hadn't realized he had such high-minded instincts but it wasn't all earnest moral principles, for he had spent a lot of time in taking cold baths, and chastising himself for acting in this most ridiculous manner.

Nikki was in charity with the world and in such superb spirits that morning that even an insistent note from his mistress, Countess Amalienborg, greeting him at breakfast did not deter his fine humor. Sophie had apparently heard of his house guest (gossip travels fast below stairs) and had requested his company at a small card party that evening. He scrawled a short acceptance across the bottom of her perfumed stationery and dispatched the message by footman.

Just as well, he reflected, Countess Amalienborg had been an enduring mistress over almost two years now, notwithstanding Nikki's occasional short flings with an actress or gypsy. However he had become faintly tired of Sophie's proprietary airs in public lately. Tonight would be an ideal opportunity to courteously break off their longstanding friendship. A skilled lover, Sophie had served well in the past as a palliative to his boredom when he craved extraordinary acrobatics in bed. She was always successful in bringing his blood up, although he thought her the lowest kind of bitch, for she'd do anything to oblige him. Sometimes Sophie disgusted him, but then there were other times when he didn't care if he lived or died and on those occasions he surpassed even Sophie's audacity in bed.

But lately, even her practised accomplishments were palling. A bank draft or jewels? Which would she prefer as a parting token. Out of innate laziness and indifference, he decided on the bank draft, called Ivan in and was assured the bank draft would be on his dressing table before dinner tonight.

"Thank you, Ivan, you're ever efficient."

Deferentially, Ivan inquired of his well-disposed employer so obviously in buoyant spirits this morning, "Did you enjoy the art catalogues you requested?"

"Immensely, Ivan, immensely! You don't know what pleasure they brought me," Nikki chuckled.

Puzzled, but cheered at his master's new interest in art, Ivan bowed himself out of the breakfast room.

Could one wonder at the cause of Prince Kuzan's enormous good humor? He had had his way after all. The object of his amorous interest, but recently outside his grasp, was now ensconced in a splendid gilt bed a mere few feet from his suite next door, and in addition, supremely grateful for his efforts on her behalf. So very convenient.

Nikki positively glided through the onerous, petty details of regimental paper work necessary to his position that fine early spring morning. Within the hour he had dispatched these trivia and had returned home only to find that Alisa was dozing once more. Not an impatient man, under the circumstances (he had all the time in the world), Nikki let Alisa sleep quite peacefully most of the day.

Sending a note round in the late afternoon he inquired if she had any preferences for dinner and informed her he would await her company in the drawing room at seven.

Nikki, elegantly attired in black evening dress and white satin waistcoat, relaxed before the open window on a large tapestry settee, one foot in its patent evening pump resting on the window sill, and slowly sipped a fine Madeira. Seeing him sitting there, all well-bred grace, one lost sight of the brute power beneath the silken raiment unless one paused to note the width of the shoulder or the thickness of wrist, unless one marked the thigh muscles flexing on the leg so casually at ease on the sill.

He turned his head at the sound of the door and automatically came to his feet, advanced across the enormous parquet floor with his customary poise and gave Alisa an elegant bow.

"My lady," he said very formally, while smiling

down at her in a most distracting fashion from under those heavy brows, "please join me in a Madeira before we dine. The weather is quite exceptional and I have been enjoying the prospect of the Neva across the quay."

Alisa was dressed in her only ensemble.

"I'm afraid I'm not adequately dressed for dinner," she stammered slightly, overawed by the magnificent rococo room, resplendent with gilt, putti, stuccoed reliefs and real Bouchers and Fragonards, as well as by Nikki's casual grace and the distinct, overt difference between the unsophisticated, natural man she had known in the country and this supremely dégagé courtier so at ease in this enormous palace, wearing his luxurious attire carelessly, as though being point-de-vice was as comfortable as old slippers. She felt like the proverbial country mouse.

"You're ever the epitome of beauty, my dear," Nikki amiably replied in a smooth drawl. He could sense she was embarrassed at her lack of elegant dress, was himself so used to dressing for dinner he hadn't considered the awkwardness it might cause Alisa. He observed to himself that he would put her wardrobe to rights immediately, and then attempted to placate her embarrassment by apologizing, "Forgive me for dressing so conspicuously, but I've an engagement after dinner I must attend, hence this attire." Alisa was surprised to feel a strange and uncomfortable jealousy at his remark.

"Come sit by me and we'll enjoy the saffron sunset. You look the picture of health once again."

Maria had bathed Alisa and washed her magnificent hair; the vibrant recuperative powers of youth had quickly restored her peaches and cream complexion and she did indeed look refreshingly glowing.

"Thank you, I feel very well."

Nikki chatted casually, never referring to anything personal, putting Alisa completely at ease, teasing and entertaining her with the trivial, innocuous gossip about town. Zacouska preceded the dinner and Nikki directed Alisa to a small anteroom where a table was spread with caviar, cheese, rusks, sardines, oysters, olives, liqueurs and vodka.

"I understand zacouska is becoming quite 'comme-il-faut' in France this year. We Russians have known for centuries that several glasses of liquor much improve that 'mauvais quart d'heure' which generally precedes European dinners. Do try one small glass of chilled vodka, my dear," and without waiting for an answer he proceeded to pour them both one.

"To your regained health." Nikki raised his glass in salute.

The dinner was superb; Nikki's French chef surpassed himself for his young master who so rarely dined in. Perhaps the new house guest would change the Prince's normal pattern, the chef reflected with a Gallic lift of his eyebrows. He would be able to serve his delectable coq au vin, his exquisite baba au rhum, his savory lobster bisque. Ah! vive la femme! he could display his skills again. Bah! he had become tired of only serving breakfasts at two in the afternoon.

Nikki came home quite late from Countess Amalienborg's card party, his brows drawn together in a lowering scowl. An evening's entertainment of charades and a bellowing Italian soprano had preceded the cards. By God! Sophie's amusements were banal. Needless to say, it had been quite late before he was able to affect a private conversation with Sophie. The amiable parting Nikki had envisioned had not been all that amiable. When he'd politely offered his adieux and his handsome bank draft, the Countess had bitterly and impertinently bearded him about his new mistress.

"Installed in the room next to yours, Nikki, I hear, and drugged when she was brought in," the countess had said maliciously. "Losing your touch, dear? Surely between your smooth tongue and big cock, you don't have to resort to force?"

"Don't be coarse, cherie," Nikki said flatly. Damn gossiping doctor, Nikki thought irritably, the news must be all over town by now. Normally he was immune to gossip concerning himself; however, he preferred not having Alisa's name bandied about.

"When I lose my touch, Sophie, dear, I'll let you know. Perhaps your husband and I will then be able to share a mutual interest in cards. Whist is all he's good for at present. I still endeavor to amuse myself in more active ways," Nikki murmured coldly.

"With your 'active' ways, next thing you know your little mistress will be handing you another brat," she sneered.

"Perhaps," he replied, quietly endeavoring to hold himself in check when he was sorely tempted to strike Sophie's spiteful mouth.

"Perhaps? Is that all you can say? You, who are near to setting some kind of record for bastards?"

"Well," Nikki continued, "these things are rather inevitable. Not every woman is in such an enviable position as you, dear, who can bed without restraint and never experience a qualm, thanks to your barren womb."

"No doubt your newest trollop is not so disposed and will soon present you with the unwelcome news of impending fatherhood yet again!" Sophie taunted.

"Whether that comes to pass or no, I fail to see how my affairs are any concern of yours," Nikki drawled, again trying to keep his anger in check.

Seeing she had pushed the quick-tempered Prince too far, and averse to losing such an accomplished bed-partner, the world-wise Sophie sensibly changed her tack.

"Stay the night, Nikki," she breathed softly, "I haven't seen you in weeks."

Glancing at his gold and champlevé enamel wrist watch, he absently toyed with the unusual alarum mechanism which upon release reminded its wearer of the hour by tapping the wrist.

"Not tonight, Sophie," he said politely.

"I don't suppose you'd say no if your newest bed warmer asked you," Sophie snapped, her brief attempt at cajolery vanishing.

The Prince raised his eyes from his timepiece and there was a glint in his eye, "That, my dear, is quite another matter."

"You rude, odious wretch!" the Countess spat.

He only laughed. "As you very well know from past experience, Sophie, my pet." Bowing infinitesimally from the waist he left the scented boudoir.

The irritating Countess had taken some of the edge from his good spirits. Arriving home, Nikki waved off the solicitous butler, let himself into his study and relaxed over several brandies, allowing the annoyance of Sophie's impertinence to wash away.

An hour later Nikki was comfortably soothed. The presence of Alisa in his own home was a powerful distraction. There might be some problems with that spiteful ex-mistress, he thought. But to hell with the problems; all he could think of was the woman upstairs; the problems could wait.

He rose from the chair near the window and slowly walked up the wide marble staircase. A small gas lamp was burning low near Alisa's bed. Nikki stood a long time and watched Alisa peacefully sleeping; she was so fragile, her breasts rising and falling gently beneath her silk negligee, long lashes resting on soft white cheeks, one arm thrown above her head, the red-gold hair like liquid copper in the mellow light, in casual disarray on the satin pillow case. Unbuttoning the silver buttons of the evening jacket, Nikki dropped it on the floor at his feet. He removed his clothes slowly, devouring her with his gaze. When he deliberately dropped his black patent shoe on the floor her eyes opened instantly.

She saw him in the soft glow cast by the lamp and for a second glimpsed the brief bewilderment of his emotions. The look was gone in a flash and the bed dipped as his weight came down on it. His head lowered and parted lips moved over hers gently, forcing her mouth open, slowly, languorously, teasing her senses, as his hands ran over her body and lifted her gown.

He could feel her beginning to respond to him. Slowly he undid the ribbons of her silk gown, and pulled it from her shoulders. He touched the hem and raised it past her softest place. Finally, her arms pulled him to her and he knew the time for their reunion of love had come.

He took her time after time that night, wanting her to need him, wanting her to cry for him, reassuring himself that she really was his, that he had her in his bed, in his house, at his demand. Perplexing emotions raced through his subconscious. He felt a need for reaffirmation of his dominant role in their relationship. A role most gratifying when she was pleading for him to grant her release in exquisite pleasure. Alisa loved him that night hopelessly, incoherently, as again and again he wakened her body to new heights of pleasure. Each touch made her feel her body for the first time as if in a new birth. And finally he filled her with all the love and warm sweetness which he had denied himself these past days.

They fell asleep coiled around each other, arms and legs entwined, the warmth of her breath on his chest, the powerful beat of his heart beneath her ear.

VIII
THE RECALCITRANT MISTRESS

Early the next morning, the bedroom door burst open and one small curly-mopped, red-gold head popped into sight, babbling excitedly in Finnish. "Momma, Momma, Look what Uncle Nikki bought—" she stopped abruptly, broke off and immediately switched effortlessly into French.

"Uncle Nikki!" she let out a squeal of delight when she spied him lying in bed next to her mother.

Katelina tightly clutched a large china doll with long flowing blonde hair in her chubby arms and flew across the marble floor, her splendid, new velvet robe and dimity nightgown streaming out behind in her impetuous dash toward the huge, gilded four-poster bed majestically installed on a dais over which four flying cupids suspended a gold and mother-of-pearl half shell. Katelina was an engaging and lively child, a beautiful little girl, with all of her mother's good looks and devastating charm.

Scrambling into bed like a frisky, rambunctious puppy, she promptly discarded her china doll and threw her plump arms around Nikki's neck, excitedly entreating, "Will you take Rakeli and me to the toyshop again today? Please, please!" she implored, her dark eyes wide with hope and expectation.

The Prince smiled amiably at the small girl clutching him and said, "You may speak Finnish to me, my pet, I too have a Finnish mother." (He had

unwittingly spoken French to Katelina the last few
days and she had responded in kind.)

In the days Alisa had been ill and recuperating,
Nikki had spent a great deal of time with Katelina.
The first time he had stood in Alisa's room and seen
the young child crying pitifully, it took several
seconds for the tableau to register as reality. A young
child crying sorrowfully in his house was so alien
that his reaction was delayed. Nikki hadn't talked to
a small child or been within touching distance of
one in years. Having heard the wailing for over an
hour since his return that first afternoon, and sur-
mising that the nanny and maid were unable to stop
the childish distress, Nikki decided to lend a hand
in an attempt to still the wailing.

Nikki was by nature kind and cheerful, as any of
his friends would agree, and altogether capable of
tenderness and gentleness as well, as any of his
lovers would concur. Nikki's phenomenal success
with women was not due solely to his remarkable
handsomeness and princely fortune, although, in
the glittering society in which he moved, those were
often attributes enough. His conquests were due as
much, if not more, to his charm, his ability to give a
woman pleasure in the drawing room as well as in
bed. He could be gay, jesting, tender, gentle, interested and concerned, as the mood moved him and
this charm was marshalled in an effort to sooth
Katelina's fear, while at the same time making his
beautiful mistress more able to recover from her
overdose of laudanum.

Nikki had offered adventures to the young child
which soon took her mind off her fears. Katelina
almost immediately adopted Nikki as a kind of vice-

uncle and behaved toward him with an uninhibited and sometimes embarrassing childish affection.

Turning quickly to her mother, as if it was the most natural sight in the world to see her with Uncle Nikki in bed and hardly pausing for a breath, Katelina rattled on, reverting back to Finnish, "Oh, Momma, the toy shop is just beautiful. Everything is most——" She stopped. "Rakeli said I shouldn't be so greedy, didn't you Rakeli?" she turned her wide eyes toward her nanny who had tarried doubt-fully by the door upon seeing Prince Kuzan. Katelina's brief regard for humble courtesies over, she rushed on breathlessly, "But Uncle Nikki said that I was a little princess and I could have any-thing I wanted. Didn't you, Uncle Nikki?" Katelina beamed widely into Nikki's amused countenance as she perched on his broad chest.

"That's right, moppet," said her benevolent "uncle."

"Oh, Uncle Nikki, could we *please* go again to-day, *please?*" she begged delightfully and gazed with pleading brown eyes into Nikki's face.

"Of course, dear, you shall have another doll if you like."

"Oh, Nikki, I would *much* rather have a train!"

Nikki's eyes twinkled gaily as he shot a sidelong look at Alisa, grinned faintly and said, "Already an independent young lady, not content to play with dolls. Very well, minx, the train it shall be," he finished indulgently.

"Oh, Momma, isn't Uncle Nikki *just* wonderful?" Katelina pronounced with all the uninhibited candor of her five years.

Nikki turned to glance wickedly at Alisa and

smirkingly asked, "Yes, Momma, aren't I *just* wonderful?"

"Say yes, Momma! Say yes!" Katelina insisted, bouncing with excitement and delight.

Before Alisa had to answer that awkward question, Katelina blithely continued her childish, gay chatter.

"Momma, I'm so *very* glad you're feeling better. Nikki said I must be *so* very quiet for *so* long. I'm glad I don't have to be quiet *anymore!*" she finished emphatically.

Unable to hold her youthful enthusiasm in check, she continued bouncing up and down as she inquired relentlessly, "When can we *go*, Uncle Nikki, when can we *go?*"

"After you eat breakfast and Rakeli dresses you," he answered patiently, "then we'll leave. Now go and get ready."

The volatile little body that gave every indication of a perpetual motion machine grabbed the doll, immediately slid off the bed and bounded across the large room. At the door, she paused, one hand in Rakeli's, one plump fist clutching the enormous doll by her blonde hair.

"May I have strawberries and cake again for breakfast? May I, may I, Nikki?" she entreated her new and generous uncle.

"Of course, dear, whatever you like."

"*When* can we leave?" she repeated again with the impatience of her five years.

"In about an hour." Nikki replied, then looking down at Alisa, warm, tousled and languid in bed beside him, he reconsidered. "Make it an hour and a half, Rakeli," he said matter of factly. The door shut behind the small whirlwind and Alisa remarked gratefully in a low, quiet voice, "Thank you for being so kind to Katelina while I was ill." Nikki took Alisa's hand in his and very simply replied, "You're welcome." He went on teasingly, with an affectionate grin, "I've had to entertain that little brat for three days while you have been lazing in bed. Rakeli was at her wit's end, with Katelina insisting on crying at your bedside and you still in a half-drugged state, unable to respond to her. Maria couldn't check the tears, either, so the task fell to Aleksei and me to devise some schemes to distract Katelina and keep her from disturbing you.

"We slid down the grand staircase on silver trays, dressed her as Empress in lace tablecloths (I was a reluctant Emperor, I might add, and Katelina manifested the true imperiousness of born royalty by ordering Aleksei and me about shamelessly), we sailed paper boats in the monteith bowls, I had the grooms bring the new kittens from the stables and Maria fetched her some new clothes from some children's modiste Ivan knew of."

Nikki was massaging Alisa's wrist absently with his thumb.

"Thank God, you began to feel yourself once again yesterday afternoon, because I'd taxed my ingenuity to its limits and had quite exhausted my meager repertoire of amusements for children. I'm afraid I'm woefully out of practice. My memories of childish pleasures are extremely dim, overborne, no doubt, by the myriad and vastly more pleasurable adult pastimes. I'm happy to see," Nikki said with a flame of passion kindling in his golden eyes, as he turned to her, "that you have been restored to vibrant, blooming health once again. I've sorely missed your warmth these last few days.

"You are my delectable, enchanting, enticing bed-warmer," Nikki said with a natural proprietary air, as he ran his finger up her bare arm. "You suit me admirably," his husky voice added.

Alisa felt panic rise within her at his words. What plot had her untutored emotions gotten her into? Each touch, each caress seemed yet another strand woven in the net that was slowly but inexorably enveloping her. She felt faint with helplessness at her situation, but at the same time she was still heavy with love.

Nikki was caressing her now with both hands, slowly running his fingers down her soft curves. He bent his head and touched her warm, inviting lips. Alisa had no further time to reflect as her passions rose to meet his demands.

Sometime later, Nikki rose from the rumpled bed.

"We must hurry and dress if we hope to meet Katelina's schedule." Saying this he turned and walked stark naked with a most unaffected composure to the door of the adjoining dressing room. Pausing in the open doorway, he reached one long arm out for the bell pull, remarking, "I'll ring for the servants to draw your bath water. I hope roisterous Rubenesque nymphs and black onyx turkish sunken tubs don't offend you, but our ancestor Platon was not distinguished for his refinement and leaned rather toward an erotic purism." Neither expecting nor waiting for an answer Nikki shouted for his valet and strode out of the room.

Fifteen minutes later Nikki sauntered back in,

the valet bustling after, easing a crisp white shirt onto the muscular shoulders.

Alisa swiftly pulled up the sheet and covered her shoulders.

"Aren't you out of bed yet? Tut, tut, dear, Katelina will be fidgeting."

"I know. I'll get up directly. The bed felt so comfortable."

"You'll like the toy shop. They have the best selection in the city," and as the valet hovered about, buttoning the gold shirt studs, adjusting the turquoise cuff links, straightening the soft collar to the right degree of perfection, Nikki carried on an easy conversation explaining the direction of the establishment where Katelina's train was to be found, noting the beautiful day, discoursing convivially of Katelina's impetuous charm, until he suddenly realized Alisa's responses to these mundane observations were rather stilted. Nikki glanced over to the bed and saw an obviously distressed and embarrassed figure clutching the bed linen to her chin.

"That will be all, Georgi," he crisply dismissed the valet.

"Yes, my Prince," said the diminutive little man and quickly left the room.

Walking over to the bed, Nikki leaned over and kissed Alisa's cheek. "Forgive me. I didn't realize Georgi disturbed you."

"It's silly, I'm sure, but, well . . . I'm not used to having a manservant in my bedroom."

"Of course, dear. I should have considered. I'll dress myself from now on."

"Oh, no! I don't want to cause trouble for your

valet . . . and . . . how will you manage?" Alisa
stammered apologetically.

"Nonsense! Georgi will find his extra leisure no
hardship, I assure you, and I'm perfectly capable of
dressing myself. Men don't have all those frippery
buttons and laces women do. Now come, my sweet,
into your bath or Katelina will complain vehemently
at the delay. I'll go and explain to Georgi."

In an incredibly short time Nikki returned through
the dressing room doorway extremely well-turned
out as usual, in a fastidiously tailored coffee brown
frock coat of exquisite fit across his broad shoulders,
a finely tucked open-neck lawn shirt, brown brocade
waistcoat and pale biscuit trousers resting the required bare half inch from the ground over his
brown kid half boots.

Alisa was being dressed by Maria while Katelina
sat upon a tufted hassock watching with a very unusual and quiet patience. Alisa was turned out in
her only dress, which had been miraculously washed
and pressed overnight; a navy and green stripe silk
serge skirt and a green silk blouse clasped high under her neck with a cameo brooch. Nikki had instructed Maria to find a wrap in his mother's wardrobe and Maria was now arranging the soft folds of
a navy blue pelisse edged in silk braid over the
voluminous skirt.

Alisa's golden coppery hair had been arranged
simply, pulled back and up on top of her head, long
curls falling down her back, soft tendrils framing her
delicate face. Studying Alisa critically from head to
foot, Nikki said, "We must see to some clothes for
you, Alisa. I'm afraid the clothes left in mother's
room are sadly out of date. However, it will do. And

you, moppet, look quite elegant," he grinned as
Katelina jumped from her seat upon hearing Nikki
speak and rushed toward him. Maria had found on
her shopping expedition a dress of white organza
with pale green ribbons that fit Katelina admirably
as well as a short green coat and an enormous pale
yellow straw sailor hat decorated with long, green
taffeta streamers.

"Shall we, ladies?" Nikki inquired with an elaborate flourish and Katelina tumbled out of the room
a full five yards in advance of Rakeli, who ran after
her impetuous young charge.

The landau, with its top down, stood ready outside the main entrance, its coachwork freshly bees-
waxed, its four horses so well groomed their gleaming chestnut coats seemed to have been brushed with
oil. After everyone was comfortably seated the
coachman, in his best livery of green velvet, set the
animals into a fashionable high-stepping trot.

It was impossible for Katelina to sit tamely on the
velvet upholstery. She hopped about asking questions, excitedly pointing out items that interested
her and demanding and getting most of Nikki's
attention. Alisa was pleased to see that adjusting to
a new environment was evidently not going to be a
problem for her daughter. With Katelina's natural
curiosity, vitality and open affectionate nature, each
new experience was avidly enjoyed. As Katelina's
father had studiously avoided her since her birth
five years ago, no emotional pangs of separation had
developed since leaving Viipuri.

Katelina had wrung a promise from Nikki to ride
to the Summer Gardens first and as they approached
the Gardens, the other occupants of fashionable car-

riages out to enjoy the balmy temperatures were astounded to see the city's most sought after bachelor riding with a beautiful young woman, a nanny and a child!

Two smartly uniformed Chevalier Gardes astride magnificent blacks rode up to the carriage as Rakeli and Katelina were disembarking to take in a short expedition to feed the swans. The coachman finished tying the horses to a hitching post and retired to the shade of a nearby tree.

Both officers bowed deeply from their saddles and the fair-haired young lieutenant remarked politely to Nikki, "Good morning, Nikki, I don't believe we've met your charming companion before."

"No, that's right, you haven't," Nikki replied rudely. "Now get about your business," he added discourteously and sketched them a brief salute. With no rebuke possible to that direct cut, they wheeled their horses and left, puzzled at his response.

"It looks like our Colonel has discovered a new bit of fluff he's jealously guarding," the young blond subaltern remarked to his companion with a chuckle as they continued their leisurely canter down the Admiralteski.

"Nikki in public with a child is enough to shock the most redoubtable aplomb. Do you think it's his?"

"Can't say. With that red hair, the little girl looks like her mother; not like Countess Souvanieff's last child that bore the stamp of Nikki Kuzan so blatantly it fair took your breath away."

As these speculations were being bandied about further down the avenue, Nikki and Alisa were interrupted once again by a passing horseman. Major

Cernov, riding up to the open carriage, doffed his hat in greeting. Nikki's face set into a scowl.

"So nice to see you *once again,* Mrs. Forseus," Cernov said pointedly with a lopsided grin, and his oriental eyes narrowed speculatively.

Alisa flushed hotly at the insinuating tone of the greeting and at the eyes that stripped her.

"Good morning," she returned coolly, angered at the bold scrutiny he was directing at her.

"Haven't seen you at the Yacht or Nobles' Clubs lately, Nikki. LaSalle Square and the Islands seem quite dull without you, but now I can see good reason for your absence."

"I didn't know my absences were noted with such assiduity," Nikki observed dryly.

"Come now, don't be so modest, Nikki; as you well know, your activities have been substantial material for on-dits and observation since you were a mere stripling."

"Surely people have better things to occupy their time than listen to absurd gossip. In point of fact, don't you have some more pressing business, Gregor? We wouldn't want to detain you," Nikki said brushing off yet another attempt at conversation.

"As you wish, Nikki. Your servant, Madame," Cernov said soothingly as he took the rather direct suggestion amiably. Taking a silk wipe from his sleeve, Cernov flicked an imaginary speck of dust from his spotless cavalry boots, pushed the kerchief back into his sleeve, so a few inches trailed elegantly below his silver-braided cuff, wheeled his horse to leave and winked at Nikki.

"If Tanya's pattern should re-occur, please inform me. I'd be interested in the merchandise."

"Don't get greedy, Cernov," Nikki quietly retorted.

The long flowing mustache only twitched as thin lips smiled faintly, "I'm a patient man, mon ami, no hurry." Cernov gently spurred his horse to a trot and disappeared into the stream of carriages and riders.

"What did that insolent cur mean by merchandise?" Alisa asked, knowing full well what he had meant, "And who is Tanya?"

"Don't get your temper up, dear. Tanya was an old friend and Cernov knows very well that you are under my protection, so he won't bother you, I'm sure."

"Under your protection?" Alisa sputtered, flushing vividly as the obvious and unmistakable clarity of his explanation struck her. Of course, she should have realized. How very stupid of her. The full implications of what the public reaction to her situation would be left her momentarily stunned, devoured with shame. She was exceedingly thankful, for the first time since her parents' death, that they *weren't* alive to see the terrible depths to which she had fallen, the sordid fate outlined for her.

All those years with that beast Forseus she had patiently waited until Katelina was older and had planned on leaving, having saved some money as she could, with the expectation of that flight. Now through nothing more than her own sensuous weakness in succumbing to the devastatingly charming advances of Prince Kuzan, she was deprived of even the comfortless life of Forseus' estate.

Irritated at the masterful certainty of Nikki's assumption and outraged to be treated once more like a piece of property, she coldly said, "I don't recall placing myself under your protection."

"Come now, love," Nikki said reasonably, "if you recall when I found you in that shed, your alternatives were surely limited; more severe beatings and possibly death if Forseus had continued drugging you. Hardly a choice of options, I should think. And consider it now," Nikki urged amiably, "plenty of advantages, especially if one has already shown a *decided* partiality for the man one has as protector. I'm not considered ungenerous and if you contrive to please me in the future as well as you have to this date, we shall deal together quite easily."

Alisa gasped indignantly, "I haven't any *decided* partiality for you, you arrogant lecher, and furthermore——"

Nikki interjected suavely, "Give me three minutes alone with you, my dear, and I feel sure I can restore my credit on that account."

Her eyes dropped shamefully before his candid regard, but she was angry enough to thrust aside the brief feeling of embarrassment, continuing belligerently, "Maria has some money of mine she brought with us."

"Not enough to buy you one decent gown, let alone support yourself, a child and three servants," Nikki disagreed bluntly with his typical disregard for tact.

"I'm relatively well educated, young and strong. I can obtain a position as governess," Alisa insisted heatedly.

"I agree in principle with your idea, but unfortunately, the pressures of existence in this world of travail serve to daunt the most optimistic hopes. For you the role of governess," the sneer in his voice was all too apparent, "is quite a pleasant conceit, my dear. You *will* forgive my speaking frankly, but I fear you are lacking in a sense of the realities of things.

"*If*—I say, *if*—any wife in her right mind would allow a provokingly beautiful young woman like yourself to enter her household, I would wager a small fortune, the master of that house would be sharing your bed within the week. Consider the folly of the notion, love. At least with me, there would be no indignant wife to throw you and your retinue out into the street when her husband's preferences became obvious. And since I have a rather intimate knowledge of many of these wives, I think my opinion is to be relied upon. And as your protector," he continued equably, "I, of course, feel an obligation to maintain your daughter and servants in luxurious comfort."

"I am not a plaything to be bought!" Alisa said feelingly.

"Ah, my dear, but you are. Confess, it is a woman's role; primarily a pretty plaything for a man's pleasure and then inexorably as night follows day— a mother. Those are the two roles a woman plays. It is preordained. Don't fight it," he said practically.

Alisa would have done anything, anything, she felt at that moment to wipe that detestable look of amused smugness from Nikki's face.

"Perhaps I'll take Cernov up on his offer after all," she said with the obvious intent to provoke. "Is he richer than you? I must weigh the advantages if I'm to make my way profitably in the demi-monde," she went on calculatingly. "Since I'm merely a plaything, it behooves me to turn a practical frame of mind to the role of demi-rep and sell myself for the highest price in money and rank obtainable. I have a certain refinement of background without the stench of the ghetto, which is surely worth a few roubles more, and I play the piano, though I must confess, with more skill than talent; of course, I embroider a fine stitch, hardly of interest in the boudoir, I fear. I dance rather gracefully, if you *will* pardon the immodesty of boasting; sketch and paint, am fluent in Latin, French, German, again, alas, of little consequence once the lights are out."

With an uncharitable pleasure Alisa noticed her words had the effect of erasing the objectionable look of smugness from Nikki's face, to be abruptly replaced by a glowering frown.

"Desist in the cataloguing, if you please," he broke in rudely and in a dangerously cold voice murmured, "Let us not cavil over trifles. You're staying with me." Alisa involuntarily quailed before the stark, open challenge in his eyes and her heart sank in a most unpleasant way.

"So my life is a trifle?" she whispered, trembling with a quiet inner violence.

"You misunderstand, my dear," the even voice explained with just a touch of impatience; "it's simply that I do not intend to enter into any senseless wrangles or debates over your attributes and the direction in which your favors are to be bestowed. Madame, you're to remain my mistress." His lips smiled faintly but the smile never reached his eyes.

Alisa closed her eyes momentarily as she reached the final point of renunciation of all the ideals of her youth. Then lifting her chin resolutely she said, sarcastically, "In that case, I suppose I must thank you for your generous hospitality."

"Not at all," Nikki replied. "I expect my generosity to be amply repaid."

Rakeli and Katelina returned at that moment to cut short the sharp retort Alisa was about to utter. They gaily jabbered on about the swans and flowers and statues as Nikki turned to speak to Alisa.

"We'll stop at Madame Vevay's. She isn't Worth, but since your wardrobe must be replenished immediately we'll settle for her." Alisa did not respond. Nikki informed the coachman of the direction and the horses broke into a canter.

Alisa coldly sat next to Nikki, her ankles crossed neatly, her hands folded together in her lap, and lapsed into an outraged, vengeful silence, answering only in curt monosyllables when he addressed her directly. After several rebuffs to his conversational sallies, Nikki leaned over and whispered teasingly into her ear, "Maybe Forseus wasn't crazy after all when he beat you. You're dreadfully provoking and singularly impertinent for a woman."

She shot him a look of black fury and hissed, "You have yet to see my full impertinence, sir."

"In that case, I look forward to the future with pleasant anticipation," Nikki retorted; and a level gaze of challenge issued from under half-lowered lids.

Rakeli and Katelina were so engrossed in their sightseeing that they were oblivious to the sotto voce contre-dit going on across from them.

Within minutes they were alighting before the fashionable facade of Madame Vevay. Nikki, in an agreeable mood, as he always was when he had his

own way, was all courtesy and easy manners as he
escorted them into the gilded establishment of the
haute couturiere of Petersburg, the interior in flattering emulation of Worth's in Paris, all green silk,
gold and mahogany.

Seeing the elegant equipage depositing its pas-
sengers, Madame Vevay came sweeping toward the
door with a finely controlled hauteur and was momentarily arrested in mid-glide when Prince Nikolai
Kuzan stepped through her delicately grilled plate
glass doors escorting a ravishing beauty, but most
startling and the object of Madame Vevay's rapt
amazement, pulling a young child in tow. The sight
was enough to stagger the most rigid demeanor, but
Madame Vevay, ever resourceful, rapidly regained
her composure and holding out both hands warmly
greeted the Prince and his party.

"Prince Kuzan!" she gushed, with an extremely
deferential familiarity, "So lovely to see you!"

"A pleasant morning to you, Madame Vevay.
May I present my—" he paused delicately, and
smiled faintly, "my—ah—cousin, unfortunately but
recently widowed, and her charming daughter." A
suitably grieved expression accompanied his mala-
pert lie concerning Alisa's "dead" husband.

Alisa flushed brightly pink to her ears and Katelina
bobbed a correct little bow as Nikki grinned broad-
ly. He was paying Alisa back for her challenge to
his authority and for her rudeness on the ride over
to the dress shop. Nikki was making certain her pos-
sibilities for finding work as a governess were abruptly dashed. Everyone would know within hours of
their leaving Madame Vevay's that Alisa was Nikki's
newest mistress. That delicate pause had peremptori-

ly put her in her place. Alisa realized this too. He is daring me, she thought, to contradict the implication, and what is more, he is quite prepared to be even more explicit if I dare. Her courage melted away and she prepared to be complaisant.

Madame Vevay was delighted at the prospect of dressing such a vivid beauty, a beauty enhanced by the fresh innocence Alisa wore without pretense. Maybe it was this tender youthfulness that appealed to Prince Kuzan's jaded palate. This mistress was scarcely more than a child herself. Her slender voluptuousness would set off Madame Vevay's most recherché creations and this "cousin's" status did not confine her to prim, demure fashions. Madame Vevay could already envision a use for that Byzantine tussah in her warehouse.

"I have a magnificent fabric that requires just such a striking beauty to do it justice," she cooed, and reflected silently, and just such a munificent benefactor to absorb the staggering cost of the rare fabric. What a delightful combination in these two splendid young creatures.

Katelina was tugging insistently at Nikki's hand, totally unconcerned with matters of fashion.

"Nikki, Nikki, *when* can I get my train? You promised!" she wailed, jumping up and down. Prince Kuzan, in a totally uncharacteristic move calculated to raise eyebrows and drop open the mouth of anyone privy to the scene, bent over kindly to the tugging and pleading little girl and in a soothing Finnish dialect quieted her tantrum.

Searching in his pocket, Nikki handed Katelina several silver roubles, stood upright and deposited a packet of roubles in Rakeli's hand.

"Now are you happy?" he asked the beaming young child. Then he gave instructions to Rakeli and explained, "If you're finished at the toy store early just have Feodor wait outside until we complete our purchases. Now have a good time. Feodor knows exactly where to go. Give your mother a kiss good-by, little brown eyes," he ordered softly.

The bouncing child threw her arms around her mother's waist and lifted her face for a kiss. Alisa smiled at her happy young daughter and bent to kiss her.

"Say thank you to Prince Kuzan," she admonished gently.

"*Thank you,* Uncle Nikki!" Katelina cried as she dashed toward the door, Rakeli in hot pursuit.

Uncle Nikki? That designation raised even Madame Vevay's unflappable eyebrows. Prince Kuzan had never publicly recognized any of his natural children. He was generous and thoughtful concerning their support, but did not acknowledge them, except monetarily, in any fashion whatsoever. His life-style, to this point, had not embraced the world of children. He simply moved in circles in which children were never seen or discussed.

His wasn't a malicious disregard, but rather a selfish indifference. Everyone in town was aware of the trust he had funded for Countess Souvanieff's last child. Bank clerks and servants were notorious gossips and no bit of scandal passed unnoticed below stairs.

So, to see the cold reserve, the unrufflable hauteur of Prince Kuzan yielding to a dynamo of childish enthusiasm was unprecedented. And he spoke Finnish to the little tyke in public; he had never even

deigned to speak Russian outside the barracks before, French being the exclusive language of society.
Surely this fresh young, dazzling matron at his side
must have some powerful attraction. Madame Vevay
was consumed with curiosity.

"If Madame will follow me, please," Madame
Vevay spoke graciously to Alisa, this obviously
clever woman who had managed to induce Nikolai
Kuzan to abandon the habits of a lifetime and actually appear solicitous in public to nothing less than a
pert child. Madame Vevay gestured toward an open
doorway into a private fitting salon.

But the imperturbable Prince showed no indication of politely accepting a dismissal from anyone.
Instead, he followed the two women at a leisurely
pace into the salon, seated himself comfortably in a
gilded brocade fauteuil, which creaked indignantly
under the impact of his weight, stretched his long
legs out before him, impeccably clad in biscuit
colored trousers and leaned back at ease. He looked
quite thoroughly at home in this elegant green and
gold showroom, as if he were frequently a visitor to
the inner sanctums of fashionable modistes, when,
in fact, Nikki normally waited, with impatient indifference outside in the anteroom while his mistresses selected their dresses, showing not the
slightest inclination to concern himself with their
purchases.

Madame Vevay, disconcerted at Prince Kuzan's
presence in the room, stammered in confusion, but
quickly recovered and enquired inquisitively, "Monsieur is interested in selecting the fabric and designs?"

"But, of course," Nikki replied blandly as though
this too were a perfectly normal practice of his. In

a pleasant tone he explained, "My 'cousin' and I don't believe unduly in the old-fashioned tradition of mourning so *I* don't want any somber black or gray crepes. Some vivid, bright colors, I think," he said consideringly flicking a leisurely glance up and down Alisa's body as she stood flushing angrily before him. With a bold crudeness he added quietly, "While the thought occurs to me, we'll order two dozen silk negligees, an assortment of colors and the usual lace and ribbon froufrous."

"Very good, Monsieur, two dozen it will be. If you will excuse me one moment I'll gather my designs and perhaps one or two dresses for Madame to try on for size."

Alisa, furiously embarrassed at Nikki's presence, after Madame Vevay left the room, hissed "I hope this charade is amusing you, Prince Kuzan!"

"You always amuse me, darling, in countless and delightful ways," he replied looking at her insolently from under half-lowered lids, his superb self-confidence evident in every word.

Madame Vevay bustled back into the room, her arms full of sketches, fabrics and dresses, and set about her business.

Nikki watched appreciatively as Alisa's blouse and skirt were removed; soon she stood blushing in corset, chemise and petticoats, the delectably lovely swell of her breasts rising above the tightly laced stays. God, she is handsome, he thought.

Madame Vevay was astonished to see multiple bruises lightly visible on the ivory purity of Alisa's flesh and considered silently. Does Prince Kuzan beat her? He had a reputation for profligacies, as well as a taste for the bizarre, but she had never heard rumors of perversions. Nevertheless, this woman had been badly beaten and not too long ago. A new quirk of his? she pondered as her curiosity about this relationship was further roused.

Slipping a white beaded silk creation over Alisa's head, Madame Vevay made a few tucks and adjustments after buttoning up the back securely. The gown was of white silk, the skirt entirely covered with white bugles. The tunic was, like the skirt, of white silk and was edged round with a rich trimming of colored silk embroidery, worked by hand on the fabric itself. The sash at the back was embroidered to match and the whole length of sash was surrounded by a deep white fringe of bugles. Vivid violet velvet ribbon outlined the flounces and ruffles terminating in bouffant bows at shoulders, décolletage and hip.

"Come closer, dear," Nikki demanded. "You look very lovely in white."

Alisa reluctantly drew closer but remained outside his reach.

"Come *here,* love," Nikki firmly said, holding his hand out to touch her as she unwillingly stepped a few paces nearer. Was the young woman that afraid of him? Madame Vevay conjectured. Well, it was safer to stop speculating about the private lives of reckless patricians like Nikolai Kuzan. He was much too rich and well connected to antagonize in any way. It wasn't her problem.

Nikki clasped Alisa's hand, straightened his posture somewhat and pulled her between his legs. He knew she was blushing.

"Turn round now so I can see the dress from all sides," he murmured softly and twirled her slowly.

The silken skirts brushed against his legs. Under his careful scrutiny Alisa turned, her slender form exquisitely shown off in the revealing gown, cut daringly low in the bodice.

"I like it," the Prince declared emphatically. "We'll take this one, Madame Vevay."

"It's much too extravagant!" Alisa whispered, Nikki's presence unnerving her. "Where can I possibly ever wear something like this?"

"Why not at dinner tonight with me? You'll quite improve my appreciation of dining en famille and I might decide to stay home this evening. Even the entertainment of the Yacht Club's gambling rooms cannot hope to match the allure you exude," he quietly replied.

Alisa raged with shame and anger at his plans for the evening.

"You can't force me to dine with you and serve as your 'entertainment'!" Alisa retorted, looking mutinous. "I'm not going to!"

"Aren't you, by God?" Nikki responded and, to Alisa's distinct chagrin, a smile of the most unalloyed amusement appeared on his face. "We shall no doubt see. Now try on that other dress." he said authoritatively and pushed Alisa gently out into the center of the salon. In a louder voice intended for the modiste's ears, he said, "The second dress, Madame Vevay."

Nikki's eager eyes watched the slender body slipping into a dark green, silk twill morning dress trimmed in green velvet and smiled lazily at her as she bent to straighten the skirt and spilled provocatively out of her corset. It was one of his favorite aesthetic diversions watching women dress. With a succulent, luxurious beauty like that she should wear sables, the natural ones with the golden vaguely foxy tint to complement her hair, he mused. He would wrap her in sables this winter.

Madame Vevay was clucking and fussing, keeping up a steady inane chatter.

Meeting Nikki's gaze Alisa quickly dropped her seductively lashed violet eyes before that unmistakable long, burning glance.

Damn her, the lure was overpowering, he thought as he shifted uncomfortably in his chair. He could just *look* at her and forget everything else.

Nikki had a disturbing impulse that perhaps this amour was not going to be like all the rest; an uneasy sensation of being drawn in beyond the usual barriers he studiously maintained against emotional involvement. Ridiculous! he snorted. He had never turned aside because of a premonition before. Nikki's resolute temperament denied withdrawal, or retreat, or too much introspection. He lived life rashly, always had, like a bold and bruising hell-for-leather rider, and if that was the quickest way to a broken neck—the consequences be damned! He led a charmed life and he knew it.

As a connoisseur of fine female flesh and style, Nikki was aware that Alisa was more beautiful than most, while instinctively, and temperamentally, one of the best women to give pleasure in bed. His feelings weren't necessarily any more involved; she was just a rarer jewel, a more precious bauble, and he'd be a fool not to react to these unique and delightful attributes. He began to understand Forseus' reluctance to let Alisa out in the world.

Raising a languid hand, he beckoned Alisa toward

him. She approached slowly, wearing her most *jeunesse dorée* look, young, petulant, sullenly beautiful.

"Smile, love," Nikki drawled. "You're supposed to bring me pleasure."

A fixed tight smile appeared.

"Now," he said equably with his usual candor, unperturbed by the grimace, "if you could contrive to behave as charmingly as you look, one could hardly ask for more."

"That's impossible, under the circumstances!" whispered Alisa, casting a glance of contempt upon Nikki's smiling face.

"One can but hope," Nikki murmured, as he pulled her down on his lap. He liked to touch her, as if it gave him some kind of ownership.

"Madame Vevay, bring your sketches. My cousin and I will select some of your designs to have made up, hopefully, very quickly."

"Oh, certainement, Prince. There will be *no* delay, I assure you."

"Please, Monsieur," Alisa whispered faintly, giving Nikki a sidelong pleading glance, but Nikki held her tightly while he peremptorily ordered a wardrobe which brought the light of avarice to Madame Vevay's greedy eyes. Nikki noted Alisa's distress and he almost felt sorry for her. But not quite.

He would have to buy her an extravagant bijou. She gave him so much pleasure he must try to erase the distress. Perhaps he could assuage the bitterness she felt at being a kept woman. That emerald necklace he had seen last month at Fabergé's. Such lavish gifts had always been highly successful in the past. All women were irresistably warmed by the brilliant sparkle of emeralds and rubies.

"That will be all, Madame Vevay. My cousin will wear this becoming morning dress and we can expect a minimum number of dresses to be delivered within two days, the rest to follow?"

"Yes, most assuredly!" the modiste promised him. She would bring in extra seamstresses to fill this order immediately, she thought.

"Thank you then, Madame, we'll see ourselves out."

She accepted her dismissal graciously and amidst effusive thanks left the green and gold salon.

"I have no doubt overwhelmed you," Nikki said teasingly, "by my generosity and superb expertise in female fashion. I trust you approve my taste and," he paused briefly, "please accept my apologies." He grinned suddenly. "This shameful conduct is quite common to me."

"Why, Nikki?" she asked quietly. "Why all this? Why me?" Alisa questioned, looking at him with liquid resentful eyes.

Because I have need for your body that drugs my mind, he thought. Because you and your charming daughter warm my spirits, he thought. "Because," he said.

Alisa, still seated on Nikki's lap, attempted to coldly stare him entirely out of countenance, but the amiable smile continued to play on his handsome face. Then with the unpredictability of her sex, she did a complete volte-face and suddenly said graciously, "Nikki, you're much too generous both to me and Katelina." Tears welled into her beautiful large eyes; a poignant smile of gratitude flickered across her mouth.

"Don't cry, darling," Nikki said in an oddly constrained voice. "You and Katelina both bring me a great deal of joy." He kissed Alisa tenderly on her soft pink lips. "Come, now, no more tears, let's go and see the child's new train."

The next week flew by. Nikki did contrive to stay home every evening and Alisa tried not to think at all; she only felt. Nikki was quite sorely missed at the Yacht and Nobles' Clubs gaming tables but when his name came up, the raised eyebrows and leering glances quite explained his sudden propensity for the comforts of home.

"If I had that beauty warming my bed, no one should see me about town until I was too old to care or dead from trying," one coarse but expressive young officer remarked.

"Nikki deigns to show up for morning reviews and immediately leaves at noon when they're over, and rumor has it he's cast off Sophie."

Alisa and Katelina in Nikki's morning absences had been squired around by Aleksei, who felt honored to be seen in the company of such an intriguing beauty. Alisa, on her part, enjoyed the pleasant companionship of Nikki's youthful cousin who generously gave up his time to escort them sightseeing. Nikki found that sort of thing a bore and Alisa would never see the beauties of Petersburg if she waited for him to accompany her. In the course of the next few days, she and Katelina saw everything of interest: They saw the Winter Palace just down the street from Prince Kuzan's pink marble palace. The Winter Palace was not yet completely restored since the fire in 1863 and was now colored brick-red by Stussov and Brullov instead of its original pale green. Aleksei conducted them not only through the Hermitage galleries with its magnificent Ecole Russe, but through suites of rooms not accessible to the ordinary visitor. They strolled through the Summer Garden with its shady walks and innumerable marble statues which Peter the Great had collected from Italy, visited the very first palace occupied by Peter the Great, the Summer Palace, built on a modest and intimate scale by Trezzini in a section of the Summer Garden. They viewed the forbidding fortress of Peter and Paul, magnificent rather than beautiful, built across the Neva. They whiled away one whole morning at the Kunstkamera, the first library and museum in Russia with its odd collection of curiosities ranging from Chinese manuscripts to stuffed birds but particularly noted for its stupendous collection of Scythian jewelry.

Another morning of sightseeing disclosed the wonders of Tsarskoe Selo with its dazzling interiors, the Amber Room,[5] its walls completely panelled in amber, pale as honey, the glass-beaded room, the Malachite Room, Cameron's Lyons Room, the walls and furniture covered in pale yellow Lyons silk woven with a pattern of branches and little birds, Catherine's own "snuff-box," which is what she called her private boudoir, panelled with opaline white glass and gilt appliqué ornament. The doors were framed in columns of ultramarine colored glass.

A further morning took them by steamer down the tideless, saltless Gulf of Finland to view Peterhof,

Rastrelli's fabulous yellow and white country residence built originally by Peter the Great to rival Versailles. On the grounds were two Imperial palaces and many little summer-houses adorned and fitted with every beauty that wealth and taste could achieve. The gardens eclipsed the finest in Europe crowned by the magnificent cascade and gilded fountains shooting glittering spray which flowed into the sea.

Color abounded in the city architecture and pale delicate hues delighted the eye at every turn: the lemon yellow and white of the Admiralty and Pushkin Theatre, the rich blue of the Smol'nyi Cathedral, the coral of Menshikov's Palace. All the rococo facades stuccoed in beautiful pastels, lilac, salmon, pistachio green served as a foil for the starkly Neo-Classic Russian Empire architecture of Alexander I and Nicholas I. Beautiful sparkling canals intersected the three main arteries which spread from Admiralty Square. Alisa was truly affected by the beauty of this Venice of the North.

Unknown to the small party of sightseers, each day, two other attendants accompanied the group. Scrupulously remaining in the background, not a difficult task in the polyglot babble of the diverse nationalities and costumes jostling each other in the capital of the Empire. The streets contained quantities of barbaric costumes. There were Cossacks from the Don, Georgians from the Caucasus, Tatars, Persians, creatures from Central Asia, Chinese, Laplanders as well as the motley crew of Russian peasants, priests, monks, nuns.

In this floating stream of humanity Forseus' trackers silently stalked their quarry, persistent as a conscience. So far, Alisa had not once ventured alone outside the marble palace, but they patiently waited, the six men changing shifts every eight hours, so one pair of men, four earnest eyes knew Alisa's whereabouts twenty-four hours a day, and only waited for an opportunity in which she was alone to carry her back to her husband. Forseus was not so foolhardy as to come to grips publicly with such an illustrious, powerful figure as Prince Kuzan. Those persons privileged to have the Emperor recognize their family in friendship were above the law and Forseus knew it.

The days of sightseeing were often concluded with a drive out to the Point, where the fashionable world went to see the sun set across the Gulf of Finland. It was a beautiful sight, the sky glowing crimson and gold, the bay as smooth as glass, reflecting the beds of rushes that rose here and there, one or two boats serenely gliding over the glistening water. Alisa stayed until the crimson faded into evening's twilight. These beauties of nature, however, were wasted on the unseen eyes, steadfastly fixed on their prey.

One morning several days later, Nikki was in his dressing room struggling into his uniform; he was already a half hour late for formation and becoming frustrated. Finally, fully attired in white tunic with red facings and dark trousers with red stripes, he sat on a low chair thrusting his foot into an immaculately polished riding boot, cursing softly.

"Where the hell is that damn valet when I need him," he muttered distractedly in the direction of Alisa who was watching him from the doorway, garbed in a pale aquamarine flower-embroidered silk wrapper.

"You distinctly warned your poor valet more than ten days ago that you didn't want to be disturbed by him in the morning until further notice, *if* you recall," Alisa chided him gently.

"I did?" Nikki asked, raising his head and lifting one eyebrow quizzically at Alisa. Breaking into a broad grin as she flushed under his gaze, he said, "So I did, didn't I?" and chuckled. "I guess I pay for my pleasures now by having to contend with dressing myself," he teased.

"Let me help you," Alisa offered as she moved toward his seated figure.

"No, no, dear, don't bother. I'm fussing for no good reason. I'm quite able to dress myself. I'm just in a damnable hurry. My late arrivals are beginning to raise comment."

"Nikki?" Alisa began hesitantly, "do you have one minute to spare?"

"Of course, love," Nikki remarked placidly as he stood before a large cheval glass and began adjusting the silver epaulets on the tunic of his undress uniform. He was buckling on his belt, and when Alisa didn't continue, he prompted her quietly, "What is it, my dove?"

"Well——" she faltered, unable to find suitable words to continue.

"Well?" Nikki rejoined, looking at Alisa intently as he noted the obvious timidity in her demeanor.

"I'm . . . that is . . . I'm quite sure I'm pregnant," Alisa blurted out and nervously dropped her eyes from the piercing glance which quickly ranged the length of her body.

"How sure?" Nikki asked conversationally, his composure unruffled by the disclosure.

"About three weeks sure," she answered, astonished at Nikki's calm reaction. Alisa hadn't known what to expect and her nerves had been on edge the last few days trying to bring herself to break the news. It wasn't unheard of to be promptly sent packing upon presenting tidings like that. And she had nowhere to go.

"Please, sweetheart, please relax, you look quite anxious. I flatter myself I am as hardened a reprobate as most men, and I indulge in numerous vices," Nikki stated with a faint smile, "but rest assured, casting pregnant females into the streets is not one of them." He looked at Alisa closely. "One must expect such things, after all," he continued tranquilly; "surely you didn't hope to escape that condition for long when one considers the diligence with which we pursue our—ah—friendship," he drawled.

"You're not angry?" Alisa asked incredulously.

"Angry? Whatever for? Come now, dear, give me a kiss good-by. I really must be off, for Cernov's jests are becoming cruder every day and I'm damned late."

Alisa felt very emotional about the pregnancy. She hadn't hoped for another child from her marriage with Forseus and had given up such thoughts. But she also hadn't wished to become pregnant by Prince Kuzan—especially since their relationship was so undefined. This child was nurtured within her body, hence a living, breathing extension of herself that couldn't be forgotten, set aside or rejected. It had filled most of her thoughts the past few days and now, she was relieved to have shared her secret.

It still didn't seem real to her, so much had happened in the past weeks.

On the other hand, Nikki accepted the fact calmly as part of the order of things, a circumstance bound to happen. For Nikki, a pregnant mistress was a reasonable consequence of their irresponsible self-indulgence. He really must buy her some extravagant toy, some bauble to cheer her up, was his immediate reaction. He perceived his obligation in this as in all other responsibilities of his rank. He had affectionate feelings for Alisa, although refusing to acknowledge any emotion more powerful. Alisa in the time-honored tradition of keeper of the womb was compelled to accept what good will Nikki offered, since she had no money, no home, no relatives to turn to. But she had other reasons, less prosaic reasons; she passionately loved this quixotic, reckless, enigmatic, oddly gentle man.

"When I return this afternoon we must keep your appointment at Madame Vevay's. She sent me a note yesterday informing me that several more of your dresses are ready for the final fitting." Nikki walked over, clasped Alisa gently in his arms and kissed her a tender au revoir.

"Until this afternoon." He blew her another kiss as he stood in the doorway. "Oh, one request, my sweet. Please for the sake of the child, would you mind not smoking cigarettes? I know it's terribly fashionable, but I have vague apprehensions of our child being born with soot on his face. Do you mind?"

"No, of course not. I scarcely care one way or the other."

"Thank you, my dear. I stand relieved. Why don't

you go back to bed and rest until I return. Aren't
enceinte women supposed to be constantly fatigued?"
he grinned.

And that was the end of that.

Fortunately the morning sightseeing trips had
been curtailed since Aleksei's presence was now also
required at his regiment, for of late, Alisa's mornings
were punctuated with spells of nausea. Perhaps she
would climb back into bed; Katelina could have her
lessons in the bedroom this morning.

After a light luncheon Nikki and Alisa arrived
at Madame Vevay's. Nikki seated himself in his
usual comfortable sprawl, blue frock coat open,
hands clasped across the middle of his embroidered
linen waistcoat, legs clad in light gray trousers out-
stretched before him. He watched Madame Vevay
slip dress after dress over Alisa's head, make a
variety of adjustments with pins and basting, clucking and chattering all the while.

"Madame Forseus!" she wailed after ripping out
the bastings on the sixth dress in a row. "I will never
be able to finish these gowns. Every fitting requires
further adjustments. Madame is putting on weight!"
she chided.

"Perhaps it is my chef's incomparable menus,
Madame Vevay," Nikki softly said. "I fear he's
been outdoing himself since my 'cousin' has been in
residence."

Madame Vevay stood back, arms akimbo, and
closely surveyed the blushing Alisa. With eyes narrowed, she replied coyly, "Monsieur and Madame,
if the chef *continues* to outdo himself, perhaps I

should put additional darts in the waistline which could be taken out as needed."

"Excellent idea, Madame Vevay," Nikki heartily responded. "Please do just that on all the remaining gowns and we'll cause no further delay in their construction. Is that all right with you, my dear?" he asked Alisa politely.

"Yes, that will be fine," Alisa answered faintly, wishing she could disappear into the floor rather than continue being the object of Madame Vevay's comprehending speculative gaze.

As they were driving back home in the carriage, Alisa fretted over the humiliation of Madame Vevay's shrewd scrutiny.

"Don't give her a second thought, love. I'll protect you from any more knowing looks, if they really bother you. Motherhood is eminently natural, and one should never be ashamed of such a state. However, if you're disturbed, I shall determinedly stare down or set to anyone in the future who attempts to disconcert you. I confess," his eyes gleamed wickedly, "I've quite a notorious reputation in that regard. Should we advance dinner by two hours today and allow Katelina to join us? Would you like that?" he asked with unwonted cajolery, hoping to distract Alisa from her wounded pride and rueful musings.

"Oh, Nikki, that would be lovely!" Alisa beamed.

"Let's talk to Pierre when we return. He could concoct some suitably childish dish with which to surprise Katelina."

"That's a marvelous idea. She is inordinately fond of rice pudding and——"

"Strawberries and cake," Nikki interposed obligingly.

"And also petits fours . . ."

The rest of the journey passed with the lovers holding hands and comparing notes on the dishes most enjoyed by themselves as children.

It pleased him to please her.

The following morning Alisa and Katelina were in the study, working on Katelina's lessons which had been neglected during their round of sightseeing, when a tall, erect, gray-haired man abruptly walked into the sun-lit room and treated them to a lowering scowl.

His glance altered approvingly upon noting the fashionable elegance of Alisa's jonquil yellow morning dress which set off her trim form and red coiffure to perfection, and determined with a practiced eye that it was not surprising that Nikki was behaving so uncharacteristically. After seeing the dazzlingly lovely, well-bred young woman, Prince Mikhail understood why Nikki had committed the indiscretion of ensconcing his mistress in his own palace. Thank God, she's a lady, he observed and quickly took in the young child at the woman's side.

"You must be Alisa," the old Prince said bluntly.

Alisa rose in confusion, immediately recognizing the unmistakable resemblance to Nikki, the same imperious air of one born to command. She colored becomingly and bowed deeply, her eyes demurely downcast. Katelina, with a glance from her mother, quickly rose and bobbed a curtsey.

"Yes, Monsieur, I am and this is my daughter Katelina."

"Nikki's newest paramour, eh? Quite unlike him, you know, to settle for one woman. Had to come myself and see what she was like," he uttered with perfect equanimity.

Alisa's emotions were thrown into complete confusion, tumultuously rushing and tumbling one over the other. Her first panic-striken thought was to get Katelina out of the room.

In great agitation, she whispered to Katelina, "Run along, dear, and find Rakeli. She'll take you out in the garden."

As Katelina skipped out of the room, after a curious look at the formidable old man, Alisa drew herself as erect as her slight frame would allow and, looking the old Prince directly in the eye, said with asperity, "Have you had an edifying look, sir, for if you have, perhaps you'll excuse me."

"Now, now, my child, don't take issue at my bluntness. I'm just not one to stand on ceremony," Prince Mikhail said kindly, the heavy brows relaxing somewhat from their normal severe expression. "Undeniably exquisite, Nikki's choice, if I do say so myself," he continued with a faint smile. "Come now, I shan't eat you. Do sit down. I'll ring for tea and sherry and we can become acquainted."

Within minutes a flustered servant brought in tea and sherry and set them on a low malachite table between the two settees where Alisa and Prince Mikhail faced each other. The Prince chatted with Alisa in his wonderfully open, relaxed way and entranced her quite as easily as his son had. Nikki's unfailing charm was most decidedly inherited, Alisa observed.

The prince, in turn, studied Alisa, which was his

reason for visiting the palace. After hearing the first smatterings of rumor concerning Nikki's newest paramour, the old Prince had immediately sent his barristers a message requesting a thorough investigation of this new "cousin."

The malicious letter sent by Countess Amalienborg had been unnecessary, as Prince Mikhail was never far removed from the pulse of gossip, but appreciated by its recipient for reasons not intended by its sender. Nikki had obviously renounced that slut after all these years. This fact was a great relief to Mikhail Kuzan who had been fearful that perhaps in a rash moment some drunken night, Nikki might offer her more than an affair, and while the old Prince would indulgently allow his only child to commit almost every indiscretion, that one he would not have allowed. Prince Mikhail had never intended to have Sophie Amalienborg for a daughter-in-law.

Then the startling news that Alisa was Valdemar Forseus' wife had required further inquiries in the Viipuri area. After three weeks the old Prince was fully informed and in control of an entire dossier on Alisa, her parents, the marriage to Forseus (which in itself raised a few questions) and her new "friendship" with his son Nikki. He kept this information to himself as he drew the young lady gently into conversation, wanting to discover for himself just what sort of woman his son was enamored of. And enamored Nikki certainly was, to have her openly living in his palace, plus, the old Prince understood with astonishment, deserting the gaming tables and keeping himself home every night.

After beholding this striking beauty before him, this extremely curious behavior was no longer baffling. Mikhail Kuzan reflected wryly, You had to give the boy credit for good sense. If Nikki was becoming serious about a woman after all these years of casual amours, he couldn't have selected a more delightful creature. Alisa's marital state was of little importance to Mikhail Kuzan. His thorough investigation had revealed the magnitude and frequency of Forseus' debauchery and his abuse of his young wife. Although Prince Mikhail was not unfamiliar with brutality in human behavior, Forseus had turned out to be rather a master of the craft and he felt no compunction to restore this young girl to that beast. A discreet word from the Emperor and the problem of divorce would be resolved.

The Prince sipped steadily on the sherry, emptying half the bottle in the course of their conversation. Soon they were getting along quite famously and Alisa had lost some of her awe and shyness. Alisa drank her sherry slowly and after having her glass filled the second time began feeling extremely nauseous. Her color waned and a thin film of perspiration broke out on her forehead and upper lip. After gallantly attempting to control the waves of sickness for several minutes, Alisa, extremely desperate that she would embarrass herself in front of Nikki's father, asked in a faint voice if she could be excused and rose carefully from her seat opposite the Prince.

After observing his wife through five pregnancies, the prince was well aware of the obvious symptoms of an unsettled stomach in the morning.

"Of course, my dear, you're excused. By the by, when are you in the way of making my son a father?" he calmly enquired.

The shock of his knowledge eclipsed the nausea by sheer horror and Alisa sat down heavily.

"How did you know, sir?" she whispered, fearful Madame Vevay's tongue had run wild so rapidly.

"I've held my wife's hand through five pregnancies, my dear, so I am well acquainted with that greenish look around the gills. The marked pallor of your complexion so early in the morning, coupled with your close proximity to my son these few weeks past, prompted me to make a calculated guess as to the inevitable consequences," he said dryly. "Prince Nikolai's amatory exploits are rarely attended by any prudence. It was to be expected," he said gently.

"Now, my dear, do you want him?" the old Prince asked flatly in his oddly abrupt conversational manner.

She seemed to ponder her reply. "It's very complicated, sir. There are several reasons——"

"You want him," he broke in quietly.

"You are very astute, monsieur."

"I have that reputation," he concurred.

"Yes, I'm afraid I do," Alisa sighed softly. Quickly rushing on in explanation, "But never, sir, if he does not want me." She continued in a subdued voice, "Having lived through one disastrous marriage, I would never wish that on anyone. It's much too terrible."

"Spoken very forthrightly. I like that. Very well, my young lady, you shall have him," Mikhail Kuzan declared with decisive, unruffled composure, with the usual Kuzan insensitivity to the delicate shades of human relationships. If Nikki couldn't find this charming, delightful, unutterably beautiful young woman compatible, he obviously had no sense and it was up to his father to mend his stupidity. The old gentleman surveyed her with distinct admiration.

"Please put your feet up on the settee and I'll ring for a cool compress. My wife will be delighted to hear the news. She had quite despaired of Nikki ever finding anyone suitable. You'll meet her later. She's traveling more slowly, having insisted on bringing several servants and eighty pieces of luggage. Perhaps you would be more comfortable in bed?" he soothingly suggested as he noticed the unnerved appearance of the young woman.

"Yes, I should, I'm sure."

"Allow me, my dear." Prince Mikhail gallantly offered his arm and escorted Alisa up the stairway to her bedchamber.

Returning down the marble staircase, the Prince crisply informed the butler that he wished to see his son *immediately* he set foot in the palace.

"I'll be in the library. Bring me a light lunch and a bottle of brandy."

"Very good, my Prince. May I say in behalf of myself and the staff, it's a pleasure to see you once again in residence." The old butler beamed happily, having served the old Prince since before his marriage.

"You'll be seeing a great deal of us in the near future. It seems I must take a hand in my son's affairs." Prince Mikhail grinned familiarly at Sergei.

"We do what we can—eh Monsieur?" Sergei responded and winked.

Upon arriving home at his usual hour, Nikki was astonished to receive the sharp message from his father. Questioning Sergei accomplished little except to warn Nikki that his father had met Alisa. Nikki entered the library slightly annoyed at the peremptory order.

His father was seated behind the polished expanse of an André-Charles Boulle desk veneered in marquetry of tortoiseshell, natural colored woods, engraved pewter, brass and ivory.

Father's eyes met son's. Both were cool and aloof, except the father's held a touch of disdain as well.

With a resigned sigh and a casual gesture of his hand, Prince Mikhail offered a chair to Nikki.

Nikki ignored the courtesy and obstinately remained standing, leaning negligently against the Palladian window jamb, looking rebellious, angered at the curt summons from his father, resentful at being made to feel like a young cub about to be upbraided for some defiance of parental authority. However because of the deep respect in which he held his father, Nikki was attempting to suppress his normally ungovernable temper. He set his teeth.

Silently, with maddening deliberation, Prince Mikhail regarded the tall, broad-shouldered, impeccably dressed figure of his only child. Under this scrutiny, Nikki's eyes lifted, met his father's and held for an instant before a lazy flicker turned his expression suddenly remote, but not before his father noted the sullen stubbornness and the barely concealed anger.

"To what do I owe this unexpected visit? It's been three years since you were last in the city."

Nikki did not really expect an answer to this flippancy and he wasn't disappointed. With the exception of one ironically raised eyebrow, Prince Mikhail ignored the remark, his attention more significantly engaged in adjusting the ruffle on his shirt cuff. The ruffle suitably disposed, he once more lifted his eyes.

Prince Mikhail Kuzan enunciated evenly, the words clear and precise in the hushed stillness of the vast library.

"I have indulged you in every way, have I not, Nikki?"

"Yes, father," Nikki responded shortly, watching his father warily.

"Have I ever said you nay, or gainsaid you in any of your desires?"

"No, father," the words rapped out, sharp and decisive.

"I have overlooked all your numerous peccadilloes and reckless escapades these many years past; never interfered except to intercede when extenuating circumstances of your—ah—affairs have occasioned the need of a mollifying or palliating presence."

Nikki stiffened at the reproach.

"I believe I have rather adequately conducted my own affairs, if you please," he replied curtly. "I don't recollect having had any need for your assistance."

"You will allow me to point out your error, my boy. An example. Perhaps you recall the dark-haired child born to Countess Souvanieff last fall. Since she and her husband are both exceedingly fair and their other three children tow-headed and blue-eyed, the conspicuous coloring of the last boy child did not go unremarked. Furthermore, if you remember, your pursuit of that fair lady was not in any way discreet. With your usual bland blindness to reason and prudence, your coach and lackeys were left waiting outside her door until dawn, time without number. That Adelaide blue brougham ornamented with silver, which you bought from the Duke of Devonshire after his state visit here, is one of a kind and elicits considerable attention, while your red and blue sledge is equally conspicuous with the golden bells and gilded, tasseled harness you affect.

"Even though I'm rarely in town, my sources of gossip are speedy and reliable. I expected, daily, to hear of yet another duel and you know how those last few contests of honor (although how the term honor comes into a fight over some woman's favors, I fail to discern) terrified your mother. I *do not* like to see your mother disturbed and unhappy," Prince Mikhail intoned ominously.

After a deliberate pause he continued softly, "Since Count Souvanieff was out of the country so often, it is conceivable that he was ignorant of his wife's affair, or perhaps your notorious reputation as a duelist may have dictated his caution. In any event, Count Souvanieff is not altogether a fool and was outraged at being cuckolded. Since you have a string of women constantly in your wake, he thought it ungenerous of you to turn your eye appreciatively on *his* wife. In this instance, you incurred the indignant displeasure of a minister not without influence and power. You were remarkably close to being summarily cashiered out of the Chevaliers Gardes for that unheeding disregard for appearances."

The old Prince heaved a small sigh.

"Fortunately my wealth and position bear some little consequence as well, and even while infrequently in town, my substantial connections prevail undiminished. In deference to our old and close friendship, the Emperor was persuaded there was no conclusive proof the child was yours."

"It appears your—er—connections are to be commended. I owe you my belated thanks," Nikki's equable voice drawled as he gave a stiff bow in his father's direction.

Prince Mikhail met his insolent glance squarely.

"Quite so. Now enough of this sparring. What do you intend to do with Alisa?"

"Do? What am I expected to do?" Nikki inquired sardonically. "I'm well satisfied with the relationship. I find Alisa delightful and charming in spite of being over-educated for a woman. As you know, I have never been overly fond of clever women."

"*That* fact has always been fairly obvious," his father replied dryly. "I am informed that Alisa is carrying your child."

"My compliments, sir, on the efficacy of your sources. I was informed but yesterday myself of the impending blessed event. May I make so bold as to inquire whether you have discovered if it's to be a boy or a girl?"

"Very amusing, I'm sure," said the old Prince with a slight lift of the brows. Prince Mikhail went on gelidly, his gray eyes snapping with contained fury at Nikki's impudent disrespect. "*Is* the child yours?"

"Apparently."

"How can you be sure."

"I've no reason to doubt her word. Rest assured, she shall be well taken care of," Nikki continued icily polite. "I'll buy her a house and set up a suitable establishment in which to rear a child of mine.

Alisa and her two children will have every comfort. As her protector, I can offer her a safe, secure and luxurious refuge."

"Is a protector enough?" his father gently inquired, frustration smoldering beneath the quiet rebuke.

"Surely I'm not to consider a mesalliance?" Nikki protested righteously.

"Remember, my boy, your mother is a Tzigane," the low voice dangerously reminded him.[6]

"Forgive me, sir," Nikki hastily apologized, an embarrassed flush coloring his neck. "Of course, I didn't mean mother. You know she's very dear to me."

"If you will recall, my pompous young cub, before your haughty airs carry you too far, our princely title is due to our ancestor Platon's prowess in Catherine the Great's bedchamber. When our noble family dispatched their fine young scion (then a mere count) to court in hopes of advancing the family interests, don't think for a minute they weren't reasonably certain his strapping good looks would attract the insatiable eye of the Empress. The Kuzan family acquired numerous properties and additional titles thanks to the good offices and vigorous stamina of young Platon. And no doubt, if we were to search far enough back in our 'illustrious' family tree, we would discover the first 'noble' Kuzan was probably nothing more than a highly successful brigand on the caravan route east.

"Scrutinize any old, prominent family in Russia and you will find, at base, a mercenary, a powerful warlord, a chieftain more shrewd or ruthless than his fellows. On such a base as that, the rank and fortunes of the first families rest, so do not speak to me of mesalliance.

"The honorable course of action would be to marry Alisa," his father admonished sternly.

"Honorable?" Nikki laughed derisively. "I'm to mend the non-existent honor of some petty merchant's wife at the altar?" he sneered arrogantly. "Since when have either you or I been unduly concerned with a fine sense of proprieties? I find it ironic in the extreme, that you should be trading little homilies with me about propriety and honor. You know, yourself, most of our recent, illustrious progenitors were loose-living, self-indulgent wastrels whose chief diversion was irregular relations with a variety of women of every class and nationality. And, with the scapegrace way you racketed around society for so many years, as rumor asserts, you'll forgive me if I find your present posture singularly out of character. In any case, it's out of the question, since Alisa is already married," Nikki finished with an easy, smug smile.

"That insignificant detail can be readily remedied." his father said curtly. "Money and influence buy most anything, as you have no doubt noted," he continued with unmistakable cynicism, "since you have had a stable of tarts both highborn and low for your convenience these many years. And damn! I like the chit!"

"Then it's a pity you're already married," Nikki smiled genially, as he once again relaxed comfortably against the window jamb and crossed his arms lazily across his chest, "for *you* could do the honorable thing by Alisa since you seem to revere her so highly. *I* am not the marrying kind, and if and when

I do reach the stage when I'm inclined to settle down and set up my nursery, rest assured, I will select some suitably docile young girl just out of the school-room who will be biddable and content to spend her time in the country raising my heirs. I certainly will not choose to ally myself with some caustic bluestocking who has shown on more than one occasion a most unsettling stubbornness of character. I would be guilty of the greatest inane rashness, it seems to me, to burden myself with a self-willed woman. Nevertheless I do feel a certain obligation to Alisa since I figured rather largely in the loss of her former life."

"This 'obligation' does not extend to marriage, however," his father jibed.

"Hardly. If I were *obliged* to marry every female who bore my children, I would have been married long ago to that lovely moujik girl you so considerately put in my way when I was fourteen," Nikki serenely remarked.

"Enough!" Prince Mikhail rose swiftly, hitting the desk with his fist as he thundered his command. He stood regally upright, his tall, spare frame still vigorous at sixty-eight; the strong aquiline features haughty, his cold gaze piercingly set on his recalcitrant, insolent heir.

"I have reached a decision!" the old Prince stated with a majestic unequivocality, flagrantly disregarding all Nikki's protestations. "You *will* marry Alisa! She is not one of your brazen sluts to be used and cast aside. I have waited long enough for a legitimate grandson to carry on the name. You are thirty-three years old and so far have demonstrated a marked reluctance to allow yourself to be persuaded to select a wife, although every tabby in town has been on the scramble for you for her daughter.

"With the spirit of folly in which you conduct your affairs, the odds for you living a long life are exceedingly slim and I want a grandson to inherit. You have, by some fortuitous miracle, finally coupled yourself with a fine, young, well-bred woman instead of the usual loose women you are wont to favor and I have a fancy to have Alisa as the mother of my grandson. Heaven knows what she sees in you, but if she wants you, she shall have you!"

"Just like that?" Nikki was no longer casually lazing against the window but standing rigidly upright, his face pale with dismay. "You command me to marry Alisa?" he asked incredulously. Nikki's eyes narrowed as he tried to hold his growing anger in check. "What if I refuse?" he inquired softly through clenched teeth.

"Let us simply say, you shall be extremely unhappy in exile on my estate in Siberia with my Finnish lukashee guarding you and no women available for your comfort. You have never felt the full force of my displeasure. Be warned. I can and will coerce you to see things my way. In this instance I will not be opposed." Each word of the last sentence was enunciated precisely, in a carefully modulated murmur as frigid as the Arctic permafrost.

In his entire life Nikki had never experienced the unconditional fury of his father's temper. For him, the wrath had always been allayed, repressed, controlled. Fate had chosen to relentlessly deprive Prince Mikhail and Princess Kaisa-leena of their other four children, each in the early stages of infancy. Nikki was, in fact, the only one to reach the age of twelve months. The small graves neatly lined one side of the east wall of the mausoleum at Le Repose, the dates pitiful evidence of the frailty of infants when pitted against the dread childhood diseases. The first-born, robust, sturdy Nikki had then become the sum total of all his parents' love, hopes and expectations. His utterly devastating charm, even as a child, endeared him to his parents even had he not been the sole survivor and only heir to the immense and centuries-old Kuzan fortune.

"You will escort Alisa to the Golchoffs' birthday dance this evening," his father stated flatly.

"Is that a command?" Nikki asked bitterly, a black scowl darkening his brow.

"Yes, it is. That will be all." Satisfied that he had settled the matter, Prince Mikhail curtly dismissed his son.

The interview was over.

Nikki left the library dazed by the unfamiliar anger of his father, but equally overwhelmed by a frustration and resentment far more dangerous. To have an indulgent parent manifest a violent volte-face was devastatingly humiliating to a grown man addicted to having things his own way.

It was not to be tolerated! Nikki seethed inwardly. To be ordered about like a minion! And now the two strong, determined temperaments of father and son presaged a clash of indomitable wills. Nikki had the disadvantage of years and a reckless brashness not yet tempered by prudence, but he had an optimistic conceit that a way would be found to circumvent the autocratic dictates of his father.

The far more experienced old Prince had a knowledge culled from an acute and cynical perception of the world and human foibles during sixty-eight years of keenly observing the machinations of society. He knew that he would have his way and *that was that*.

Nikki left the house in a high pitch of anger and spent the rest of the day at the Yacht Club rather moodily gambling.

Earlier that afternoon, Prince Mikhail's wife had arrived and, after seeing to her unpacking, had waited in the east drawing room for Alisa to present herself. Prince Mikhail had alerted his wife that this was not Nikki's usual choice of paramour and thus she was prepared to like and accept Alisa before even meeting her.

The ladies spent a delightful hour together—talking of their homelands, exclaiming over Alisa's forthcoming child. When Alisa begged to be excused to rest for dinner, Princess Kaisa-leena went in search of her husband to tell him she too approved of Nikki's choice.

That evening, Prince Mikhail entertained both his wife and Alisa at dinner and explained to them that Nikki would join them for the Golchoffs' party. Prince Mikhail received a note just as they were finishing the meal.

I have been unavoidably detained. Please accept my apologies. I shall join you at the Golchoffs'. N.

The note was a direct challenge. Nikki's father smiled faintly. The boy had spirit—that he had known for years and was not naive enough to anticipate a compliant, dutiful son. Nevertheless, he could afford to play a waiting game for the moment. One must not press one's authority with foolhardy zeal. No doubt Nikki's regard for his parents or at least his consideration for Alisa would overcome this initial resistance. Prince Mikhail felt sure Nikki would appear later in the evening.

"Nikki is detained and will join us later," he noncommittally explained. "Ladies, allow me the pleasure of escorting two such charming beauties. We have time for a hand of cards before we leave."

At ten thirty the trio walked out of the drawing room into the hall and through the double doors swept instantly open by two footmen in Kuzan liveries. The tall stately Prince in black evening dress, its severity solely relieved by the prestigious Order of St. Andrew suspended from its pale blue ribbon, was flanked on either side by a slender woman, each beautifully garbed in rustling silk, their dainty stature further enhanced by the majestic size of their escort.

The small "intimate" birthday celebration consisted of a crush of three hundred guests. Alisa, presented as a relative of the Prince, was accepted graciously by their host and hostess, ever ready to accommodate any of the whims of Prince Mikhail.

Gossip had of course preceded Alisa's introduction into the restricted exclusivity of the creme of Russian society and some disapproving glances were cast at the exquisite red-haired beauty, but no one dared cross swords with Prince Kuzan or his equally arrogant son. Their credit guaranteed every door would open to their protégé and she was now surrounded by a veritable, if spurious, fog of respectability.

"A formidable assemblage of support, I'd say," one guest sniffed. "Prince Mikhail hasn't breathed the city air these three years past."

As Alisa was being introduced to one rather erect, forbidding matron arrayed brilliantly, if not garishly, in purple silk and plumes, she had a taste of the old Prince's commanding power. When the intimidating purple-clad female cast a baleful eye on this "cousin" and offered a frigid greeting, Prince Mikhail said very suavely, "I do not in the least understand Anna Feodorovna how you can afford to stand there risking my displeasure with your censorious expression when you know as well as I do that not so much as one arshin of the 70,000 tons of steel rails just ordered from the Creuzot works will be laid in the area of your husband's wheat fields without the approval of the Minister of the Interior, who is a very old and dear friend of mine. Now curtsey prettily and bid a pleasant evening to our cousin," he smiled thinly.

The grande dame acceded to his wishes. Alisa received a rather strained good evening.

"You are excused, Anna." Prince Mikhail murmured. As the woman's stiff back receded, the old Prince observed. "Damn hen-witted female. She was never a woman of intuition—eh? Kaisa-leena?" and he peered down at his petite dark-haired wife and grinned widely.

"I think you have enlightened her somewhat, Misha," she smiled back at him.

"Come now, Alisa, who else haven't you met? Bah! I'm not going to introduce you to any more old hags."

Many of the women watched this new beauty with undisguised, malicious envy, noting each detail of Alisa's appearance, but they prudently held their tongues, while the men took full advantage of

Alisa's first essay into public free of Nikki's jealous presence. Everyone did agree, though, this newest mistress was in Nikki's usual style: beautiful, provocative, sensual. Alisa was immediately surrounded by a phalanx of charming, solicitous men, each attempting to flatter, praise and please her. She danced endlessly, thoroughly relishing the gay party and the attention of admirers, although she quietly and regularly searched the crowd for a sign of Nikki. He had not given her any explanation of his absence that afternoon.

Alisa was seated facing the door, looking delicately beautiful in a ball gown of two shades of lilac silk, patiently waiting for the six gallants who had rushed off to satisfy her request for a glass of champagne, when she saw the tall, unmistakable figure, of Nikki. Unhurriedly he strolled across the vast expanse of the room, quite as if he were not four hours late to act as her escort. Alisa was unable to check a rising resentment at his bold impudence.

He seemed oblivious of the hundreds of eyes swiveling to regard the encounter between Nikolai Kuzan and the new "cousin" with whom he was consorting; who now, with the imperious audacity only old Prince Kuzan was capable of, had been taken under the wing of the family. To have Nikki appear at a ball would have been a rarity enough to occasion their stares, but this gesture for the obvious sake of his newest inamorata was not to be missed, for Nikki Kuzan never did anything to oblige anyone.

No one believed for a minute that Alisa was a "cousin," but in society one soon learned the necessity of never "noticing" in public. The Kuzan's, as one of the oldest and most powerful families in Russia, pre-dating the Romanovs by several centuries, were above the normal conventions; hadn't the old Prince married a young gypsy girl eighteen years his junior with total aplomb during the reign of Nicholas I, and forced society to accept her? And even if one would have liked to demur, one did not dare aggravate Prince Mikhail's obstreperous temper which had been famous throughout Russia for 50 years.

Nikki's languid stride slowly brought him face to face with Alisa, who was seated on the brocaded Louis Quinze settee. The brittle glitter of considerable drink shone from his golden eyes.

"You have deigned to make an appearance," Alisa mockingly stated.

"As you see, Madame." He bowed elaborately with his usual self-composed air which made her want to strike him, "I have a distinct feeling that not only my father, but these hundreds of curious, gaping people, will be supremely dismayed if I do not take a turn with you, so please," he continued in a lazy drawl, "do me the honor."

He reached out for her hand in a graceful gesture.

Alisa burned with annoyance and attempted to decline the obviously acid invitation. "I'm sorry . . . Major Khreptovich and Count Soltikoff and several others have gone off to bring me champagne and . . . will be back directly." To her vexation, she felt herself blushing under the intense scrutiny of his glittering, inebriated eyes.

Nikki in one swift movement grasped her hand in an iron grip and spat through tight lips, "They can wait my convenience."

Pulled unceremoniously to her feet, she felt a muscular arm around her waist and her right hand clasped in a strong hold that offered no opportunity for further resistance. She was swept forcibly off onto the floor and gliding into a waltz found herself dancing with quite the most adept partner she had ever had. He danced superbly, as he did all things, but with his usual bored elegance.

After avoiding his eyes with deliberate coolness and concentrating instead on the third button of his collar, her silence was interrupted by Nikki remarking rather grimly, *"Well?* Mrs. Forseus? What are your plans?"

Alisa's eyes lifted in response to the icy tone and met his cool stare. She lifted her chin belligerently as the uncivil inquiry raised her fighting spirit. "What are *my* plans? What a monumentally censorious tone, Monsieur, as if the responsibility is exclusively mine. Without your damnable wager I should never have had the misfortune to make your acquaintance, and had you not so assiduously 'wooed' me once again in Petersburg, I would not now find myself in the unenviable position of carrying your child!"

"As I perceive, Madame, you would hardly be classified as an innocent after having lived with that perverted lecher Forseus, and do not forget, my dear, that my attentions were rarely repulsive to you. Why as recently as last night, your response was, shall we say—er—selfishly demanding?" he finished with silky malice, one eyebrow raised sardonically while a parody of a smile creased his lean cheek.

Alisa's indignation rose at the ignominious truth of his statement, for she was mortified at the ready response Nikki's bold and passionate advances invariably drew from her. She always succumbed to his consummate skill and experience, her senses betrayed by the exquisite torture of his touch.

The creamy skin of her cheeks glowed rose at the direct cut and she endeavored to pull away from his grasp and leave the floor. She dropped her hand from Nikki's shoulder and twisted her fingers from his grip. Undeterred, Nikki only tightened his hold on her slender waist and quickly regained her right hand, this time in a viselike grip so ruthless that tears of pain sprang into her eyes. He pressed her closely against his tall frame and calmly continued twirling expertly down the long ballroom, scarcely having missed a step in the smoothly flowing rhythm of the waltz.

"That's better," Nikki said approvingly. "Really, my love, aren't we offering enough of a spectacle already without resorting to childish tantrums? For me to be on a ballroom floor should keep the matrons' tongues wagging for quite some time. It must be some four or five years since I have graced a polite social function. Consider yourself quite the belle of the ball to have captured my attention in such an unusual public display of my regard."

By this time the musicians were staring rather fixedly at the combatants with disastrous results to the tempo of the dance; half the waltzers were also quite obviously staring, while the other half were politely pretending they hadn't observed Alisa's flushed face, Nikki's grim expression and the tempestuous dialogue passing between Prince Kuzan and his newest paramour.

"Rest assured, Prince Kuzan," Alisa said formally, "I do not solicit your public displays, or as a matter of fact, your private displays either."

If Nikki chose to eschew his responsibility in a typically masculine fashion, she refused to plead or grovel for aid.

"Once it is discovered I have a husband living, my reputation will be ruined, and an illegitimate child can hardly further damage a reputation already sunk below reproach. You can cease directing your tender and public attentions toward me and I will with great pleasure rudely repulse you, in which case you will be absolved from any further tiresome dangling after me."

"Nothing would suit me better, Madame, but curiosity impelled me to ascertain if perhaps your intentions were in the opposite direction. After a rather candid conversation with my father this afternoon, I was not altogether certain of your earnest desires," he said with suspicious emphasis.

Nikki's irritation was further provoked as he uncomfortably recalled the confrontation with his father and the express command issued him.

Alisa gazed at the Prince, almost speechless with indignation. Presently she collected herself, still trying to glide with the music.

"Do I understand, Monsieur," she said in glacial tones, "that you envisioned me clinging to you? What monumental arrogance! I fear I must disappoint your expectations. Unfortunately, you see," her soft whisper held a world of fury, "that is a dramatic tableau I find myself incapable of enacting even to save the child from some unknown fate. Recourse to you as some permanent but unwilling protector I find wholly repulsive!" She fixed her basilisk eyes on his.

Unexpectedly, this snappish diatribe resulted in a bright, boyish grin, a most engaging smile that was immediately followed by a deep, relaxed chuckle. Nikki's formidable, glowering countenance was overcome by a benign amusement.

"What a lovely spitfire you can be; most engaging," he murmured softly as he gazed into the seductive beauty of Alisa's flushed face, the violet eyes glowing with anger, her breathing irregular from the violence of her emotions.

Feeling relieved he said, "I should have known you were not behind the damnable fiat delivered by my father."

Alisa's eyes opened wide in astonishment as she stared incredulously into Nikki's now placid gaze.

"What fiat?" she demanded hastily.

"An unequivocal command to marry you." He smiled lazily at the surprised face, lips parted in wonder. "Now I can inform father that his coercion is unnecessary since you are as antagonistic to the union as I am," he explained amiably.

"What an utterly preposterous notion in any event, since I am already married. His idea surely cannot signify." Yet, her heart was beating rapidly at the thought.

"On the contrary, my dear, father is not one to be contradicted or nonplussed in any of his idiosyncrasies, as I discovered for the first time today," he said tranquilly, his self-assurance restored.

"Well, in this instance, he must. The idea is absurd."

"Agreed!" Nikki unchivalrously replied.

The music stopped and the dance ended.

Nikki stood looking down at Alisa, lightly holding her voluptuous warmth in his arms.

"Monsieur, you may now be excused from my unwelcome presence. Please feel free to grace the dance floor with some other fortunate object of your attentions," Alisa said sarcastically.

"Very well, dear, as you wish." Nikki released his hold, honored her with a weak inclination of a bow and, to Alisa's chagrin, very ungraciously accepted her petulant suggestion, as he moved away with the easy stride of a cavalry officer and spent the rest of the night dancing with Countess Amalienborg. The Countess preened with unmitigated pleasure at receiving Nikki's attention. Now everyone could surely see that Nikki was still enamored of her and that little bitch didn't mean anything to him, she gleefully noted to herself.

Alisa felt her spirits sinking with a sudden odd pang, as she watched them. Only the twin fiends of stubbornness and pride kept her from succumbing to the unhappy feelings generated by the spectacle of Nikki and his old mistress dancing across the room. They were a picture of handsomeness, for the Countess was a tall, dark-haired beauty, with a classic profile, a noble body of Venus most admirably displayed in black lace with a daringly cut décolletage, and Nikki's attractive dark looks and magnificent size suited her to perfection.

I hope her dress is ripped to shreds by those spurs, Alisa hatefully thought.

Prince Mikhail was furious with Nikki's behavior, and after seeing Alisa's distress he insisted they leave. That ungrateful whelp would pay for this discourteous display, he reprovingly vowed. Could he have that slut of a Countess sent to Siberia? It was a thought.

In the early hours of the morning, Nikki reluctantly accepted the Countess' invitation to accompany her home and with a perfunctory preoccupation fondled and caressed her in the carriage when she slipped his hand under her skirt.

Now he lay on his back on her bed, the Countess' head resting in his groin. He watched the reflections of what she was doing, in the mirror above his head, with a certain detachment—as if he wasn't involved in the activity. Her head shifted and her mouth began to move once again with a soft, sucking sound. She had one of the most magnificent bodies, he observed, and one of the most degraded imaginations he had ever known. He rated her on a par with Cora Pearl,[7] an encomium of the first order, but by and large, he was a man of normal proclivities, a sensualist fastidiously indifferent to the practices of the deviates. Within seconds, these casual musings ceased as the whole nervous system of his body was forced to concentrate on Sophie's delicate manipulations. A little later, the flickering mirrored vignettes of Countess Amalienborg's movements had stilled, she had swallowed and Nikki closed his eyes and breathed deeply. He relaxed in the silence, not wishing to see or talk to her.

The black-haired Venus slowly eased across his body, running her hands up and down his torso, cupping her fingers gently around his testicles. He shook off her hand.

"Not now, Sophie."

"I want you to dominate me, Nikki!" she moaned. Those damnable long fingers of hers were perversely effective. Her skill was remarkable. He was rigid already.

"Hurt me, Nikki!" she pleaded, pulling at him to enter her.

Christ, tonight he didn't like her in this mood and she was irritating the hell out of him, Damn her! He took her then like a dog and forced her to do his bidding. Nikki's black mood only served to further excite her. Minutes later he rose from the bed.

Why did he always get involved with women like Tanya and Sophie who wanted tyranny in the bedroom, although they were both masterful technicians in bed?

"Nikki, where are you going?" she cried, attempting to cling to him. "Stay with me!"

Three times was too much. He was feeling tired and hadn't wished to see Sophie again in the first place. If it wasn't for wanting to spite his father and Alisa, he wouldn't have even addressed a civil hello to the Countess at the Golchoffs.

"I'm fatigued and long for my own bed," he replied curtly as he dressed rapidly.

"You just long for that harlot sleeping in your bed!" the Countess screamed in anger. "What about my pleasure?"

Nikki was pulling on his boots and closed his eyes in disgust and weariness. He eased himself slowly from the chair, turned to the door and as he walked out of the room said coldly, "I'll send your wolfhound in for your pleasure. I understand he is one of your special perversions. Adieu, Sophie."

On the ride home he rested his head gratefully

against the velvet squabs and attempted to rid himself of the loathing Sophie engendered in him. He reminded himself that Sophie's perversities had not always disgusted him—in fact her extraordinary expertise had been a major element in her attractiveness. What was happening to him? All he could think of was Alisa. Day and night, her beauty, her artlessness, even her stubborn temper. He chuckled. God, he missed her. After tonight Sophie was definitely off his list.

Arriving home, he slowly walked up the stairway and down the long marble hallway into his rooms. Without pausing, he continued through the adjoining doorway into Alisa's bedchamber, wanting to look at her peaceful beauty and rid himself of Sophie's taint. He had expected Alisa to be sleeping at this late hour, but she lay wide awake, propped up against a bolster of pillows, the faint light of a single lamp dancing her shadow across the wall. Before he had time to speak she acidly remarked, "You positively reek of a woman's perfume!"

"Countess Amalienborg's," he replied candidly, unused to the necessity of explanation. He walked closer to her bed.

"How dare you!" Alisa retorted in affront, drawing away from him.

"How dare I?" Nikki's eyebrows rose in genuine perplexity. The idea of explaining his actions to a mistress was unthinkable.

"It's unspeakable! Coming here warm from another woman's body! You're despicable, insufferable, detestable!" she cried in rage, her eyes blazing.

"Is that a fact, Madame," he responded almost gently as his goaded frustration began to build. His eyes held a distinct menace. "Mistresses should not harangue. It isn't wise," he quietly reminded her.

"I did not choose to become your mistress and I do not choose to conduct myself wisely at this late date!" Alisa snapped back, unabashed by those dangerous eyes, for frustration and indignation were making her reckless. It had been a long sleepless night with images of Nikki and the Countess prevalent in her thoughts.

"It seems, then, that you need some schooling in the duties and behavior of mistresses," Nikki remarked with narrowed eyes glaring.

"I need no instruction from the sordid likes of you, *if* you don't mind!" the haughty, undutiful mistress replied.

"*If* I don't mind? But I *do* mind, madame," Nikki returned silkily, "You see, I dislike acrimonious contre-dits when I'm in the humor for an amenable mistress to comfort a black mood."

"Get your 'comfort', you whoremonger, from that whore Sophie! As you may have noticed, I am not in an amenable mood!" she hissed angrily.

"Please, Mrs. Forseus, don't be vulgar. Vulgar women I can find by the score." Nikki's lips curled into an unfriendly smile while he thought resentfully: Two bitchy women in one night. By God, it's too much! First the lingering bad taste over Sophie's tantrum and now totally unnecessary goading from this indignantly aroused woman was enough to quickly ignite his ready temper.

"You just do as you please, don't you?" Alisa continued, angrily clutching the bedclothes to her heaving bosom.

"As I please!" Nikki snarled, the black rage and

irritation of the long day, his interview with his father, the long afternoon and evening drinking at the club, his required appearance at the Golchoffs' party, the unwanted ministrations of Sophie and now this screaming shrewish virago all finally burst into an uncontrollable fury. Needless to say, twelve hours of drinking brandy did little to curb or tranquilize his foul disposition.

"Perhaps I can persuade you to alter your 'mood,'" Nikki enunciated evenly as he walked slowly toward the bed, beginning to unbutton his tunic jacket. "Move over," he said unpleasantly through gritted teeth, continuing to strip off his clothes. Lifting first one foot and then the other onto the silk counterpane he unbuckled the spurs and dropped them on the floor.

"Damnable boots!" he cursed, sitting heavily on the bed; it was impossible to remove them without help. He turned to Alisa and pulled the bedclothes from her.

"Put your back to these boots, madame, or I'll ride you shod. At least Sophie knows enough to help me off with them."

"I suppose that whore serves you gladly!" Tears sprang to her eyes.

"Yes and now *this* whore will serve me, gladly or no. Bend to the task, my dear."

He lay on the bed and flung one foot into her lap.

"Pull, dammit, I'm in a hurry!"

As Alisa struggled with first one tall, slim patent leather boot and then the second, Nikki stripped the leather breeches from his hips and slid them onto the floor. Lying back on his elbows at the foot of the bed, he surveyed his seething mistress with a cold, predatory gaze.

"Don't you dare touch me!" she cried, finishing her task.

"Dare? I dare? Mrs. Forseus, you bait the wrong man tonight." His tone was dangerous. "Now, my sweet, take off that negligee or it will be in shreds in seconds."

Alisa lunged for Nikki's face with bared nails as he came at her, clawing instinctively for his eyes. He snapped his head back and the vicious nails raked one cheek, leaving deep furrows which immediately sprang red. A new shock of anger surged through him.

Lashing out, he slapped Alisa across the face, sending her reeling onto her back.

"Don't scratch my face." The voice was soft with an unnatural calm. "I abhor having to give explanations." There was a strange light in his flashing eyes and a cruel twist to his mouth as he ripped the filmy gown from her body.

"Now, my dear, come here and service me in the way of mistresses," he demanded as his hard, mocking eyes roved over her quivering form. "It seems my misfortune to be plagued tonight with unpaid whores who suddenly have principles. Really, my dear, isn't it a bit late for these theatrics of affronted honor?"

Alisa uttered an infuriated cry and again flung herself upon him. Nikki caught her hands in one swift movement, deceptively casual but cruelly tight, wrenched them behind her and bent her back on the bed beneath him.

Violently her knee came up and he arched back

just in time, loosening his grip on her wrists. For a brief second Alisa twisted free and swung both legs over the side of the bed. Plunging his fingers into the heavy waves of her hair, Nikki savagely pulled her back, rolled over her, pinning her arms at her sides. As he forced a knee between her legs, they found themselves in close contact, and they glared at each other, both panting, incensed, blood running down Nikki's swarthy cheek.

Tears of frustration rose in Alisa's eyes as she lay exhausted, pinioned helplessly despite her struggles. With a sardonic quirk Nikki lowered his blood-stained face and sought her trembling mouth, kissing her long and insolently. Alisa's efforts at resistance were futile against such strength and brutal determination. With a stubborn perversity Nikki held her immobile and caressed her, forcing her to kiss him, filling her mouth with his thrusting tongue, slowly, lingeringly, destroying thought or opposition. Soon she no longer wished to struggle, she ached for him, longed to embrace him, but the animosities of the long night alone, while he was with another woman, still rankled and she would not grant him the satisfaction of responding. She lay inert beneath his touch, knowing this servile passivity annoyed and frustrated him.

"Am I discharging my duties properly?" she taunted. "Is this befitting subservience, my Prince? A tame enough mistress, my lord?"

With a superhuman effort he kept from slapping the audacious wench and, cursing softly, swore to himself that he would hear her beseech and plead for him soon. The skilled hands roved her body while his lips followed and caressed each tender fount of pleasure. He cupped her full breasts and lowered a mouth to tease and warm each soft nipple until they peaked proud and rigid, then moved down her satin smooth belly into the down beneath, and further still until his hands and tongue had probed and titillated the soft regions of pleasure and the inert woman moaned softly and moved fitfully and arched in search of his pleasing tongue. Raising himself up and over her body he glided slowly into her wet, lubricated warmth, then moved gently backward and forward, slowly forcing himself deeper with each gentle stroke. Her legs gripped and she lifted to meet each sensual thrust; her heavenly violet eyes fell back voluptuously. The fire of passion threatened to consume them both but Nikki deliberately restrained himself. Alisa wrapped her arms tightly around Nikki's muscular back and pulled him to her. Suddenly Nikki withdrew.

Alisa cried out in dismay, as suddenly she was empty and alone.

Lifting himself up and leaning both hands on the bed, Nikki looked into her startled, confounded eyes and said softly, "Ask me."

"You do this to humiliate me," she whimpered, trying to pull a sheet over her naked throbbing thighs.

"Ask me," he repeated inexorably.

"Please," she sobbed quietly.

"Please what?" he questioned mercilessly.

"Please," she caught her breath, faltered, then whispered, "make love to me."

"Say, fuck me."

She did not answer.

"Say, fuck me or I'll leave."

A pause, then she whispered, "Fuck me." Her lips burned at the word.

"Does it matter that I have come from another woman now?" he persisted. He began again to tease her damp soft crevice, moving his fingers slowly, gently.

She hesitated. "No, Nikki," she said at last. She moved her legs to make herself wide for him.

"Are you ready for me?" he cruelly continued, stroking her harder. Almost hurting her most tender flesh.

"Yes," she murmured, her eyes closed, too ashamed to look at him. Nikki exhaled a deep breath of satisfaction. His desire for vengeance was gratified.

Dropping down, he took her then, no longer in fury but in hunger. She drew him deeper and deeper into herself, shuddering in ecstasy with each plunging stroke, holding him fiercely against each withdrawal. She was wild, begging him with her body to stay inside her. He brought her to a tumultuous climax and lay quiet in her as the waves of pleasure died away then brought her up to the peak again and then allowed himself to reach fulfillment.

"My compliments to a bewitching, dutiful mistress," he whispered teasingly, kissed her tenderly and fell asleep cradling Alisa in his arms. Alisa couldn't sleep for a long time, mortified by her body's traitorous desires.

IX
THE BEGUILING BELLE

Rising early the next morning without disturbing Nikki, Alisa dressed and went downstairs to breakfast. A melancholy pervaded her thoughts as she regretted the passions that put her so mercilessly under Nikki's domination, while a slow anger remained over Nikki's gross perfidy in coming straight from Sophie's bed to hers. She toyed with her breakfast in an abstracted silence, only responding mechanically to the friendly conversation of Nikki's parents as they attempted to restore her normally cheerful spirits. Kaisa-leena sympathized with her son's lovesick mistress and sought ways to comfort her; she was not too old to have forgotten the torment of loving with the despairing gloom of youth. The old Prince fulminated blackly, personally disposed to thrash his son if it would do the least bit of good. Sighing resignedly as he viewed the folly of that useless endeavor, he decided instead on a course of action which might be more successful. He wanted Nikki to marry this fascinating young woman who was bearing his grandchild but balked at the use of naked power to achieve his ends. He could, of course, quite literally compel Nikki to wed the girl but preferred less harsh measures. But he would not be gainsaid; he would bring his recalcitrant son to heel, one way or another, by force if necessary, but first—a more subtle attempt.

"Alisa, my pet, after that disgraceful spectacle created by Nikki and Sophie last evening at the Golchoffs' ball, might I hope to persuade you to move your quarters to our wing, at least temporarily. I think that scapegrace son of mine deserves a set-about. Would you be receptive to the idea? Kaisaleena and I would be delighted to have you in our apartments." (And in a palace boasting ninety-two bedrooms, the distance factor was considerable, from the parent's east wing to the son's west wing.)

Alisa's eyes lit up in relief. The perfect solution to her dilemma. She could not control herself when Nikki was pressing his suit, and it would serve him right for his arrogant, dominating attitude. She would simply remove herself from the temptation of Nikki's soft lips and practiced hands. Memories of last night's tempestuous, degrading act of union outraged her whenever she recalled the humiliation he had forced on her. She lifted her chin determinedly and smiled mockingly.

"An excellent idea, Monsieur, for I fear your son has very little use for me after all." Would this retaliation even suit? Indeed, would Nikki even care? She knew with a desperate hopelessness that she cared very much if he missed her. A pang of great loneliness, even amidst the devotion and friendship of Nikki's parents' concern, enveloped her. She was alone as she had been for the last six years. One could ultimately rely on no one but one's self in this world and sometimes the emptiness of that solitude was overwhelming.

"We shall see about that, my dear child. I think the young fool will find your absence provoking."

* * *

SEIZED BY LOVE 195

Later in the day after Nikki had gone out, the change was effected. That evening at dinner, when apprised of the alteration, Nikki did not rage or threaten. In fact, Alisa noted with consternation, he scarcely evinced any noticeable sign of acknowledgment. The drumming pulse in his temple would have been visible to only the most astute observer as Nikki casually drawled, "I see, father, you're up to some scheme. Pray do not be disappointed if I fail to rise to the lure."

He consumed his meal with his usual careless indifference, perhaps imbibing one or two more glasses of wine than normal, politely asked to be excused when the third course was served, declaring he had recalled an urgent matter requiring his attention, rose unhurriedly to his feet, drew himself up to his full six feet four inches, courteously bid his adieux and strolled in immaculate evening dress out of the dining room.

Prince Mikhail accompanied Alisa and Princess Kaisa-leena to a dancing party that evening and when Alisa caught sight of Nikki walking in with a very young lady dressed demurely in pale pink organza, the shock was like a dagger in her heart. Her despair was not improved when, later in the evening, Countess Amalienborg with her customary disregard sat down next to Alisa and, leaning confidentially close, began inquiring in an apparently polite fashion of her relationship with the Kuzans. Alisa was too disconsolate to parry the swift ripostes.

"Come, come, my dear, the green-eyed monster is too apparent. Your heart is in your eyes, cherie." Without pity the worldly, smiling woman continued, "It is only natural he should have wanted you, you

are quite a diverting little beauty and he is after all
a healthy young animal, but my dear, please do not
pine so openly. He is an incorrigible rogue and has
affairs without number, all of which are very short
lived. Nikki is the most notorious rake in town, has
a horrid temper, and every scrap of scandalous
rumor you hear of him is true. But because of his
outrageous charm, wealth and breeding he is still
the most eligible parti in Petersburg and received in
even the most reserved drawing rooms; in point of
fact, I have just learned that he paid a morning call
today on sweet little Emilie Belkenkoff on whom he
is dancing attendance tonight. This remarkable visit
quite effectively threw Emilie's mother into delighted
speculation. Nikki simply never calls on sweet young
chits in the daytime."

The significance of the timing of that visit was
very clear. He had not even known she was moving
from her room that morning. The transfer had not
taken place till late afternoon. She was evidently
only another of his short-lived affairs. Her temper
blazed, the melancholy burned away in a fire of
resentment. The violet eyes under her heavy lashes
turned royal purple to match her royal rage.

"This morning?" she inquired coldly.

"This morning," Sophie cooed.

Had Nikki taken the notion in his head to court
the pink frosting confection? He had always declared his intention to settle on a biddable school-
room miss, and if he chose to pay addresses no
young miss could remain entirely indifferent to his
practiced charm and handsome good looks. Someone
like young Emilie, who couldn't be over seventeen,
must be in love at first sight. Alisa glanced up to see

Nikki across the room, bending solicitously over a seated Emilie, talking quietly with an admiring attention upon that sweet upturned face.

Soothingly patting Alisa on the knee as she rose to leave, her malevolent intentions fully realized, Sophie said with an air of benevolent condescension, "I am sure, cherie, that you will find a very suitable husband from among these young blades panting after you. Someone eminently more suitable to your station in life. Nikki can, after all, as a Prince of one of the finest families, look much higher than a poor obscure young widow with a child, and young Emilie's antecedents are impeccable."

"No doubt it will be refreshing. After Nikki's usual dalliance with, as you say, obscure widows and," Alisa pointedly continued, "jaded sluts, a bonbon of such obvious naiveté as Emilie will be a welcome change."

The thrust hit home, for the Countess turned swiftly on her heel and left in a huff without replying.

Alisa watched Nikki dancing with the dainty young girl, a sugar plum kind of female, all pink and white and softly rounded, dressed in multitudinous pink ruffles adorned with creme roses. Her pale cornsilk hair had been fashionably arranged, pulled up high and bouffantly in front, while glossy golden curls cascaded down the back of her neck and onto smooth white shoulders. Indeed, it would have been hard to find fault with her appearance. Nikki was carrying on his customary charmingly insouciant conversation to which the innocent young girl could only blush or giggle in reply.

For the twentieth time that night Nikki made one of those bland social remarks necessary to occasions such as this, "You waltz quite enchantingly, my dear." He waited patiently for the inevitable. It came, after half a heartbeat—the trilled little flight of nervous laughter. Nikki gritted his teeth and glided into a wide turn. He felt sorry for the nervous sweet thing. She was out of her league, unpracticed in elegant badinage, but sympathy did not necessarily behoove obligation, he abruptly decided. Smothering a yawn, his attention wandering to contemplate a ripe brunette with shiny ringlets and a practiced eye who was scrutinizing him. Through force of habit he gave the blooming brunette a wicked wink over the cornflower blonde head.

Thankfully, the waltz ended and he returned young Emilie to her beaming mama, who was probably already measuring him for the marriage bed, then sauntered slowly across the floor toward Alisa. As he approached the swarm of young swains milling around Alisa, the crowd parted and quickly drifted away under the steely gaze Nikki bestowed on each and every one of them. After curtly nodding dismissal to one of Alisa's lingering admirers more foolhardy than the rest, Nikki drawled, "Must you, madame, constantly surround yourself with such lovesick pups? I should think you would find the conversation tedious."

Alisa did not speak and Nikki with a comfortable smugness perceived that his deliberate attendance on Emilie had not gone unnoticed, thus he would count one point for his side in this three-way war of wills between father, son, and mistress.

"You should talk, Prince Kuzan. Aren't sweet witless young misses equally tedious? I swear, that little blonde appeared to do nothing but blush or titter," Alisa finally answered him acerbically.

"Alas, Madame, quite true, and while she's not entirely witless, as near to it as makes no difference," Nikki sighed and shrugged eloquently, "so I think my duty dances for the evening will now suffice. I fear my background of vice and dissipation has little acquainted me with the pleasures of virtuous young women."

The direct cut was blunt and deliberate.

Alisa's eyes sparked in anger as she purred spitefully, "Perhaps what you need, Prince Kuzan, is an introduction to more virtuous pursuits. Who knows, you may not be totally sunk beyond redemption. A few evenings or afternoons in the company of that pink and white miss might be rewarding."

"Egad, woman, are you mad? Two dances was enough to give me the headache. I'm off to take the perfect remedy for a headache, a bottle of brandy. Would you care to join me, my sweet?"

"Thank you no, I shall continue to converse with these young gallants in hopes of raising myself somewhat from the depths of depravity, as you so frankly put it. These young blades have a refreshing youthful charm."

Nikki had no idée fixe on women's morality, but his views on his mistress' morality were decided.

"As you wish, just so long as you offer no more than conversation. Remember. I prefer your charms to remain exclusively mine," he finished. His eyes twinkled mischievously as he saw how angrily Alisa responded to his directive.

"We are not all indiscriminate whores like Countess Amalienborg, Monsieur."

"How *very* reassuring, my love." Nikki raised her hand to his lips and brushed Alisa's fingertips with his warm breath while he gently massaged her palm. "Adieu, my love, until later," he murmured imperturbably as Alisa flushed pink at his touch and tried to snatch her hand away. Deliberately holding her hand a few moments more before relinquishing it, he grinned faintly, gave a swift bow, turned on his heel and began strolling toward the card room.

Alisa willed herself to control the rising pulsations Nikki's touch had evoked. Damn him! His merest touch set off sensuous ripples through her veins. She shook herself mentally and looked up smiling lightly at Lt. Polovtsev who was the first to reappear at her side.

X
THE ANGRY LOVER

For the better part of a fortnight now, Alisa had been squired around a frantic whirl of parties, dances and dinners by Prince Mikhail and Princess Kaisa-leena; the father determined to see that Alisa was enjoying herself regardless of Nikki. Removing Alisa from Nikki's embrace was not without a shrewd intent on the part of his father who knew his son's need of women. For Alisa, it was pure anger and revenge; she would show Nikolai Mikhailovich Kuzan she was quite capable of having a marvelous time without him.

In spite of Alisa's vengeful intent, she woke up one morning after a particularly grueling evening, and decided she could take this no longer. She must get away. She was exhausted, sick and nauseous again. The ball last night had lasted until four. After returning home she had slept poorly. All this feverish round was taking its toll; she found polite enthusiasm more and more arduous to summon. One must always appear cheerful, vivacious and interested when the only person she was interested in scarce recognized her in a crowd. This just wasn't working; no matter how kind Nikki's parents were, she resolved to leave, out of a combination of fatigue, despondency and grief.

Alisa sent a footman with a message to Aleksei requesting him to escort her shopping in one hour.

Hastily dressing in a sedate walking costume of brown silk, a coarse straw hat lined with velvet perched on her curls, she gulped a cup of tea in an attempt to ease the nausea. Then she went to her jewel box and, with only a moment's hesitation, plunged the splendid emerald necklace Nikki had given her into her reticule and rushed downstairs to find Aleksei already in the front hall waiting.

"Thank you, Aleksei. You're always to be depended on."

"You know I'd do anything for you, Alisa," and in his nineteen-year-old puppy infatuation, he sincerely meant it. She explained in the coach what she intended to do, and they set off for 28 Morskaija, the street where the finest shops were situated. Aleksei promised to help; he could find an apartment for her; of course he would be delighted to assist her.

The jeweler who had sold the necklace to Nikki was more than obliging about buying the emeralds back.

"Certainement, Madame, we would be more than willing."

The price offered astounded Alisa; she could live three years on the proceeds if she were frugal. Profuse thanks were exchanged and the business was concluded.

Alisa returned to the palace in prodigious fine spirits, sustained by thoughts of thwarting Nikki. She would leave and fie to him! Aleksei said she had but to ask and his time was hers.

"In a few days, Aleksei, we'll go apartment hunting. You can help me find my new home. I'll drop you a note."

* * *

The idea of living alone did not hold as much pleasure as the day progressed. Alisa lay on her bed that afternoon moodily contemplating life without Nikki. Could she do it after all, now that her pique of anger had passed and she was not as irritable and tired as earlier this morning.

These musings were interrupted as a sharp rap sounded on her door and in his normal way, Nikki walked in without waiting for a reply. Still dressed in buckskins and tweeds from an afternoon ride, he strode, ill-humoredly glowering, over to the bed and tossed the emerald necklace at Alisa's feet.

"Mrs. Forseus," he said in a glacial murmur, a wintery smile on his face, "I wish you wouldn't be so ready to dispose of my gifts. It smacks of the mercenary, designing professional. If your need of pin money has reached these proportions, I'm sure you could have easily approached my father or myself."

"How . . . how did you find out?" Alisa stammered, since no more than four hours had elapsed since her visit to the jeweler.

"Mr. Fabergé and I are acquaintances of long standing, so he informed me immediately when the necklace I purchased so recently had been resold. With all due sincerity he felt I should know that my inamorata was quite desperate for funds. Have you gaming debts, my dear?"

"No!" she snapped, "I'm leaving and I need money."

"If it's Cernov, I'll . . . His scowl deepened and he glared at her.

"Don't be ridiculous," Alisa tartly replied, giving him back look for look. "I'm simply getting my own apartment."

Nikki's brow lifted as a flicker of relief shone in his eyes.

"If that's all you want why didn't you say something?" The tense crease between his brows relaxed.

"You have not been exactly available these many days past, Monsieur."

"Rest assured, my love, the oversight will be remedied. I'll have Ivan find you something suitable tomorrow. This damn living in my parents' apartments has been hellishly inconvenient."

A smile broke across his handsome face. "It will be pleasant to have you for myself again without my parents' affronted breath constantly on my neck."

"I think you misunderstand, Prince." Alisa flung up her head defiantly. "I wish to live alone. Alone!" she screamed, her lips trembling.

The smile disappeared in an instant.

"In that case, Madame, you will stay here. I'll not have you available for all the lecherous acquaintances of mine to patronize. Keep the money, but if you attempt to leave, I'll have you locked in . . . and to hell with father!" he yelled.

"Remember now, I mean what I say," he said ominously. "If you try to flee I'll run you to ground within the day and if I am put to that irksome exertion, you will find my temper disagreeable. Dammit, Madame," he exploded, "You *will* do as I say!" and so saying, he turned and left the room.

A damned bird in a gilded cage, that's what she was. Why was she so unhappy, so desolate. If he would just say he cared. Why couldn't he say he cared?

The party-going resumed, both Alisa and Nikki

perhaps even more deliberately provoking to each other. Just out of spite, for the effort was excruciatingly boring, Nikki did occasionally pay homage to young Emilie, preferably at a ball or a party where he did not have to endure long stretches of her undiluted company, but by and large, Nikki had returned to spending his evenings at the club. His gambling and drinking were deep and heavy, his remarks often bordering on the insulting. A defiant recklessness spurred his actions and even his closest friends judiciously chose to tread warily, not anxious to provoke his sarcasm or find themselves at the other end of his dueling pistol.

Precisely at two each night Yukko would appear at his side, the cards would be discarded, regardless of the hand, irrespective of his gains or losses; Nikki would rise slowly, offer polite excuses to his partners and stroll out of the club followed by Yukko.

Each night, in turn, curious, watchful eyebrows were raised as Prince Kuzan's late appearance was duly noted at the parties, routs or festivities graced by his beautiful "cousin."

Invariably, he would sullenly lean against one of the walls, drink in hand, nursing his anger, and follow with glowering eyes the slender figure of Alisa as she whirled past in a waltz or flirted brightly with the young officers. He felt insulted and very angry, but he pretended a methodical detachment.

One evening an old tabby approached Nikki and remarked injudiciously, with a gay little titter, "It appears your cousin is quite surrounded by admirers and just when it had been rumored that you had developed a tendre for the poor creature." (The "poor creature" in this instance was laughing gaily at some sally from young Count Berzlov, arrayed in a sumptuous creation of green gauze and diamond brilliants, decorated with sprays of silk apple blossoms tied in place with green velvet bows, her ripe luscious bosom a foil for the magnificent emeralds.) Nikki watched her and seethed.

"It seems you are most alarmingly hindered by rivals. For one must admit your cousin is beautiful as sin."

"Countess," Nikki replied as calmly as his inebriated mind was capable, "my 'cousin,' " he purred the word maliciously, "occasionally lacks discrimination in her friendships. But let me suggest, Madame, that in future perhaps I shall remedy her shortcoming," he finished acerbically, bowed insolently and walked away.

Since being locked out from Alisa's bedroom, Nikki's temper hadn't been improved by his unaccustomed celibacy. Emilie was untouchable, had he even felt the inclination, which he didn't. There was little challenge in such a simpering child, and little pleasure, too, he would imagine. The four incidents with dancers hardly counted; merely a perfunctory performance briefly engaged and as rapidly forgotten. Other women simply didn't look interesting anymore. Damn Alisa's alluring ways. He could not shake from his thoughts the beauty and sensuality of this unique, infuriating minx.

It had been a long, frustrating, exceptionally irritating two weeks. With a palpable, but losing effort, he was attempting to maintain some semblance of control over his growing irritation.

They met quite by accident one evening, two nights later.

Alisa, having been left by her partners who went solicitously to fetch her an ice, heard a familiar chuckle and whirled around. Nikki was standing almost directly behind her, lounging against a pillar.

For over a fortnight he had treated her with coolness when they met at a social affair or in the rooms of the Kuzan palace. The golden eyes that stared into hers were both insolent and admiring.

"Merde, you look demure. A creditable feat for a whore clothed in that gown. Are you displaying your wares for the highest bidder? The gauze of your bodice almost reveals more than it covers." The sarcasm coiled around her, silky smooth and faintly menacing.

"At least should I choose to accept one of the bidders, I can offer him warmth in bed, which is more than you'll get from that pale confection of a mechanical doll you have been squiring around." "How is she in bed, by the way?" Alisa retorted angrily.

Nikki said, "Not much good, the bitch. But one can always find someone else to warm my flesh, my dear, should I tire of the giggling," he coldly stated as his eyes lingered on her pretty breasts which were almost completely exposed. "May I compliment you on the effectiveness of your ensemble. Never have I seen wantonness so beautifully unclothed. One's imagination quite runs apace. You fairly invite ravishment dressed in such a fashion," he bluntly declared as his bold glance swept Alisa's form in the blue silk ball gown draped with a tunic of tulle trimmed with cut-outs of lace appliqué. "We're all waiting breathlessly to see if your gown will contain those luscious breasts so precariously balanced above these wisps of tulle," the sneering voice intoned as his long, lean index finger insolently flicked the offending blue tulle ruffles.

"Don't touch me," Alisa whispered hoarsely.

"They're probably taking bets in the card room right now as to whether you stay in or out of your dress tonight. May I offer my services in helping you out of it?" Nikki leered, "Although, no doubt, every man in this room will be equally anxious to offer you the same assistance."

A red flush rose up Alisa's slender neck and flamed on her cheeks.

"Blushing, my love? Outfitted in this gown which leaves so little to the imagination? I would have conjectured you were beyond maidenly blushes and soon into a new bed."

Alisa's eyes blazed fire as Nikki's calculatingly insulting remarks blandly continued. She wanted to run from him but she couldn't make a scene.

"And thanks to your excellent tutoring, Prince Kuzan, the new bed partners will not be disappointed in my accomplishments," she spitefully cooed.

"Did I remember to teach you everything?" Nikki paused in mocking thoughtfulness, "In any event, I'm sure your resourcefulness will prevail, but just a word of warning. Although your lovers, no doubt, won't be disappointed, you might be," he grinned.

It was too much Alisa turned forthwith and flounced away in a furious rage damning his insufferable arrogance.

The next several of Alisa's partners were nervously disconcerted to find their waltzing even more carefully followed by the coldly watchful eyes of Prince Kuzan, who was now holding up another pillar and refreshing himself rather regularly as the footmen went by with champagne. One might almost think he was trying to get drunk as he tossed down a glass, reached for another and repeated the action.

Lt. Bobrinski in the deep throes of infatuation made the mistake of waltzing Alisa through the large arcade into the conservatory. Nikki with apparent calm drained his champagne glass and followed the impertinent young officer. Alisa and the lieutenant were seated on a delicate iron bench under the brilliant display of a blossoming gardenia tree. Lt. Bobrinski was ardently pouring out his love to an embarrassed Alisa, offering her his hand, his heart, his rather considerable wealth.

With a baleful eye and a temper goaded beyond civility, Nikki surveyed this tender scene and then walked boldly up to the couple, interrupting Alisa in the midst of her confused acknowledgment of the deep honor she felt in having Pavlov regard her with so much affection.

Nikki's imperturbable voice finished Alisa's flustered statement by drawling, "Tempting as your offer is, Pavlov, my friend, I'm afraid Mrs. Forseus rather counts on having me for a husband."

The Lieutenant began protesting.

Quite pleasantly Nikki told him to be quiet, then continued, "If you will excuse us, Pavlov," Nikki said coolly, fixing him with a look of such cold malevolence that the young lieutenant stammered his adieux and hastily retreated.

"Must you always interfere?" Alisa flashed angrily, feeling hopelessly a prisoner.

"You wouldn't really consider marrying the pup, would you, my dear?" Nikki drawled.

"A lot more than I would ever consider marrying you," she retorted rudely.

"Ah, may I disagree with you, my love? But then, as the saying goes, since nobody asked you," he murmured dampingly, "I fear we shall never know. And then, darling, think what a shock Pavlov would have if you were to give birth to a child before you had time to marry or shortly after the ceremony. Now if the child was Pavlov's there would be no problem, even if it was born six months prematurely. As he well knows, being a direct descendant of Catherine the Great and Orloff, there is no stigma attached to illegitimacy if one's rank in society is lofty enough. But his family might frown on unanticipated progeny."

"Pavlov knows me as a widow just recently bereaved. A posthumous child is not without precedent," she spat irritably at Nikki's smug countenance.

"Not, however, when the child is born bearing my stamp," he quellingly retorted. "These black, wolfish features have an embarrassing inclination to reproduce," he softly murmured. "So you see, a

posthumous child in my image might require a bit
of explaining. Am I not right?"

Petulantly Alisa refused to answer.

"Maybe I should just not bring this pregnancy to
term and put a stop to all these senseless arguments,"
Alisa replied, wishing to wound as deeply as possible.

"Do not," he said in an awful voice, "even consider it." The tawny eyes smoldered, "It's too damned
dangerous. Illyich's little actress bled to death last
year because of a botched abortion. Let me assure
you it was not a pretty sight."

His words had the desired effect as Alisa paled
visibly.

Thoroughly annoyed at Nikki's checking her
riposte, Alisa retorted, "At least these men treat
me with respect and courtesy," allowing the obvious
comparison to hang in the air.

"Everyone has their own approach to the citadel,
my love," Nikki returned brutally. "Don't delude
yourself, cherie, they all have their tongues hanging
out for the same thing, but some cloak their desires
in a soothingly deceitful address."

"May I disagree with your coarse intimations of
my suitors' intentions. I have received several proposals of marriage. This is not the first. Is that a fine
enough indication of my beaux' regard for the
proprieties?" Alisa smiled smugly.

Nikki's eyes were very cold as he met her mocking gaze.

"Other marriage proposals? You have? Married?
Married?" he repeated. "If you were to be so foolish,
I would make you a widow soon enough, by God!"

He swore softly and long. "Married? By Christ, we'll see about that!" Nikki snapped contemptuously.

She was his, by God; he had wakened her to womanhood, had drawn the female from her shell of naiveté. She was not fair game for every drooling callow youth, every lustful eye, every practiced man about town. Wasn't his mark on her, wasn't she carrying his child? How dare they address marriage proposals to her, he thought with the unmitigated audacity of a Kuzan born and raised. He would tolerate this charade no longer! Locked out of her bed, her person guarded by his parents like an unblemished virgin, an untouchable holy relic. He *would* have her again. His anger was dangerously roused.

"I've watched you flirt and entice and coyly cast out lures for the last two weeks. My charmingly acquiescent temperament has reached its limit. You will flirt no more!" the quiet voice growled.

Alisa ignored his tone as her temper rose.

"Acquiescent!" she snorted. "Sooner try to convince me that the world is flat or that the sun rises in the west, you arrogant bastard!"

"Acquiescent," he whispered through clenched teeth and meant it, for what else had curtailed his rising fury these last weeks if not that sterling trait. He was not unfeeling and could understand the angry motives which prompted Alisa's light amorous bantering these several days past, but when marriage proposals resulted, he drew the line. Nikki's altruism never stretched so far as to sharing his mistress.

To hell with them all! He would take Alisa away tonight to Mon Plaisir, his estate north of Lake

Ladoga. Remote, sequestered, irrevocably off the beaten path, a summer with Alisa in that distant fastness of forest and kallio brought his blood up.

"You've permitted every whoremaster here tonight to ogle your bounteous charms. I think it's my turn," Nikki said, his face contorted in fury, his breathing deep and heavy.

"Come now, dear, we go. Your flirtatious days in society are over. I've put up with all the interference from father I will tolerate. My independence from his control ceased years ago."

"He'll stop you!" Alisa warned him, a rising note of hysteria in her voice as Nikki took her arm and began forcing her toward the door.

"I wish him luck in that endeavor," he coldly replied and then unexpectedly broke into a warm chuckle. An exhilaration raced through him. The inaction and restraint, the stifling protocol of society he had labored under for weeks were cast aside. He was his own man again! His old mad recklessness invigorated him. One could be prudent only so long and then must break away.

Taking Alisa's hand in a vicious grip that made her sob in pain, Nikki pulled her violently protesting through the conservatory, thankfully empty of people at the moment. He slammed through double French doors, dashing them aside with a powerful sweep of his arm, causing them to shudder indignantly on their metal frames. Oblivious to the shocked stares of partygoers on the terrace, he tossed up the now kicking, screaming, abusive Alisa and flung her over his shoulder. In this embarrassing position her pummeling fists uselessly bombarded

Nikki's strong back while he held her feet firmly in his left hand, concerned with protecting his manhood from her kicking toes.

"Put me down, you monster, you brute!" Alisa screamed, beating ineffectually against the broad back, cursing him furiously.

Blandly ignoring her screams and sobs of outrage, he did not even break stride as his long legs carried him and his rambunctious burden across the sweeping lawn, toward the waiting carriage.

Walking purposefully down the long row of carriages, Nikki found his equipage, opened the door and unceremoniously dumped Alisa onto the floor. Climbing in behind her, he curtly directed Feodor to drive back to the palace and slammed the door shut with a crack.

Immediately he was set upon by a scratching, clawing, screaming wildcat. For days now, he had been forced to contain his fury, his resentment, his frustration. There was a limit, diable, there was a limit! Screaming termagant! his mind thundered, I have my limits!

The horses had hardly begun to move when Nikki seized Alisa in one sweeping motion and shook her viciously by the shoulders. When she cried out, he hit her across the face with the flat of his hand. She sprang at him wrathfully, but he caught her arms in a relentless grip that left bruises on her flesh.

"I will not tolerate having you trifled with by other men!" he roared, the suppressed vexation of watching Alisa flirt and laugh and dance and posture before other men's frankly lustful gaze finally released.

"You're mine!" he thundered, "No man will trespass on my property! Do you understand?" He gripped her tighter and, struggling to regain his composure, spoke in a low, hard voice, "Do you understand?"

Alisa's eyes narrowed, her nostrils distended in anger, her lips bruised where he had struck her. He shook her again.

"Answer!" he roared, the brief moment of control snapped.

Alisa spat on him and laughed raucously at his discomfiture.

Nikki cuffed the laughing mouth and flung her across the carriage.

"Christ's blood, I'll have the taming of you yet," he said thickly.

He grabbed a handful of her copper curls and pulled her head back until her eyes were wild with pain and fear. Then he savagely stuffed his silk handkerchief into her gasping mouth, muffling her whimpering to a whisper, then tied his neckcloth around her head as a gag. Her wild eyes watched him rip the blue ruffles from the hem of her gown and truss her hands and feet together. Finally he flung her on the seat and sat smiling sardonically at her attempts to free herself.

When the carriage reached the pink marble palace, he grimly alighted from the carriage, closed the door and issued orders rapidly to Feodor.

"Mrs. Forseus fell asleep, please don't disturb her. Make ready a second carriage, bring along another coachman and four grooms; two outriders on mounts are also needed. Have everything ready in fifteen minutes."

Being neither deaf nor blind, Feodor didn't believe for a minute that Mrs. Forseus was sleeping but, inured to the idiocies of his young master, he only presented an impassive face and an affirmative response to his orders.

Nikki sprang up the stairs to the front door, anxious to be packed and off before his parents discovered Alisa's absence from the party. The startled butler was the recipient of numerous and curtly barked orders. Footmen were to carry down the luggage to the waiting carriages outside, maids were to be sent upstairs to help with the packing. Get Ivan his secretary immediately, he needed money and a letter sent to his regimental commander requesting leave, have the chef pack some food, vodka and brandy. Everything to be accomplished in no more than fifteen minutes. Understood? Sergei quailed before the dangerous look in Prince Nikolai's eyes.

Nikki bounded up the stairs to waken Katelina and whisper to her that they were going to the country. She was, always to him, a vivid recollection of the bright freedom and wonder of youth. Katelina, ever amiable to her favorite Nikki, had already tumbled out of bed and was collecting her toys.

"Uncle Nikki, will you teach me to ride a horse as you promised and take me hunting like you said?"

"I certainly will, lapsikulta," he pronounced solemnly, for he treated her with the courtesy of an equal, never condescending to patronize her childish delights. "I'll let you ride a horse, take you hunting with me and even teach you to drive your own pony cart."

"Uncle Nikki! What fun! I'll dress very quickly," she promised.

Nikki gave her a kiss and a quick hug, imparted instructions to Rakeli and Maria to have Alisa's and Katelina's clothes packed in ten minutes, and walked to his room to settle affairs with Ivan and select some of his favorite old clothes for hunting.

Within an incredible twenty minutes the small caravan was on its way, Katelina, Rakeli, and Maria settled comfortably in the second carriage, Arni riding guard outside, Nikki and Alisa traveling in the first carriage with two outriders in the vanguard.

As the carriages left the outskirts of the city behind, Nikki silently untied Alisa and removed her gag, neither gentle nor repentant.

Alisa closed her eyes as the gag was taken from her mouth. Gasping, she tried to speak, but her mouth was too dry. Slowly she sat up, breathing deeply, trying to gain some semblance of composure for what she was about to say. They eyed each other coolly.

Finally she was able to speak. She pronounced each word slowly and distinctly, having, in the angry solitude of her wait, discarded numerous and varied epithets and invectives. She was furious at being inhumanly treated as an object.

"I am not your baggage to be trussed and ordered about."

"You are now," he said grimly and unequivocally, not a flicker of tenderness in those tawny eyes. "At Mon Plaisir *I* am lord and master. *Everyone* obeys my bidding," he continued icily, emphasizing the pronouns. Steeling himself in an effort to remain reasonably calm under the strain his willful temperament had undergone this last fortnight, he said, "And now we'll have our first lesson in obedience, my lovely baggage."

He felt himself harden with lust.

"You will not flirt with Lt. Bobrinski or any other man again, will you?" He reached for Alisa and pulled her resisting body to his.

"I will if I choose," she spat, still defiant.

"You will not." In one motion he had thrown her face down across his lap, tossed her skirts back and pulled down her lacy drawers. Her lovely bottom was exposed. Hand poised above the soft, pink flesh, he mildly asked, "Will you now?"

Alisa shook her head affirmatively, stubbornly refusing to give in to his demands.

His hand came down and struck her brutally, leaving angry red welts on the smooth circles of flesh.

"Speak up, darling. I can't hear you," and the hand descended again to raise more finger marks on the tender skin.

She could feel him stiff and rigid against her belly and trembled at his anger.

"We'll return to this question later, my love," he sighed softly, his passion rising fast, a throbbing stiffness hard against his trousers. "It's time for your second lesson in obedience. The very motion of a carriage is enough to rouse my passions and you're so conveniently close." He slapped her again lightly.

"Off with your clothes, now. Let me gaze upon my property. I feel a need for your services."

Nikki turned her over and began pushing his and her clothes aside, too much in a hurry to undress. His two large hands held her face while his lips fiercely found hers, his open mouth demanding, insulting, his face dark with passion.

"You dirty lecher! You're just like the worst of all men!" Alisa rasped breathlessly as he released her lips.

"*Just* like?" inquired Nikki sardonically as he settled her with a casual effortlessness beneath him, adjusting her position precisely as he wanted her, his strong arms holding hers against the hard carriage seat.

"Worse!" she panted, unable to move against his powerful strength. His excitement was so intense now he shuddered at the seconds' delay in his rape. But rape her he would, for nothing else mattered.

"Or better, mayhap, my dear?" he smiled arrogantly and faintly as he mounted her and without any sympathy for her dry, unprepared passageway rammed himself in clean up to the hilt.

Alisa gasped in pain as Nikki viciously had his way. Despite an effort to steel herself, a cry was torn from her lips as a particularly fierce thrust ripped into her. He finished in seconds, leaving her wet too late to ease the pain, withdrew, wiped himself off on her petticoats and adjusted his clothes. Then he resumed his position on the seat opposite, and stretched out comfortably, leaving Alisa lying in pain and anger.

"A dog could do better!" she panted in disgust.

He turned his head with a slow, deliberate motion, his eyes cold and blank. A brief second elapsed and then the familiar derisive expression played across his face.

"My dear," Nikki replied softly in mock dismay, "I do hope you don't consider taking up Sophie's perversions. So very vulgar, you understand," and so saying, he shut his eyes wearily and with an infuriating, calm indifference proceeded to fall asleep.

Alisa pulled her clothes around her naked bruised body, turned over on her stomach and wept hysterically.

They traveled steadily for the next five days with only brief stops to rest the horses and break their fast. Nikki did not touch her again, he barely acknowledged her existence, further exasperating Alisa who longed to stir up some reaction when she railed at him in anger. For most of the journey Nikki slouched low in the seat, his long legs propped up on the seat opposite occupied by Alisa; a bottle of brandy was his constant companion.

On the evening of the fourth day, after having traveled with Katelina in the second carriage entertaining her with tales of fairies and elves most of the day, Nikki climbed back into Alisa's carriage and lay back against the seat.

Alisa immediately began hurling denunciations at his head, trying to ease some of her resentment at being so arrogantly and tyrannically abducted. Further adding to her anger was the fact that Katelina looked upon the whole journey as another delightful adventure being supplied by her darling Uncle Nikki, and even Alisa's old and loyal servants were quietly pleased to be going back to the country; they much preferred their familiar pine forests to the bustle and dirt of the city. Even Rakeli and Maria seemed to be on Nikki's side, and they would look uncomfortably away in embarrassment when Alisa would deliver some malicious remark to Nikki in their presence. She could not bring herself to tell them the extent of his brutality to her.

After patiently and quietly listening to the string of invective for several minutes, Nikki held up his hand wearily in an attempt to stay the tirade directed at him.

"Please, my dear, no more." He heaved a small sigh. "Your virulent sentiments do not stimulate my interest. I am by nature a very mild man," (Alisa snorted derisively) Nikki continued unperturbed, "and actually, dear, I prefer considerably more passivity in a woman. So do try and be slightly more silent. In fact this constant heckling may be dangerous, don't you see? My restraint is not unlimited and it has been four days now." His heavy lids rose slowly, revealing a gaze suspiciously sardonic. "I'm surprised you have such a penchant for soliciting abuse. It must be your long apprenticeship under Mr. Forseus' tutelage. Does it develop a certain masochism, love? I must admit, I personally view with odium my rather brutal attentions directed at you that first evening in the carriage. Most unprecedented; perhaps I could be excused as having been under unique pressures and then, of course, you are decidedly provoking with your tempestuous tantrums. Forgive me. It will not happen again."

"At least, I suppose that's something I have to be thankful for," Alisa snapped.

Ignoring the sarcastic retort, Nikki continued in his calm, equable tone, which explained but neither petitioned nor beseeched its listener.

"I must warn you, however, as soon as we arrive

at Mon Plaisir, if you continue to remain recalcitrant to my ah—demands, some methods of persuasion will be necessary, although, rest assured, they'll be more pleasant and subtle than those I so hastily and imprudently resorted to five days ago."

"You're all kindness to be sure, Monsieur," Alisa retorted angrily, "but I shan't be long at Mon Plaisir. You can't make me stay."

With a husky laugh which indicated that he thought otherwise, Nikki replied quietly, an ironic smile in evidence, "I disagree, but do, by all means, put it to the test. In my present humor," he went on grimly, "after having listened to your insults for four days and five nights, I feel extremely inclined to let my mild, chivalrous nature lapse momentarily and add some fresh bruises to that creamy white body of yours. Even *my* benign patience is not interminable."

The cold steely look in his eyes restrained the angry retort Alisa was about to make and she lapsed into silence. The rest of the journey passed in a frigid hostility. They reached the estate late that afternoon.

In 1796 Nikki's grandfather decided to build a wooden country villa on his forest tract far north of Lake Ladoga, a retreat from the frenzied pace of court life. Using hundreds of serf artisans, this large structure was built completely of wood, with the ax alone (saws, chisels and drills were used only for decorative details) and had not a single iron nail or other metal part. It was built "by the eye" and became a remarkable demonstration of the spontaneous expression of the folk genius.

The central eighty-foot-long, three-story block

was flanked by two wings extending the overall length of the facade facing the lake to one hundred and sixty feet. Elaborate openworked eaves projected over the log walls cut flat on both exterior and interior. Intricately carved moldings framed each window and doorway, vast carved panels were inset in walls, delicate spindle-railed balconies projected from the second floor bed chambers, while a huge baroque pediment flanked by carved whole tree trunk pilasters distinguished the main entrance doors.

By the spring of 1798 the villa was completed, the interior as beautifully crafted as the exterior. Chandeliers, mirrors, door frames, the parquet were all made of wood; some gilded, all of superb execution. The scrollwork on furniture, frames and candelabra: incredibly carved garlands, roses, cornflowers, figures, animals, all were made of wood by men unable to write their own names.

The rooms all bespoke the quiet charm of the hand craftsman; softly waxed floors, fur and woven rugs, tapestries, handwoven linens, crocheted lace, embroidery in the traditional tomato red stitchery (in Russian the words "red" and "beautiful," both 'krasnyi', were identical), while fresh flowers were arranged in huge vases throughout the house.

All these splendors were only briefly glimpsed by Alisa as Nikki immediately carried her up to his chambers in the East Wing, laid her on the bed, turned without a word, walked out of the room and locked the door.

Returning back downstairs, Nikki directed the servants and Katelina into the West Wing where they were to be housed. Seeing that the little girl was settled comfortably, he explained to her as well as to Rakeli and Maria that Alisa wasn't feeling well because of the arduous trip and she would remain in her room for a few days until she felt stronger. He promised Katelina to take her riding the next day and told her to come and see her mother in the morning and wake him up. The servants did not resist Nikki's suggestions that Alisa be afforded seclusion for a few days, because he had charmed them as well as Katelina and they did not view him as anything but kind and generous to them all. He was courteous to them and politeness itself to Alisa and Katelina in their presence. He had even accepted Alisa's spiteful remarks during the long journey with a benevolent, restrained calm.

In fact Rakeli annoyed Alisa by her constant praises of Prince Kuzan. He is so much nicer than old Mr. Forseus, she would say with a completely unassailable simplicity.

Nikki returned to the bedroom in the East Wing after having ordered some supper sent up. He found Alisa pacing agitatedly back and forth between the huge bed and the bay windows which overlooked the acres of lawn sloping down to the lake shore.

"Don't wear a path in my Carabagh rug, love. You might as well relax. You're here for the duration."

"How long will that be, pray tell?"

"As long as I desire your services. If you contrive to amuse me I may let you out sooner."

Her mouth dropped open in astonishment.

"You're going to keep me locked up?"

"Precisely."

"You can't! I'll scream, I'll tell Rakeli and Maria what a monster you are; I'll make your life a hell!" she cried in high dudgeon.

"Upon further contemplation, my dear, I think you won't. Now," he said briskly, "let us be practical. You are 300 versts from the nearest town. I am the master of this estate and its employees. If you attempt to inform Rakeli or Maria or Katelina or anyone else of your, shall we say—'retirement for health reasons,' I'll lock you up in an isolated cabin which is two miles deeper in the forest and inaccessible to anyone but me. I'll inform Katelina and your retainers that you have returned to Petersburg for a short stay and venture to entertain Katelina myself, which shouldn't be too difficult. You may have noticed, we're great friends. After she goes to sleep in the evening, I shall slip away to your forest cottage and have you entertain me for the night."

Alisa's heart sank in dismay as she listened to Nikki's voice explaining her alternatives.

"Now, if you should, instead, choose," he continued amiably, "to remain here in this room and obey me, I'll allow Katelina to visit you every morning as you are both in the habit of doing and I will also allow you to sit on the balcony outside the bay windows and watch me tutor Katelina in riding and driving a pony cart. She is delightfully pleased with both prospects. If you undertake to be biddable and obedient, I'll permit you to see Katelina and your servants. If you disobey me, you shall be locked in my cabin. I'm sure you will agree to my terms when you consider the great advantages to seeing things my way."

Alisa sat on the bed, her mind racing to find some

alternative, some way out of the trap she was caught in.

"Really, dear, I don't like to press you, but do come to a decision soon, for if you choose to be obstinate, I must spirit you away to the cabin tonight. You understand, with morning," he said deprecatingly, "the difficulties would be endless."

She had no choice, Alisa reflected bitterly. She couldn't think of a single pathway out of this tangled web. If she stayed at the villa at least her opportunities for escape would be greater and Katelina would be close.

"Very well," she said sullenly. "I'll stay here."

"Marvelous. I thought you would accede; after all, you are a clever woman. Now, unless you plan on sleeping in your dress I suggest you wash off the dust of the road and get into something more comfortable."

As if on cue, a timid knock was heard; Nikki unlocked the door and a procession of servants entered. Two footmen carried an enormous ceramic bathtub which several more servants then filled with steaming hot water. Stacks of linen towels were left on the dresser and the cavalcade withdrew as silently as it had entered.

"Madame, please be my guest," Nikki gestured grandly.

Alisa would have liked to curtly refuse the offer but after five days in a dusty, rocking carriage, the temptation of a warm, soothing bath was too much to resist. One searching glance around the room indicated neither dressing room nor screen. A mental shrug dismissed the issue. Surely it was a little late to be unduly concerned with modesty. Alisa kicked off her high-heeled yellow kid slippers and reached behind her neck to undo the countless buttons marching down the back of her lemon yellow traveling costume.

"May I offer my assistance as lady's maid?" Nikki drawled softly as he leaned back against one of the enormous carved posts of the bed.

"Thank you no!" Alisa snapped. "I'll manage."

Several minutes later despite all attempted efforts, she was unable to reach all of the succession of minute covered buttons. Nikki watched her contortions, a slight smile playing about his mouth. Alisa looked up once and shot him a murderous glance, whereupon he quickly composed his features into a sham solemnity.

Several seconds later: "Please dear, do accept my services or your bath water will be disagreeably cool. Since we must out of—er—necessity dispense with personal servants, I beg you forget our differences and permit me to valet you these following days. I hardly relish the idea of seeing you in that same dress day and night."

If looks could kill, he chuckled to himself as he viewed the fuming, piqued woman opposite him.

Alisa did not deign to reply but merely flounced around offering her back to his ministrations. Several minutes of cursing later, which uncharitably cheered Alisa, the tiny buttons were all released.

"My God, Madame, those hellish loops are surely not meant for masculine fingers. A greater deterrent to lust I've never encountered."

"If I know you, sir," Alisa said with sweet malice,

"you wouldn't let such trivial defenses arrest your passions."

"It presents a certain dilemma, I will admit, though, and leaves one with only two choices. To make love to a clothed woman or to send a lady back home with her dress ripped in two. Now, the former course, unless excessively drunk, I abhor on principle; so very crude; and the latter I abjure out of prudence, for husbands and servants are apt to notice small matters such as tattered dresses when ladies return from afternoon visits or rout parties."

"Surely sir," Alisa couldn't prevent herself from saying, although she knew better than to provoke, "you'll understand if I find it singularly difficult to see you as either refined or prudent."

Not particularly goaded by Alisa's acrid remarks, since he had her exactly where he wanted her, quite literally under his fingertips, he yet had an irresistible compulsion to nettle her, as retribution for five days of vituperation he had suffered on their journey north.

In spurious anger, he growled, "Crude like this, cherie?" and he ripped the ties of her petticoats, which fell to the floor on top of the folds of lemon yellow silk. She stiffened.

"Imprudent like this, Madame?" and he swung her around to face him, reached out one powerful arm, forced his fingers between her full breasts, firmly grasped the material of both chemise and stays, gave a vicious wrench, and silk and lace ripped from top to bottom. They too joined the garments on the floor.

"Any more provocative remarks, my dear?" he

arrogantly demanded as Alisa stood crimson with shock before him, clad only in delicate, gossamer drawers. Then he laughed softly, saying, "I see, my dove, your temper is at its usual fine pitch. Have a pleasant bath." He flicked aside a red curl that had fallen across her breast, bent over slowly and sought a soft pink nipple between his fingers. He pinched gently, then harder. A wild tremor drove through Alisa and Nikki smiled triumphantly, pleased with his power over her. "Reluctant as I am to leave you just now, the dust of the road offends me, so I'm off to bathe in the lake. In deference to your—ah—delicate condition, I knew the 45 degree water temperature would not appeal to you."

With a blown kiss he was gone, the quiet click of the lock echoing in the silent room. Alisa burned with shame at her treacherous body and Nikki's recognition of her response.

Within the hour both Alisa and Nikki were refreshed from their baths and together in the large room, mauve and golden rays of the sun striking through the thick atmosphere of silence. Nikki was sunk deep in a down-cushioned chair, calmly reading while Alisa moved restlessly about, her thoughts in a confused turmoil, her emotions warring within her mind; all conflicting considerations ultimately overridden by anger at Nikki's arrogant mastery over her. Damn him, she wouldn't put up with this treatment. There must be some way out!

The servants knocked on the door at that moment and dinner was carried in. Two footmen set it out on a table near the tile fireplace.

"We will serve ourselves, thank you, Anastasia,"

Nikki said courteously to the beaming peasant woman who was directing the placement of the dishes.

"Is there anything more your lordship will require tonight?" she asked.

"No, nothing. I'll ring for you in the morning and Mrs. Forseus will select a menu for the day."

The servants cast surreptitious glances at the sullen beauty who was standing near the window tapping her foot in exasperation, scowling till her brows drew together over dark heavily lashed eyes. The door closed behind the retreating backs of the cook and footmen. Nikki walked over to the door, locked it and replaced the key in his waistcoat pocket.

"Don't be so foolish as to contemplate stealing the key while I sleep. I warn you, you would find the cabin extremely lonely when I caught you and brought you back there. And catch you I would; my Finnish trackers are nonpareil in their trade and have taught me since childhood a certain degree of proficiency as well."

Moving over to the table, Nikki lifted the covers on the silver dishes tastefully arranged on a hand-woven beige linen cloth; the crystal and china sparkling in the candlelight of four tall tapers.

"A magnificent meal. Come, dear, sit down. Look, I ordered all your favorite foods, although I apologize for not offering sterlet.[8] We left in such a rush, you'll forgive the oversight." A flicker of a grin appeared.

And indeed he had bespoken her food preferences, Alisa noticed, as she sat down and glanced over the sumptuous array before her: mushroom soup Madeira, duck au bigarade, brook trout in white wine sauce, cucumbers in sour cream, buttered baby carrots, wild strawberry tarts, large crusty rolls of dark rye, and almond dragées to complete the repast.

Nikki lounged comfortably in a large bergère that had been pulled up to the table.

"I would like a glass of champagne," he quietly ordered, adjusting the cuffs on his well-fitting chamois jacket.

"I'm not your servant," Alisa snappishly replied.

"You are now, my love, for you see, if you don't do as you're told, you don't eat. It's very simple, très simple," he breathed softly. (Having watched Alisa's healthy appetite increase due to her pregnancy, he had thought himself diabolically inspired to have devised such an affable form of persuasion. Alisa couldn't go long without eating; that he knew for a fact.)

"You wouldn't!" she gasped in horror.

"Try me," he said flatly.

Her eyes blazed in anger.

"I would like a glass of champagne." he repeated.

Alisa stubbornly sat where she was, seething with indignation, telling herself she'd starve before she did what he commanded.

"Dear, dear, I can see you're going to be difficult. I was so looking forward to a pleasant evening." Nikki helped himself to champagne and drank several glasses as he relaxed in his chair, watching the firelight, refilling his glass, occasionally offering an idle bit of gossip as conversation, which was pointedly ignored by the tight-lipped, seething beauty opposite him. In this same tranquil, easy manner he drank two bottles of Clicquot and was opening the third when he apologetically remarked, "I can't wait for you any longer. Please excuse my discourtesy; I believe I'll eat." He helped himself lavishly to each of the foods, pulled his chair slightly closer to the table and began eating slowly, resting between mouthfuls to drink his champagne. Nikki maintained a steady, quiet dialogue praising the flavor of the duck, remarking on the delicate hint of fennel in the trout sauce, activating the saliva glands in Alisa's mouth so she had to swallow often. He pretended not to notice.

Alisa hadn't eaten much that day, in fact, the entire five days had been pick-up meals and cold collations as they journeyed into this wilderness. She was inordinately hungry, bombarded now with the sight and delicious aromas of all her favorite dishes, and as Nikki had surmised, even more ravenously hungry due to her pregnancy. Damn his black soul, she was starving and he sat there chewing his food so slowly and carefully, you'd think he was a taster for some foreign potentate. She swallowed hard once again.

After twenty minutes of leisurely dining, Nikki softly reiterated, "I'd like some champagne," and he held out his goblet.

Alisa hesitated a long moment——then forcing aside her pride, she rose and poured the stemmed glass full of the bubbling liquid.

"*Now* may I eat?" she inquired sarcastically.

"Soon, dear. I'd like you to feed me first. It will teach you obedience. *My* comforts come first."

Gritting her teeth on the reply which sprang to her tongue, Alisa stood beside Nikki and dutifully fed him. He smiled up at her encouragingly between bites, blandly disregarding the glares she returned.

Much later when he deemed himself finally satisfied, she returned to her chair, sat down and reached for the food.

Nikki rapped her knuckles lightly with the hilt of a silver knife, arresting her hand in mid-air. Alisa gasped at the unexpected pain.

"Forgive the delay, but I'm afraid there is one more lesson yet, my sweet. I never quite received the proper replies to my questions that first night in the carriage. Perhaps you have reconsidered your answers. I stated that I will not tolerate you being trifled with by other men. Do you recall?"

Alisa sulkily shook her head and peevishly replied, "That hardly remains a problem out in this desolate part of the world. I'm 300 versts from the nearest dance or party."

"You may not be here forever. I want an answer," he said shortly, fixing her with a steady look. "Are you going to flirt with other men in the future?" he patiently inquired.

She looked at him woodenly, refusing to answer.

"Are you?" he questioned, a scowl darkening his brow.

"I may," she replied yawning, her devil of a will still recalcitrant.

"You what?" he roared furiously and swore roundly. Reaching across the small table he took her face between his two powerful hands and, glaring at her, whispered, "What did you say?"

She tried to glare back belligerently but her eyes fell before the fury in his.

"No," she gasped softly.

His hands slowly relaxed their cruel grip and he

released her face, leaned back in his chair, while a faint smile lifted his lips.

"You're learning to be sensible, my dear. Come here and sit on my lap; I'll feed you now."

"I can perfectly well feed myself," the soft lips spat, her violet eyes filled with resentment.

"Come," he commanded quietly, and she went.

Nikki fed her slowly as he held her on his lap. She ate and ate, the flavors delicious, the variety magnificent.

"I'm full. I would like to return to my own chair."

"A little more," Nikki insisted patiently.

"No." Alisa clamped her mouth shut obstinately like a small child.

"Come, love, a few more bites. I want my baby to be fat and healthy and I delight in your rounded curves filling out," Nikki murmured as he slipped his hand into the bodice of her negligee. "Such full, soft breasts," he whispered. "They fairly cry to have someone suck them. Take off your gown, cherie, and I'll caress those divine breasts."

"No, Nikki," she protested, drawing back from him, "they're so tender lately."

"If I promise to be gentle?" he murmured huskily as he lowered his head. Her protestations were immediately quieted as pleasure surged through her senses when his lips touched her nipples.

"Ah, love," he softly sighed, lifting his head briefly as he ran his hands over her swelling hips and looked into her languorous eyes, already sinking into sensuality. With an indrawn breath, she felt the world drifting away and experienced a shivering thrill as his fingers glided between her legs.

"You've changed your mind. I know you better

than you know yourself," he whispered. "You've learned well but still resist admitting you were made for love. It's no sin to acknowledge your desires and respond to your instincts." His long, lean fingers were probing, caressing, making her wet with passion and desire. "Your body needs me as much as I need you." He lifted her in his arms and carried her to the beautifully sculptured pine bed, lavishly decorated with carved flowers and leaves.

She didn't argue at all, as he lowered her onto their private bower of love.

XI
THE STALEMATE

There was little sleep that night, for the Prince after almost three weeks of missing Alisa in his bed had an immoderate need for her. She always offered her initial resistance but he wooed and inevitably prevailed. Her senses passionately responded each time and she hated herself after for that betrayal. By dawn, Alisa was sore and tender and swollen.

"No, Nikki, please, no, you're hurting me," she whimpered. He caressed more softly but he did not stop. His long legs spread her wide and within minutes he had once again brought them both to a frenzied ecstasy. Kissing her gently as he withdrew from her warm body Nikki whispered apologetically, "Forgive me; you bring on a fever in me that won't be quenched."

Later that morning in an atmosphere once again heavy with hostility, for in the cooler moments, removed from Nikki's passionate embrace, Alisa still raged at her bondage, he silently began opening Alisa's trunks and portmanteaux, pawing through clothing with a fine disregard for wrinkles.

"Leave them, Monsieur," Alisa said icily from the huge bed. "I'll unpack them myself."

Ignoring her, Nikki continued in his search until he found the articles he wanted. All twenty-four of the assorted negligees and peignoirs ordered from

Madame Vevay were there. Taking out only the peignoirs, Nikki hung each one in the armoire, shut the trunks, unlocked the door and in one swift motion shoved the luggage out into the hall.

Walking back into the room, he scooped up the yellow dress and petticoats still in a heap on the floor, threw them over his arm and proceeded to move toward the door.

"What in the world are you doing? You can't leave me without any clothes!" Alisa protested aghast, rising from the bed, a silken sheet clutched to her full breasts.

"Au contraire, my dear. I can and I do."

"I need my clothes!" she cried in frustration.

"Let me assure you, my love," and a wicked leer lit up his wolfish yellow eyes, "your activities will require no clothing. I leave the peignoirs merely in deference to modesty should you care to take some air on the balcony."

"You—you're despicable, loathsome; I hate you!" Alisa sputtered, sinking back to her pillows.

"My, my, how soon we forget," Nikki murmured in mock dismay, "Why, no more than two hours ago I recall you crying rather plaintively for my presence."

Laughing heartily at Alisa's discomfiture as she flushed pink to her hairline, Nikki turned and left the room. And she hated him then, hated him for making her melt in his arms, making her forget all his iniquities forced upon her, with only the touch of his lips.

The situation remained thus for almost a week. Alisa was confined to the room. Battle lines were drawn, heated words exchanged; a stalemate between two tempestuous, willful temperaments. The only reverses were those suffered by Alisa when Nikki skillfully, patiently roused her senses to a passionate need for him. As soon as the sexual skirmish was over, the advance was beaten back. He gained ground only to lose it once again when her sensibilities calmed, when her tremblings ceased.

One afternoon, Nikki was seated reading in one corner of the large bedroom, while Alisa sadly stared out the windows at the beautiful lawn and garden, the sparkling surface of the lake in the distance dancing in the light breeze; an outside still refused to her. She had been locked up in this room for six days now, forced to accede to Nikki's wishes, and her nerves were taut.

Nikki glanced up from the page and quietly watched the stubborn set of Alisa's back as she stood immobile before the windows, barefoot, her shapely form wrapped in a sea green lace dressing gown, silhouetted against the brilliant afternoon sunlight.

Within seconds his erection was rigid. My God, he only had to look at her and he wanted her. She went to his head like a drug. He was going to push himself into insensibility in a few more days at this rate. Well, it was a pleasant way to go, he reflected lecherously.

"Chattel," Nikki said provokingly, "come here."

Alisa spun around, eager for combat to release her animosities. She threw up her chin, glared at the lounging figure in the cushioned chair, and stood defiantly erect, refusing to move.

"Go to hell!" she spat.

Why did he taunt this woman? Nikki wondered. It was unprecedented for him to want to so totally possess any female. In all his former liaisons Nikki had remained deliberately aloof, never wishing to satisfy more than a casual lust. This independent, strong-willed creature was a challenge to him, a piquant change from the accommodating, insipid women in his past. That fierce determination was like a tossed gauntlet he could not ignore. It raised his blood. He *would* possess her totally; she *would* bend to his will. An irrational impulse drove him to tame this spirited, bold woman.

"Come here," he repeated softly and crooked a finger. She still did not move, favoring him only with a silent, poisonous look.

"The cabin deep in the forest waits you," Nikki reminded her in a mellifluous murmur, the sweet tone belied by the dangerous glitter in his eyes.

She came then, eyes downcast, walking slowly across the room and stopping several feet distant from the sprawled legs.

"Reconcile yourself, Alisa," he said gently, "for I mean to keep you near me."

She opened her mouth as if to speak and he stayed her with a raised finger. Shaking his head slowly in a sort of baffled self-disgust, his voice dropped to almost a whisper.

"Don't ask me why again; I don't know. I can't tell you. All I know is you're in my blood; I need the taste and feel and scent of you. I want the warmth of your skin next to mine in the morning when I wake; I want to know you are here to welcome me whenever I return." He glared almost in bitterness at Alisa. "I want to fuck you day and night." She shuddered before the crudeness of the remark and the piercing savageness of those fierce eyes.

"And," he laughed a short bitter rasp at the painful, unfamiliar sense of possessive jealousy she raised in him, "I feel an unaccountable need to keep you for myself. No other man shall touch you. Stay willingly or unwillingly. It scarce matters to me, but rest assured, my little dove, you *will* stay. Now, take off your clothes. I have need of you." Her hand reached up and began unbuttoning the front of her dressing gown.

He had won another round.

Nikki drew Alisa to him and caught her in a brutal embrace; his fingers grasped the curls at the back of her neck, tightening, forcing her head back, as he pressed ruthless, demanding, bruising kisses on her lips, her throat, her trembling breasts, branding her as his in a savage assuagement of the uncomfortable, compromising sensations she engendered in him.

One swift gesture slid her robe aside, off her shoulders, and it fell to the floor. Scooping her high against his hard muscular chest, he carried her to the bed, settled her beneath him and cruelly penetrated the soft, warm flesh which held him in thrall with silken bonds of mindless desire. He fiercely resented his passionate bondage and brutally thrust, each powerful stroke an exorcising of his frustration. Alisa's soft, whimpering cries of pain finally pierced the confusion of his black anger and he was aware of hurting her. Taking her face gently between his hands, he tenderly kissed her tears away, murmuring apologies, whispering quiet entreaties, gently rocking in a slow rhythm that caressed and stroked and roused.

She wanted his love but he gave her passion. In the dark recesses of her soul she wanted to be his wife; he wanted only a sensuous mistress.

Soon they both forgot all else but their need for each other as the driving ecstasy reached consummation and they met once again on the only common ground that offered them both surcease.

In the mornings Alisa watched from the balcony as Nikki patiently taught Katelina to ride her pony and handle the reins of the small red pony cart. A warmth of feeling would rush over her then; he was so good to Katelina. If only he didn't insist on owning *her* in such a feudal display of masculinity, leaving no dignity or pride. Damn him, damn him, for making her want him, for after six days of continuous lovemaking, morning, afternoon and night, Alisa's passions were roused by Nikki's merest touch, her body addicted to the titillation of its senses; a brushing hand, a soft caress enough to instantly activate the sensuous nerves which cried for, yearned for the exquisite torment and pleasure of satiation. Her need grew no less with indulgence.

That night was no different from the rest; a war of words and thoughts but never deeds. Deeds, the act of doing for each other was the only harmonious chord they possessed. Alisa, at the moment, was persisting in her verbal assault.

"Why do you insist on humiliating me? Women aren't simply things, playmates in bed. We have feelings too. We're equal."

"Equal?" he retorted in astonishment. "Nonsense!

Why would a woman want to be equal? Isn't it enough to be normal and happy? You're beautiful," he murmured reaching for her. "Come here." The audacious thought was summarily dismissed from his mind as Alisa's seductive image provoked his desires.

She resisted his advances as she always did since they had adopted their lines of battle. Within seconds Nikki pushed her aside in disgust.

"Sacrement!" he exploded, "you're an insufferable shrew. Why do you always fight me? Why do I always have to force you? Can't you admit your desire for me? Do you think I don't know when a woman wants me? Alisa, you wanted me from the first day I met you."

I know, she thought sadly. But she did not answer.

"There is nothing more gratifying or flattering to a man than to have an irresistible woman want to be his lover.[9] You, it seems, are incapable of confessing to these natural feelings."

He glared at her lying beside him. He took a deep breath and exhaled. "You win. I'm leaving tomorrow. You can stay or go for all I care. I'll not bother you again. Take your damnable pride and dignity and I hope you find them good company! Ivan will set up a trust in your name at the bank in Petersburg for our child. It will be adequate to cover your wants and offer the child financial security. I trust you will eventually find some accommodating man to bolster your insufferable ego."

Nikki turned his back to her and immediately fell asleep.

Alisa lay frozen beside him. How could he? How

could he be so unfeeling? He was leaving her in the morning and he could sleep like a baby.

Alisa tossed fitfully as her awful pride waged a battle against her love for Nikki. How could she love a man who only used women, who ridiculed and railed against clever women, who spoke of setting up a nursery someday with some compliant young chit. How could she love him? Had she lost her reason? She meant no more to him than the droves of women who had been dogging his heels since he entered manhood. And when he left her, she would be desolate, life would hold no joy, no meaning, her future would stretch bleak and empty. Is your hellish pride worth all that desolation and unhappiness? Is your body so inviolable and precious that you can't give it freely to the man you love? But he doesn't care for me, she cried piteously to herself. He only lusts after my body; I need him to love me.

Silly fool, her confused mind would remonstrate, he has given you much; his time, affectionate attention to your daughter, gifts beyond belief and tenderness in making love to you. Is that not enough? You must chain his independence as well? Must you ask for more than he can give when he has given so much more of himself than he ever has to anyone before? If you want him, learn to give of yourself. Learn to do for him as he does for you. If all he wants is your passion, at least he wants that.

Then the nagging dissenter in her thoughts would whisper devilishly. Had she no sense? Was she oblivious to the inner voice that screamed she was a fool? Had she no pride? she would severely lecture herself, and then, looking at the passion and love Nikki evoked, she confessed, sadly—no. With Nikki she had no pride.

Her ego would flare up in anger but her greater need for him ultimately reduced her pride to humility. Humbled before a man—by love—when she had stubbornly retained her pride; her independence had survived for six long years with the unholy monster, Forseus.

Love is to blame. It conquers all, levels the qualities dearest to a willful mind, even humbles arrogant pride.

But what good was her pride if she lost Nikki, she asked herself with a brutal honesty. She could not give him up. She loved him. Could she make him stay?

She finally realized, just as the early glow of morning touched the room, that she wanted him anyway she could have him, unconditionally, on any terms he chose. A restless sleep finally overcame her tortured thoughts and she dreamed of demons tearing her away from Nikki's arms, of dark wastes and lonely vistas in which she sat desolately alone. Full morning at last brought relief from the nightmares if not the anxiety prompting them.

Alisa rose just as the sun crept around the linen draperies, determined to keep Nikki here if she could. Standing before the wash stand, she deliberately banged and clanked the china pitcher and basin in the spurious act of washing.

When Nikki's easy breathing changed from sleep to wakefulness, she wiped her hands, slowly raised her gown and seductively stripped it from her body, lifting her arms high above her head and stretching languorously like a cat waking in the sun.

The early morning rays shining through the coarse linen draperies bathed her body in a soft, golden, iridescent glow.

Nikki, watching, thought her, in that pose, as beautiful as Rosso's nymphs in the Gallery at Fontainebleau. Lithe, sensual, the morning sun gilded her soft curves of breast and hip and thigh, warmed the pure, white flesh, and accentuated the bloom of womanhood. By God, she was deliberately seducing him. He willed himself to resist the provocation.

"It won't work," he said evenly, the simple statement dropping ominously in the quiet room. "I'm leaving this morning." He paused briefly, running his eyes boldly over her luxuriant curves. "And I don't like you performing like a whore," he finished coldly.

Hands on her hips, lips petulantly pursed, Alisa murmured softly as her violet eyes held his, "You're always telling me I must learn to accept my passions, my sexuality. I'm simply taking your advice," she said softly, advancing toward the bed, slowly melting over his supine form and kissing him lingeringly, searingly, on his lips, brushing her hand against his stiffening prick, caressing the powerful muscular chest with light fingertips.

"Take me one last time before you go. I'll leave you something to remember me by." She breathed the soft words into his ear.

Nikki strangled a curse, inveighing his faltering willpower to prevail, but losing his fight against Alisa's passionate lips. She bent her head low, gentle lips touched the red engorged head, a moist tongue drew him into her and all resistance ended.

He groaned and gathered her up into his arms.

"Come here, my wanton nymph. My leave-taking can wait," he whispered hoarsely as his tongue ravished her mouth. Alisa clasped Nikki to her with a frenzy of hope and desire, withheld nothing, giving her love with a wild, reckless abandon; wanting him to stay with her, wanting to make him need her as much as she needed him. For the first time, their mating was a complete union of two hearts, two spirits, as well as two passions; a yearning for each other totally fulfilled.

She drew him deeper and deeper into her as if she could hold him to her forever, chaining him to her with bonds of warm flesh. He brought her to climax after climax, marveling at the ardor she contained; the final relinquishing of her heart as well as her body reflected in the intensity of her passion. During her convulsions, he lay rigidly still inside her, affording her the maximum of pleasure, letting her feel the full impact as each trembling wave washed over her. Finally he could no longer hold himself back and poured himself shuddering into her, his heart pulsing violently. In that final moment he experienced a feeling of fulfillment, contentment and blazing sensation beyond his wildest memories of pleasure.

At last he kissed Alisa tenderly and pushed the tousled, red-gold curls back from her forehead, gently cradling her in his arms. The scent of mating hung heavy in the room.

Quiet tears filled her eyes and lashes.

"Don't cry, Alisa lemmikki, I won't leave you," he promised softly.

She smiled faintly and brushed his lips, so close to hers, with her fingertips. "Thank you," she murmured low as the tears overflowed, and she cried for herself, for her slavery to this man. She would do anything to lie with him, to have him near her, and thus she cried for the loss of her will.

Nikki was all gentle kindness. She was his now, completely, wholeheartedly. He was joyfully triumphant. He sent for breakfast and her trunks of clothes. Her imprisonment was over at last.

After they dressed and breakfasted, Nikki had a swing hung under the rose arbor near the house so Alisa could sit in the warm sun and watch Katelina go through her paces with the pony on the large lawn.

Katelina jogged along happily on the small pony as Nikki spoke encouragingly to her, prompting her to hold her hands lightly, to remember her seat, to keep her elbows in. The tousle-haired youngster successfully followed all his instructions letter perfect.

Nikki adored Katelina in a casual way. He had provided money for Katelina's lifetime with his usual careless liberality; an act which served also as a sop to silence his conscience which chided him to provide some measure of permanence in Katelina's life. Insistent, nagging remonstrances that urged him to commit himself legally to his lovely mistress, the expectant mother of his child.

Mother and "Uncle" applauded loudly as Katelina's mischievous face lit into a beaming smile of joyous glee when she completed the circuit of the lawn in fine form.

"Mother, dear," Nikki murmured as he sat next to Alisa on the wide swing, "Katelina is charming," he said with pride, "If your second child is as delightful you will have doubled my pleasure."

Alisa's heart melted at his whispered affection. He cared for her and Katelina and also for his yet unborn child. He made no promises, never, never even in the height of his lovemaking did he tell her he loved her, offered her no future, only a passionate present. But he did care and she clung to this small compensation for giving herself up completely to him.

"And I intend to keep you pregnant, at my side, populating this glorious wilderness," Nikki whispered playfully. Then he realized what he'd just said. A new unfathomable sense of the future with Alisa seemed to stretch out ahead of him. He immediately rose and paced beside the swing so she couldn't see his face, so she wouldn't raise false hopes within her heart. Resolutely he sought to shake off the unfamiliar feeling. He struggled for control. Mon dieu, it would never do, this giving way to emotion.

How *did* he care for her (he dared not use the word "love")? Love was anathema to him. Love for a woman, the deep, lasting monogamous kind of relationship he had seen in his parents' marriage. That feeling had never touched him. He felt a love for his parents but that was filial and far removed from what he considered the destructive love a woman could engender in a man. He would never allow himself to be pierced by that arrow again. He reveled in his independence and fiercely clung to his singular existence. It suited him to bow to no one, man or god, and certainly never to humble oneself for a woman, never again. He would not allow himself to dwell on these unfamiliar sensations Alisa stirred in him. He would not permit a woman to breach his inner private citadel again, although the storming was exquisitely acccomplished with soft words, soft lips, and soft thighs.

She pleased him, that was all, so he would keep her, but only until such a time as she no longer pleased him.

"You think of me only as a brood mare," Alisa pouted prettily. Now that their war was over, she enjoyed being openly flirtatious, seductively suggestive. "You are imperious, and peremptory to even suggest such a thing as keeping me pregnant."

"But not excessively repugnant, for all that." His eyes twinkled a little, as he stopped pacing and joined her at the swing.

"No, not completely, my lord," she posed demurely.

Nikki smiled lightly at the soft mouth fixed in a pretty moue, delighted with her obvious attempt to gratify his wishes, to appeal to his stated preference for a soft passivity in a woman.

"Not only as a brood mare, love; you enchant me in a variety of ways, but I'll admit, the thought of you nurturing my child within your body warms me with a pleasant conceit." He bent low over her to place the palm of his hand against her rounded, swelling form. *His child.*

Katelina was squealing for Nikki's attention and he rose to stroll over to the insistent little girl on her pony. He spoke a few words to her and walked back to Alisa while Katelina kicked her chubby legs into the pony's ribs in an effort to make the animal move. At the moment, the pony was more interested in cropping the daylilies and Siberian wallflowers on the edge of the flowerbeds.

Nikki glanced in Katelina's direction as he stood

near Alisa. "I promised Katelina I'd take her squirrel hunting this afternoon and she's holding me to the promise. Will you be all right alone for a few hours? I reluctantly leave you but must honor my word to that persistent little brat." He grinned, "And I won't ask you along, for I don't want you riding. You must be very careful of our child. Shall I call Rakeli or Maria for companionship while we're absent?"

"No, I'll be perfectly fine alone. Perhaps I'll stroll down to the lake. The only glimpse I've had of it until today has been through the bedroom windows." She smiled mischievously through half-lowered lashes.

"Sorry for my damnable temper, love. I'll endeavor to bridle it in the future. The entire estate is at your disposal," he indicated with a sweeping wave of his arm, "but don't wander too far into the forest. You might become lost."

"I won't, Nikki."

"Now you're sure you'll be all right, alone?" he asked anxiously as he bent to kiss her.

"Of course, dear, and don't shoot too many poor squirrels."

"No, we won't be gone that long. Au revoir." He blew her a kiss as he strode away, extricated the pony and rider from the flowerbed and disappeared around the corner of the West Wing heading toward the stable block.

Alisa sat on the swing for a half hour after the hunting party left. It consisted of Nikki, Katelina, Arni, Yukko and three trackers. The sun was comfortably warm and Alisa day-dreamed blissfully. She walked around all the flower gardens, beautifully cared for by an army of gardeners, then moved in the direction of the lake. On reaching the sandy shore she strolled along the soft white sand of the bay that swung away in an easterly direction from the house. Within minutes the house disappeared from sight behind the tall, dark pine trees lining the shore. Alisa stooped occasionally to select a small flat piece of shale and skipped the rocks across the luminous sparkling water. She walked for some ten minutes, careless of her distance from the house because there was no chance of becoming lost out in the open of the lake shore.

Finding a large flat boulder, Alisa sat on its broad expanse and gazed out on the lake, knees drawn up under her chin, arms clasping her legs, letting the lassitude of the warm sun and light lake breeze bathe her; contentment filled her soul.

Hearing an unexpected sound behind her, she whirled around, fear gripping her mind.

Valdemar Forseus was standing five feet away, his small, deep-set eyes peering with a dangerous mockery at the terrified face of his young wife. She froze in horror at the sight of those fanatically piercing eyes.

"So, Mrs. Forseus, you have led me a merry chase," he breathed softly. "We were beginning to despair of ever seeing you outside the house. That whoremonger of a Prince guards you well. But, alas," he sighed, a sinister smile playing across his grotesque face, "not well enough. And, of course, I am a patient man."

A rapid flash of his arm and two gigantic men appeared out of the trees and strode swiftly to his side. "My trackers," he conversationally remarked, "my sweet young wife. Men, the object of this long

and diligent quest," he politely introduced them,
his wrath barely concealed beneath his rigidly controlled demeanor.

Alisa was dumb with alarm, as wave after wave
of silent terror flooded her consciousness. Why had
she wandered so far from the house? Why had she
so stupidly assumed Forseus would accept her flight
from him? God, where was Nikki? She began to
tremble in the sure knowledge that Forseus would
kill her, certainly if not now, later, after he had used
her to suit his devilish will. He was insane, sadistical-
ly taking delight in causing pain. Help Nikki, Help,
she sent up a silent plea, her nerves stretched taut
in panic. Flashing, blinding spots of light danced
before her eyes and oblivion took pity.

She crumpled in a swoon at the feet of the three
men.

"Pick her up," Forseus ordered sharply. "We
must make haste."

One tracker effortlessly lifted her body and the
three men walked back to their horses tethered in
the pines. The men mounted, Alisa was settled
across one man's chest and the party spurred their
horses. Once back on the road, neither quirt nor
rowel was spared as the riders furiously pressed their
horses south.

Mercifully, Alisa remained in a faint for several
hours, the agonizing terror of Forseus' proximity
locked outside of her unconscious mind. A temporary respite to the numbing fear of her most certain
future—death.

She regained consciousness in the late afternoon
when they were forced to stop and change horses.
They mounted her on a small bay, her hands tied to

the saddle pommel. Forseus spoke scarcely more than three words to her, carefully restraining his anger in front of the two trackers. To bring back a runaway wife was legal enough; he could expect their help, but even these primitive men would not accept the punishment he was going to inflict on his contrary wife once he had returned her home.

"You will rot in hell, jezebel, and your carnal urges will be punished as you deserve," he whispered evilly that evening as they stopped briefly to water their horses at a stream. "I hope you last long enough. I wouldn't want my pleasure curtailed." As if to prove his point he cruelly tightened the cinch on his horse's saddle and heaved his great bulk back onto his mount.

Alisa trembled involuntarily and prayed for courage and strength to sustain her. The full horror of the day's happenings was beginning to overwhelm her. She told herself sharply to remain calm, but her panic was reaching nightmare proportions.

The squirrel hunt lasted longer than anticipated since Katelina was enjoying the excursion. Shadows of twilight were slowly creeping in from the forest as the small group rode back into the stable yard; a tired but satisfied little five-year-old nestled in Nikki's arms.

Walking into the large hallway carrying the fatigued child, Nikki hallooed for Alisa, cheerfully anticipating a welcoming kiss from his lovely mistress. He handed Katelina over to Rakeli and strode up the broad wooden stairway to the bedroom. He was so anxious to see and hold her he didn't even stop to shake the dust from his boots and clothes. This morning had been magnificent. God, *she* was magnificent; beautiful, sensual, intelligent, and she loved him. His world was near perfection at this moment.

"Alisa!" he called out. "Alisa, we're back!" Nikki called as he opened the door into the bedroom, lit now with the last rays of sunset glow. "Katelina is becoming a very excellent rider for——" He paused on the threshold as his eyes swept the room, searching for the familiar form, the auburn hair.

The room was quiet and empty. The muscles in his jaw tightened. Turning sharply, he retraced his steps down the main staircase, shouting for Alisa. The housekeeper came running from the back hall and explained quickly, "I haven't seen Madame these last hours. She was walking in the garden last I saw her."

"You mean you haven't seen Mrs. Forseus all afternoon?"

"No, sir, I haven't," she answered fearfully, for the Prince was scowling mightily.

Nikki thanked her gruffly and proceeded out the front door, racing down the steps of the entrance in three long strides, the tiniest twinge of apprehension beginning to mar his perfect mood. Within seconds he had turned the corner of the West Wing and peered across the broad flowerbeds, all gaily blooming, a few bees still busily humming from flower to flower.

No Alisa.

A larger fragment of doubt replaced the vague apprehension as he walked purposefully back to the entrance, thundering loudly for the housekeeper. He ran up the stairs two at a time. Having heard the roar of Prince Kuzan's voice in the kitchen, she was at the door to greet him.

"What is it, my lord?"

"Assemble all the servants—immediately! I can't find Mrs. Forseus." Within the minute a glowering Nikki was addressing a long line of maids, gardeners and footmen.

"Has anyone seen Mrs. Forseus since I left for my ride?"

The answers came in a confused babble but when all were sifted and deciphered, apparently no one had seen Mrs. Forseus since early afternoon when she was strolling in the yard.

A fierce rage began to smolder in the quick-tempered Prince. So all the theatrics this morning, the tears and sighs, the loving words had been just that—theatrics. She had probably coolly plotted the drama and he, driven as usual by his genitals, had fallen for her scheme. How else would she have ever been released from the prison of the bedroom. Very clever of her; the oldest female ploy; when all else fails, use your body.

He swore to himself and then aloud as the servants huddled in a group glancing nervously at their distraught master. There was no more to learn from them so he curtly dismissed them, charging them to keep out of his way.

"Yukko, bring me two bottles of brandy," the incensed voice demanded. Nikki stalked off into his study, infuriated at having been deceived by the seeming sincerity of that loving scene this morning.

Damn her, damn her lying tongue. He'd drag her back by the hair! He'd beat her black and blue! He'd show her not to trifle with him! But even as he

stormed and raged, the more pragmatic side of his
nature came to the fore. Why bother? Why bring
her back? He had been ready to leave her this morning anyway; the decision had simply been taken out
of his hands. Maybe that was what piqued him most.
Was his pride pricked because Alisa had chosen to
leave him and taken away his prerogative, and he
was made to look the fool?

The bottles of brandy appeared. Yukko attempted
to raise a question about Alisa, but Nikki was only
able to conceive Alisa's disappearance in terms of
deceit. He sat there condemning her duplicity,
censuring, damning her provocative sensuousness,
castigating himself for the thousandth time for his
childish credulity. Cunt did that to him. He forgot
all else.

"Nikki, what of Katelina? Alisa would never
leave——" Yukko braved his master's wrath.

"Silence!" Nikki bellowed and put the bottle to
his lips, draining a third of its contents in one huge
swallow. He looked up with a deadly glare and said,
"Are you championing that bitch?" He lapsed into
Finnish. "I don't want to hear that trollop's name
again! Do you hear? Do you hear?" Nikki snarled.
"Now go. Leave me in peace. Bah! Women. Who
needs them!"

Yukko lifted his eyebrows in resigned disbelief at
the last statement. If there was ever a man who
couldn't do without women, it was his master.

"Very well, Nikki," he sighed, as he watched the
hand grasp the bottle again and pour another long
draught down. Leaving the study, Yukko resolved to
look for Alisa himself. She wouldn't run off now
when she was carrying Nikki's child. Everyone

below stairs knew that. But then when Nikki's temper was up he didn't listen to reason.

It took Yukko no more than twenty minutes to find why Alisa had disappeared. He raced back to the house to where Nikki lay slumped in his chair, his face an unreadable mask. Having finished the first bottle of brandy, he was approaching the mood when all the world was of no consequence.

Yukko pulled the second bottle of brandy from Nikki's sullen grasp and said, "Alisa's been abducted. Three men on horseback took her from the east shore of the lake about three quarters of a mile down the beach."

Approximately three seconds elapsed before the news penetrated Nikki's senses. Then he shot to his feet, clapped a fierce grip on Yukko's shoulder and tersely questioned, "Abducted? You're sure?" he asked sharply. "She didn't run away? You're sure?" His eyes were eager.

"I'm sure, Nikki," Yukko answered positively.

"Thank you." Nikki's eyes lit with a hungry hope.

Yukko turned away in embarrassment from his proud young master. The Finnish brotherhood of trackers and woodsmen were by nature and training taciturn, proud, laconic of speech and disinclined to showing emotion. Nikki for a brief moment had exposed his vulnerability and Yukko, with a delicate courtesy, chose to avoid the sight.

When Yukko looked next Nikki was out the door, dashing down the outside steps and halfway down the path to the lakeshore. Yukko and Arni hurried to catch up with him. The three men ran down the soft sand, darkening now in the swiftly growing twilight, following Alisa's small footprints.

An awful obscenity exploded from Nikki when they reached the additional footprints around the large lakeside boulder where Alisa's footprints abruptly terminated.

"Are you positive there's three, Yukko?" Nikki asked curtly.

"Yes, three," Yukko replied decisively as he knelt to scrutinize the tracks more carefully. "Two big men and one average size."

Rising, Yukko followed the trail into the woods to the place the horses had been tethered.

"They're carrying Mrs. Forseus," Yukko said, glancing compassionately at Nikki striding beside him. Yukko had been with Nikki ever since he was a small boy given as a serf-companion to the young master. He knew all his moods, knew all his pleasures, knew all his idiosyncrasies, so he had watched with almost unbelieving amazement as Nikki had altered his life for this young woman. Yukko reached out a sympathetic hand and touched Nikki's shoulder.

"We'll catch up with them, Nikki," he solemnly promised. "They can't have more than a four-hour start on us and won't be able to travel as rapidly as we will since they have Mrs. Forseus. She can't sustain a headlong pace."

Nikki cast a swift glance around the small clearing that had sheltered the horses, shutting his eyes briefly in despair. There was no doubt in his mind who had abducted Alisa, and the knowledge of Forseus' cruel sadism shook his composure, brought back memories of his own recent mistreatment of her. He resolutely dismissed the awful visions and started back to the house. He ran full out, his long legs outdistancing both Arni and Yukko. Dashing into the stables he ordered the grooms to saddle six horses, then he swiftly returned to the house and explained to a fearful Maria what had transpired. He warned her not to alarm Katelina.

"We should be back in two days. Tell Katelina anything, anything at all to pacify her until we return."

He strode into his study, lifted down an ivory-stocked Winchester model 1866, lever-action carbine, the best in the world, purchased in Paris, as well as a serviceable Belgian Colt Navy Model Revolver, crammed his hunting jacket pockets full of shells and shouted for the cook as he ran back outside to the stables.

The horses were almost ready; the cook breathlessly appeared and Nikki ordered food to be packed for three days' travel.

"You've five minutes to prepare it before we leave," he snapped. The cook scurried back to the house crying for the kitchen maids.

"Empty the stables," Nikki commanded sharply. "I want every horse with us. Two grooms will be needed to return the fatigued animals. Vite! Vite!" He snapped his fingers.

Arni and Yukko were checking their harness, the mounts dancing and sidling in the nervous activity of the stableyard. Horse after horse was led out and strung together with long braided leads.

Nikki slammed the rifle and revolver into his saddle holsters, took one look around to determine everyone's readiness and flung himself up into the saddle. Koli pawed in sensitive anticipation, anxious to be off. The cook and her helpers came flying out from the kitchen carrying rucksacks which were hastily fastened to the saddles.

Within seconds the party thundered out of the stableyard, Nikki setting a dangerous pace in the early evening darkness.

XII
THE CHASE

The horrible possibility of some injury befalling Alisa kept running through Nikki's distraught mind as he leaned into the wind. If Forseus had harmed Alisa or his child in any way he would see him burn in hell before another day passed, Nikki vowed as the dreadful fear for Alisa's safety rode with him. He knew Forseus' mind was not normal. He derived pleasure from subjecting Alisa to indecent aberrations, from hurting her. God, what if he killed her, what if she were dead already? His pulse rate soared while his heart plummeted. A suffocating despair gripped him. Nikki dug in his spurs, furiously pushing the horses, forcing them unmercifully, until they were unable to go on, their mouths foaming, their coats glistening with sweat. Without pausing for more than three minutes, the beaten horses were unsaddled and left with a groom, the tack transferred to fresh animals and Nikki, remounted, was three hundred yards ahead whipping his new mount to pick up the pace.

The damn fool will kill all his horses, Yukko muttered as he threw himself onto his vigorous new mount and put spur to horseflesh. Thousands of roubles of prime bloodstock were being driven into the ground.

The largest horses were needed to support Nikki's

weight and they, in their brute strength, had a stamina and endurance beyond an average horse's powers. Nikki was well ahead, picking up and following a glaringly obvious trail. Forseus was traveling in headlong flight; no care was taken to cover his escape. He was either confident no one could overtake them or too frightened to take the time and effort to be cautious. It didn't matter. Either way, he would die, and soon, Nikki promised himself.

They watched for signs of change or splitting up.

One horse had faltered—a light track—the horse carrying Alisa. She must have been remounted, for a different animal was now supporting her slight weight. They were gaining on the fugitives. At the wicked, reckless speed Nikki was urging, it was just a matter of time. Nikki's party were all mounted on Strylet horses now which had been left for last, having the stamina to cover long distances without flagging. They counted on the fact that Forseus would have to stop for food and rest, however briefly, and Nikki would gain valuable time, for no one in pursuit remotely considered rest. Nikki would not stop until Alisa was safely with him once more, or— merciful God, no, he didn't dare think.

He dug the bloody rowels into the horse's ribs.

By four o'clock in the morning, waves of exhaustion were sweeping over Nikki, regularly, overwhelmingly. He hung on to wakefulness with stubborn determination. He mustn't close his eyes. Darkness pulsed around him, the rhythm of the horse was soothing. Had he dozed momentarily? With effort he levered his eyelids open. It wouldn't be long now. He had to remain awake. They flew southward in the velvety night, the blackness of the forest pines flashing by.

As the sky lightened, Nikki knew that Forseus couldn't be far ahead. The fugitives didn't have the advantage of fresh horses and their mounts had to be exhausted, maintaining no more than a slow trot.

Nikki and his trackers came up on the encampment in the gray mists of early dawn. Frantically his eyes searched the glen for Alisa, for some sign of her. Finally his glance caught her dress lying beneath a rock outcropping and his heart almost stopped beating. Was he too late? Had Forseus beaten her beyond endurance. Horrible visions of her lying in a pool of blood, her child come early from the terror and brutality of her abduction, flashed through his mind as he leaped from his horse and bent to retrieve her torn dress. He barely heard the voices of Arni and Yukko threatening Forseus and his men into submission as he prowled from place to place looking for Alisa.

"Alisa," he called her name, but barely a whisper passed his lips. Panic was tightening his stomach. He heard a rustling in the underbrush and turned thinking to tell Yukko to help him in his terrible search for her. And then he saw her.

She was bound and gagged, her eyes wide with fright. Her chemise was the only covering she had left, the blanket having slipped off her immobile form long ago.

"Alisa," he cried, relief flooding his veins. Quickly he untied her and pulled her sobbing into his arms.

"Are you all right?" he asked anxiously.

She nodded speechlessly against his chest.

"Did he . . . the babe . . . are you . . ." He couldn't say the words, but he had to know.

"There was not time," she gasped. "Thank God, there was not time."

"Your dress is torn as if . . ."

"He ordered me to undress in front of him. When I refused, he tore my clothes from me and then he tied and gagged me." The words rushed from her as if to exorcise the horrible memory. "He sat drinking, watching me, as if planning his next assault. Then I think the journey and drink together proved too much for him and he passed out." She closed her eyes.

Nikki kissed her and pulled the blanket around her trembling shoulders. "Wait here. I will be with you soon." He now had work to do.

He followed the voices of his faithful servants until he came to a camp clearing. Three men stood together under the guns of Arni and Yukko. Nikki immediately recognized the evil countenance of Forseus.

He could think of nothing now but killing the man who had stolen his mistress. In a low savage voice Nikki said, "Prepare to meet your maker, Forseus."

Forseus stared at Nikki with a bestial ferocity, his eyes flecked with insanity, and when he spoke his words were uttered with the finality of the deranged. "The jezebel deserves to die for her sins," he intoned, the fire of a zealot burning in his eyes.

Nikki's precarious hold on his monstrous hate broke. He leaped into the clearing, drew his pukku and drove Forseus helplessly down upon his back, forcing his advantage of size and strength ruthlessly.

Nikki was wild with loathing, his eyes enraged with venom. The point of his hunting knife flashed in the air.

Yukko instantly sprang into action and stayed Nikki's knife hand, talking rapidly while he held back the shuddering strength of Nikki's hatred. But his master was too much for him to contain. Nikki shook him off and once again leapt after Forseus who had risen to his feet. Just as he was about to strike a murderous blow, Alisa came running toward him, her blanket clutched tightly to her, her eyes wild.

"No, stop," she cried, "I don't want that man's blood on my conscience. I cannot have you kill for me. Oh, please stop."

It was the only voice which could have stayed Nikki's hand, and even then he hesitated before pulling back from Forseus' chest. His awful face of rage relaxed. He rose abruptly, releasing the man he had held helpless beneath him, almost as good as dead. Then he pointed his knife at the man's loins. "I will not kill you, but if I should see your face again you might not survive what I will do to you."

With the fanatic courage of insanity, sustained by an aberration he termed religion, Forseus screamed wildly, "God will punish you for your sins!"

"Will he indeed?" said Nikki icily. He picked up Alisa and mounted his horse. Then he wheeled around and rode out of the clearing followed by Arni and Yukko.

They traveled home slowly, Nikki holding Alisa closely to him, both filled with an enormous sense of relief. The miles passed in a silence of contented exhaustion. Several hours later, Nikki looked down on the red-gold curls, the delicate face dozing lightly on his chest and said softly, "I love you," very simply and without emphasis. The raw terror of almost having lost Alisa was still brutally fresh in his mind.

Through the mists of a light half-sleep Alisa responded faintly to that staggering statement with a small satisfied smile.

Nikki placed a gentle kiss on her tousled curls. Home—they were going home.

XIII
THE HALCYON DAYS

The first evening back at Mon Plaisir, Nikki and Alisa retired contentedly to their bedchamber after putting the lovable child Katelina to bed. Nikki had ordered a sumptuous dinner to be served to them to celebrate Alisa's homecoming. Numerous sterling candlesticks illumined the small table à deux, lending a lyrical poetic brilliance to the scene. Alisa perceived with wonder the rich and varied display of wealth and comfort.

Arranged before them in precise rows on Lanerschy decorated china plates were unbelievable quantities of succulent, lightly scraped asparagus. In Nikki's usual arrogant manner, instructions as to their preparation had been stipulated: no more than seven minutes of the plunged stems in boiling water or heads will roll, he had teasingly commanded of his beaming cook.

Finger bowls were laid out, and a large sauceboat of melted butter rested between the two services. Nikki silently reached across the small table with his long arms, rolled up the sleeves of Alisa's dressing gown, did the same to his linen shirt sleeves and admonished her in a thoroughly relaxed drawl as he reached for his first spear, to please forget etiquette and enjoy the pleasure of the delicious vegetable.

Alisa hesitated momentarily as she contemplated launching into the plate full of asparagus as Nikki

269

was doing. As she paused, one hand daintily raised above the plate, Nikki muttered, typically heedless of decorum, "Yes, I know asparagus is a great stumbling block in a refined ladies repertoire" he said smiling, "but, à propos shoddy table manners, I must confess, they would never cause me to reject such a charming companion."

Alisa, already consuming her first tender spear, chose to acknowledge this reassuring statement by a full-mouthed, muffled comment to the effect that she agreed.

This harmonious, calm, pleasant, comfortable companionship continued through the entire four courses of superbly prepared food, and Nikki, in a gentlemanly fashion, forwent the lonely port and cigars and directed his attention to the lady's entertainment. This friendly gesture was pleasing to both of them. When have the singular qualities of port and a cigar, however fine the vintage or leaf, been able to compare favorably to a warm, wanton, thoroughly aroused female?

And later that evening, as they sat by the fire, he pulled her to him and looked deep into her eyes. "I love you," he said again.

Alisa looked up at him in tearful disbelief. "I thought it was a dream. But now I know it was true. You did say those words before, when we were coming home."

"And I'll say them again, many times." Nikki smiled as he lifted her into his arms and carried her to their waiting bed, "But now is not the time for words."

* * *

In the following days, these lovers, so similar in their volatile temperaments, and yet so dissimilar in the outward appearances of their past lives, settled into an intimate companionship. They slept and ate and laughed and talked and *agreed*. They entertained Katelina and read together and walked the estate hand in hand. The rhythm of their days was serene and languorous; the rhythm of their nights passionate and intense. They lived in a cocoon of love, preoccupied with their own concerns, oblivious to the outside world.

The summer nights were very short now and many evenings after a sauna they would sit on the porch of the bath house perched over the shore of the lake and watch the pale iridescent colors of the setting sun far into the evening hours. Even the land of the midnight sun seemed to be presenting an extravagant, sumptuous backdrop to these glorious halcyon days. Often on these evenings, when it was warm and still and heavy with the scent of grasses and clover, they would sing together, all the old Finnish folk songs. Nikki's bass and Alisa's soft soprano in concert with Katelina's lilting, high-pitched child's voice blended in a pleasant harmony.

Their relationship, at one time so turbulent and violent, was in these days without flaw. Late one evening, after putting Katelina to bed, Nikki and Alisa were sitting in the library; Nikki was drinking his way to sleep as was his custom but slowly now and with none of the reckless intemperance of the past. The Prince was happy, not the usual frenzied exhilaration that had often passed for enjoyment or the satisfied lust that offered a certain consolation, but truly a deep, contented happiness. He watched

Alisa from under lowered lashes as she sat across the turkish carpet on a small settee, engrossed in Winckelmann's 'Excavations at Pompeii.' Her peaceful beauty reached out and struck him afresh. She was his, proud now to be his, and she was to have his child. A strange sense of fulfillment soothed his mind. He actually looked forward to the event. He was not just happy because she was happy but happy within himself.

Could he have stopped the passage of time he would have then. He was content. Before, he had always lived for the uncertain future, hoping to find tomorrow an assuagement of his restless ennui. But now, he wished for neither past nor future. He was experiencing a happiness that had eluded him for twenty years and he wanted to halt the progress of time.

Alas, it could not be.

Morning brought an abrupt and decisive end to these perfect days.

Unknown to the participants of the sunny, contented household at Mon Plaisir, Nikki's father had been informed by his servants of the dangerous abduction attempt by Valdemar Forseus.

Prince Mikhail was in a fine choler, storming and cursing as he paced around his study in Petersburg one warm summer morning. Damn, insolent pup! He could wait no longer for Nikki to come to his senses. Alisa could have been very easily killed by that insane lunatic, Forseus.

I have waited long enough, biding my time while he thinks only of his amusements, the old prince muttered impatiently. I even *explained* to him my firm desire for a legitimate grandson, he fumed. I don't have to request. He will obey, he furiously raged.

Prince Mikhail stalked from his study bawling for his barrister, his secretary, his Finnish trackers; he raved and fumed.

"I want an audience with Alexander II as soon as possible," he commanded his secretary curtly. "Alisa shall have a divorce before the next sun sets. Send for my barrister. He must inform Valdemar Forseus of the divorce and offer him a settlement to sugar the action," he snapped briefly.

"Johanos" he turned to the leader of his trackers, "I want Nikki back here as soon as possible. Go up to Mon Plaisir and bring him back. I don't care how you do it. I'll write a note informing him of my wishes while you're saddling your mounts."

Prince Mikhail turned and disappeared into the study, while Johanos raced out the door and toward the stables crying for his cohorts. Within a few moments a group of trackers were in the saddle and hurtling out of the courtyard while Prince Mikhail stormed about the hall, raging still.

Princess Kaisa-leena came running down the stairway, roused by the noise and commotion. "What's going on, Misha?" she inquired breathlessly as she reached his side, searching his tempestuous face for some answer.

"That damnable son of yours, that's what's the matter!" he roared. "He's coming home. He'll be less impudent soon, by God!" and he gave her a terse outline of his plans then stalked away, cursing still.

Kaisa-leena sighed resignedly. She could envision

the embroiled household already. Father and son, both with indomitable tempers, at each other's throats. She must do her best to sooth the ruffled feathers but she wondered this time whether she had any chance of success.

XIV
THE RELUCTANT BRIDEGROOM

Three days later, Nikki stood in the library at Mon Plaisir, holding his father's note in his hand.

He had read with mounting horror the short, crisp missive.

Alisa's divorce is being "accelerated" [10] *by the Emperor while your marriage plans proceed. Please be so kind as to return immediately. My trackers will expedite your removal.*

I'll bet they'll "expedite" my removal, Nikki reflected with a ghost of a laugh. The barest civility was accorded when his father used the word "please," but the implication of coercion was eminently plain as Nikki glanced out the window and noted the fifteen men dismounting and stretching their limbs after their three days of hard riding.

He had never truly believed that his father would have the audacity or ruthlessness to dragoon him and had felt quite safe and content at this remote northern retreat. But no, here it was—simple, direct and certain. He was to be married.

He sighed and slumped into a soft, leather chair, kneading his brow with his left hand and getting into a fine sweat at the thought of his father's plans. Nikki had been successfully avoiding this tender trap for half his lifetime, and had considered himself quite proficient at the art. Now he could see that his efforts had prospered only because of his father's sufferance.

Sweet Jesus, he had no inclination or partiality to spend the rest of his life playing checkers with the Governor of Archangel. He knew his father's warning about a future at his estate in Siberia was no idle threat now.

So here he was on the brink of marriage; you can see what can come of an apparently harmless diversion. He'd like to wring Illyich's neck. But he did love Alisa, he supposed, in a way that was not entirely carnal and he felt quite sure she was in love with him.

There was no point in wasting his wits and digestion ruminating over his folly, Illyich's evil wager, or his father's astonishing new sense of priorities. Mon Dieu, if his father wanted a grandson, he would happily round up any number of those, but not, unfortunately, legitimate ones, and that seemed to be the kernel of the immediate problem. Why all of a sudden had his father developed such a fine taste for propriety?

He was snared, not a damn thing to do about it but grin and bear it; either that or molder in Siberia for forty-odd years. A wife need be no great encumbrance if one has money, and they do have their conveniences; but all the same, it was a distressing abominable piece of madness. He kept swearing to himself as he rose from the chair and walked upstairs to inform his mistress of her imminent change in status.

Alisa was seated at the mirror brushing her hair and smiled at Nikki as he walked into the bedroom.

"My father has obtained your divorce and I have

been commanded to marry you, and, it appears, Madame, that we are to be married post haste." Nikki stated, a note of grimness apparent beneath the lazy drawl.

The smile died on Alisa's lips and she turned to face him. Her red lips trembled in anger. "Please inform your father that no one has to marry me. Having endured one unsatisfactory marriage, I do not care to venture into a second that has all the prognostications of being a disaster, with an unwilling husband to boot. As you well know, I do not wish a forced marriage!" Alisa exclaimed indignantly.

"Ah, my dear, I am of a like mind," Nikki declared with unfeeling candor. "Our new relationship is so agreeable lately that I scarce believe it possible," the carefully modulated voice remarked with its old derisiveness. "But, alas, neither of us, my dear, has any choice in this matter." He continued, "If I refuse, my future entails a dreary life on father's estate in Siberia, which I am in no mind anxious to pursue. He will, no doubt, treat you more tenderly for the sake of this grandchild he is bent on having. Certainement, he will remove you to his dacha on the Crimea so the little tyke will have the creature comforts of sun and beach." He paused thoughtfully. "Although, if one must be shackled to someone, I daresay you will suit." Nikki flicked a bold glance over the beautiful face and form of the affronted woman standing opposite him in deshabille, a filmy morning robe but imperfectly covering her. The future child was just beginning to make his presence known; Alisa's belly rose slightly beneath voluptuous, trembling breasts as she haughtily regarded the arrogant, lean figure confronting her.

"I'm afraid, I cannot return the sentiment, for you do *not* in the *least* suit me!" she snapped.

Nikki shifted his weight and advanced menacingly. Alisa involuntarily shrank back to the dressing table as the cool, golden gaze stared caustically into her own mutinous eyes. Forcing her against the edge of the table, Nikki leaned forward slightly to within three inches of the flashing eyes and murmured, "I beg to differ with you, Madame, for in one area, at least, we suit to perfection or else you are capable of the most artful pretense since Delilah gulled Samson out of his hair."

"I will not marry you!" she cried.

"It is customary to wait to be asked, Madame," he snapped, at which point he ground his teeth in exasperation and hurled the dressing table mirror through the bedroom window.

Alisa burst into hysterical tears at Nikki's violent display of anger. Where had their peace and contentment gone? She ran to the bed and collapsed face down, sobbing into the pillows because she wanted him, and then didn't want him because he no longer wanted her.

Nikki stood in the center of the room, rankled and incensed, clenching and unclenching his fists as he gazed at Alisa tumbled on the bed. Her robe had been pushed up as she fell and her beautiful white body was exposed to the waist.

God, what a beautiful roses-and-cream exterior and a passionate nature underneath, he mused as his ungovernable temper was slowly being pushed aside by sensual desires. Nikki walked slowly to the bed and pulled the robe from Alisa's shoulders. She shuddered beneath his touch. He lay down and kissed her cheek. She turned away. Nikki unbuttoned his pants and turned her towards him; she lay quivering against him for a moment, then lifted her face for a kiss. His lips came down on her parted lips and he climbed on top of her, boots and all.

Several moments later, Alisa lifted a provocative glance and whispered seductively, "Do you find me a nuisance to have around?" and moved her bottom deliciously beneath him.

"A nuisance I am persuaded to retain," he groaned softly, as he fell to making love with a will and in that moment decided marriage to Alisa had its advantages. Soon they were both lying exhausted and content in each other's arms.

Jesus, this passionate creature would soon be his wife. An alarming distressing thought crossed his mind. If she had lain so easily with him, had there been others before—or since?

A fierce jealousy possessed him. Would he be justified in keeping her locked in her apartments in Petersburg? Even though the civilized niceties were often paper-thin in Petersburg, such medieval techniques would cause a damnable scandal. On the other hand, would it matter to the noble Kuzan family if one more scandal were added to their long list? But it was perhaps antiquated in the bustling, modern capital city of the Empire. Wives weren't locked up any more; sent away to remote convents, perhaps, but that recourse, he very selfishly decided, would deprive him of Alisa's companionship and warmth in bed.

Lifting himself on one elbow, he slid out and fixed Alisa with a piercing scowl of censure. Her face was softly flushed, her eyes dreamily abstract.

"Listen to me, woman," he said evenly and shook her gently back from the depths of her passion.

"If I ever catch you seriously flirting, I will shoot your gallant. And if you compromise my name, I'll shoot you." He had no intention of playing the cuckold; he would have to keep an eye on her; she had tumbled easily enough for him. "I presume I am perfectly plain?" he inquired sharply.

"Perfectly." she murmured complacently and sighed, blissfully sated. Moments later however when reality was more real, she was not entirely happy with his capitulation.

"But, you don't love me." Alisa pouted.

"I love you, dear. See, I've said it again and I've never said that to any other woman." (At least not in sixteen years, he thought.)

"You only desire my body. You command me to obedience and yet you promise nothing of yourself," Alisa insisted pettishly.

"I won't deny I desire your flesh, I'm a man, after all, and you a lush flower of love and if I promise you nothing, I cannot change. I'm not prone to sugared sentiments and fanciful absurdities. I will give you shelter and food and the luxuries of life; I will see our child wants for nothing. He or she shall have everything money can buy. I can't promise more. I can't promise you I will love you forever when I don't know. Don't cry," he soothed as tears fell from Alisa's eyes. "We have, right now, more happiness than I have ever dreamed possible. But, don't ask me to give up my independence. I cannot."

And remember for both of us, he thought to himself as he tenderly kissed her tears away, remember these blissful, unutterably happy days, these golden summer weeks; remember for both of us because I can't promise for myself.

This will never come again, he mourned, for no pleasure can be twice repeated, and he was fearful even these golden, happy memories would be fleeting.

Nikki was able to momentarily forget the daunting prospect of marriage while involved in the throes and immediate aftermath of making love, but that evening, Nikki resorted to several bottles of brandy to escape the impending demise of his bachelorhood. Such finality, it was appalling. Alisa nervously sat beside him reading as he gloomily drank himself into oblivion.

The next morning he felt shaky as he hauled himself into the saddle and in a state of philosophic resignation began the journey back to town; two carriages carrying Alisa, her daughter and servants, the grooms and outriders, fifteen trackers and a reluctant bridegroom rode forth with two of the trackers flanking him the whole way. They even followed when he stopped to relieve a call of nature.

"Really," Nikki protested. "This 'protection' is quite unnecessary."

"Sorry, Lord Prince," the taller one solemnly intoned. "Orders from Prince Mikhail."

It appeared the old boy was dead serious and Nikki finally resigned himself to the constant com-

282 SUSAN M. JOHNSON

pany of the two enormous men. They even slept on
either side of him with a light leather braid knotted
around his waist and their wrists.

Arriving back in town five days later, Alisa was
immediately whisked away by Kaisa-leena for dress
fittings and other womanly pursuits necessary to or-
ganize a gigantic wedding.

Prince Mikhail summoned Nikki to his study
within minutes of their return and flatly informed
Nikki that he would be married in two days' time.
The invitations had been delivered and even on such
disastrously short notice the responses were all in the
affirmative. No one ever declined an invitation
from Prince Kuzan and furthermore this wedding
had all the indications of a delicious scandal. It
would have been humanly impossible to keep the
curious away. Prince Nikolai Kuzan actually marrying; all the servants' gossip hinted at an exceedingly
recalcitrant bridegroom and an enceinte bride only
one week divorced. How delightfully titillating.
Whom would the child look like? Most assuredly
Nikki, for one could not contemplate for a second
his marital capitulation to a woman carrying another man's child. And yet——speculation ran on.

For two days Nikki's two bodyguards followed
him everywhere; discreetly, of course, in order to
arouse as little gossip as possible. On the eve of his
wedding, Nikki descended the marble staircase
splendidly attired in white linen mufti, for the summer heat had settled on the jewel of the Baltic. His
faithful companions at his heels, Nikki stopped on
the last step, turned and glared at the two guards

who had stopped respectfully three steps higher, their pleasant faces tranquilly composed in spite of Nikki's obvious displeasure.

"Good God!" Nikki complained irritably, "enough's enough. I'm just going to my stag tonight and promise on my mother's soul that I'll be back in time for my wedding tomorrow."

Johanos just shrugged his shoulders and spread his hands in apology.

"Sorry, Lord Prince, your father's orders," and he stared impassively into space.

"Damnation!" Nikki exploded. "If you say 'father's orders' one more time, Johanos, I swear, I'll do you bodily harm," and he strode cursing out the door into the summer night, vowing to drink them under the table. Then he would be free of their unwelcome company.

He should have known better than to attempt to drink a Finnish woodsman under the table. The brandy and champagne flowed freely. All Nikki's fellow officers and friends were bent on teasing him remorselessly as Nikki, whom everyone considered the least likely to succumb to wedded bliss, was about to leave the ranks of bachelorhood.

With a drunken earnestness and a maudlin sentimentality over losing one of his drinking cohorts to Parson's mousetrap, Illyich cornered Nikki late in the evening and whispered conspiratorily, "I never thought you'd do it, Nikki. Why in hell's name do you consider marrying your mistress? I thought your greatest fear was the marriage block."

"That, my dear Astrakan," Nikki replied smoothly, "is my second greatest fear. The first is that of freezing my vitals off on my father's estate in Siberia."

Illyich's eyebrows rose.

"So you perceive perhaps, my friend, how things go on at the Kuzans. Although when one considers that half the genius and energy of Russia has been interred in Siberia for two centuries, it is entirely possible that its domestic society has improved, but I prefer not to be put to the necessity of discovering whether this is true," Nikki finished, and the unwelcome thought induced him to refill his glass once again.

"So that's it. My sympathies, mon Colonel," and in his usual kind humor Illyich attempted to cheer his friend. "But she is very lovely, eh? And warm in bed I warrant. Things could be worse, Nikki. Think of the advantages."

"Somehow, at the moment, I can only see the disadvantages," Nikki muttered "A pox on the female sex, Astrakan," he stated sourly. "Here, you need a drink."

Both glasses were refilled and tossed down.

Several hours later one of the youthful officers in Nikki's regiment who was not fully apprised of the true feelings of his colonel, made the gaffe of offering his felicitations on the coming nuptials.

"Go to hell!" snarled the Prince.

The following afternoon, a pale and silent Nikki faced his father across the library desk.

"You returned home after dawn. I trust you enjoyed yourself at your bachelor party," Prince Mikhail said in a polite distant voice.

Nikki lifted his shoulders in an eloquent shrug and remained silent.

"I won't keep you long so you may retire to gather your strength for the ceremony and festivities this evening. However I have a few simple remarks I wish to leave with you.

"You are to see to Alisa and to that other life. I trust I can with confidence leave them in your hands. I hope it is unnecessary to tell you that I expect a tighter bridle on your excesses. I do not care to hear rumors like those already circulating about Vladimir. The Emperor is quite irritated." [11]

Nikki did not deign to respond.

"I advise you, Nikolai," his father continued unperturbed, "that I would be pleased if you did not amuse yourself with Sophie again. Although I am certainly worldly enough to understand that faithfulness is not a necessity in every marriage, indeed in few apparently, may I remind you that Sophie is brazen enough to possibly cause public embarrassment to Alisa."

"Sophie is not one to be easily put off, father."

"I wish you to make the effort. She is a decadent slut at all accounts; une femme facile, in contrast to Sophie, takes on the aura of saintliness."

"You speak from experience, no doubt?" Nikki's eyebrows rose as he flashed his father a questioning glance.

"Naturally." The Prince did not lower his gaze.

In spite of himself, Nikki grinned. "I'll be damned! You must admit, sire, she is non-pareil in her bawdy role. A damned fine cunt."

"I am relieved to learn," the old Prince said mildly, "that your heart is not involved."

Nikki laughed harshly, raised a lazy eyebrow and commented rather caustically, "Hearts are not in Sophie's style, mon père, only stiff cocks."

Blandly ignoring this vulgarity, Prince Mikhail tranquilly resumed his tuition. "Your mother and I will retire to the country immediately after the festivities. Take care for the mother of my grandchild." His voice was all the more deadly for not bearing the slightest trace of emotion.

"While I am all for family, father, I fear I don't have the dynastic instinct as strongly as you, "Nikki replied with a quiet contempt.

"I do not need your impertinence," Prince Mikhail said in that same chilling murmur, "simply do as you're told and reflect on the consequences of my wrath if you don't."

He waited patiently for perhaps ten seconds and upon receiving no answer, rose from his chair, saying, "Please be on time at the chapel; we are curtailing the service in order to alleviate any unnecessary standing for Alisa." He walked from the room leaving Nikki slumped in his chair.

Nikki sat there for almost half an hour, his mind blank of any thoughts or emotions, his body fatigued from the long night of drinking. Hauling himself to his feet, he retraced his steps to his room and fell into a deep, exhausted sleep. The next thing he knew, he was being shaken awake. His bath had been prepared and all his silk finery spread out ready for dressing.

Within the hour Nikki was traversing the nu-

SEIZED BY LOVE 287

merous hallways and passageways that led to the
family chapel. His cousin Aleksei and Aleksei's
brother were standing as witness for him and followed closely on his heels as he strode rapidly and
mindlessly to his wedding. The chapel was small,
holding no more than 200 persons. When Nikki
entered the gilded and stuccoed room flooded with
the flickering light of thousands of candles and perfumed with the scent of tens of thousands of flowers,
a sigh broke from the assembled guests. He was
fifteen minutes late.

Nikki strolled across the front of the chapel and
took his place under a large canopy of trelliswork
interwoven with orchids. That moment Alisa reached
the main door and began to walk down the aisle. A
beautiful chant began.

She was quite breathtakingly flawless in a creme-
colored silk overlaid with deep flounces of magnificent lace, her pregnancy perfectly concealed beneath
the current fashionable tunic which draped yards of
material gracefully across the skirt front and pulled
it all in successive folds to the back of the waistline.
The increasing waistline, which had been the despair
of Madame Vevay, was hardly evident to anyone
who had not known Alisa's original lithe slender-
ness. A small tiara of diamonds set with cameos (a
gift from Prince Mikhail) crowned her red-gold
coiffure and held in place the yards-long hand-made
lace veil, valued at one thousand roubles an arshin.
The veil was of the most exquisite texture, the design
of roses and lilies so truthfully wrought that the
flowers seemed raised from the surface. Full twenty
feet trailed gracefully behind. Nikki's pendant neck-

lace of emeralds was around her neck and Aleksei's gift of diamond earrings hung from her ears.

Nikki caught his breath and paused to absorb her beauty, then stepped forward boldly and took her hand in his, drawing a quiet, subdued bride to his side. They both stood on a strip of satin and were given a lighted candle to hold which they retained throughout the service. The priests wore dark blue velvet, much embroidered in silver, and began reading the ceremony.

Nikki and Alisa both put rings on their right hands, a glass of wine was given them, out of which they both drank in turns three times, the priest holding it. Then elaborate golden crowns were brought in, which the officiating priests waved before them and which were then held over their heads by the best man, who became very tired and had to change arms. The priest began to deliver a long and beautiful recitative portion of the service in a magnificent bass voice, but abruptly cut the anthem short after a meaningful curt nod from Prince Mikhail. Nikki's father had been keenly observing Alisa and noted a slight weariness and pallor beginning to appear.

The ceremony was blessedly abbreviated, and after intoning the benediction, the deep voice of the Russian Orthodox priest pronounced them married before the eyes of God.

Alisa clung to Nikki's arm as they passed from the chapel, feeling faint from the closeness of the small room filled with people and heavy with the pungent sweet odor of flowers and incense. Nikki had not exchanged more than a dozen words with Alisa in the last two days, for despite his attempt to graciously accept the imperious commands of his father, a nagging anger continued to surface in his consciousness.

Rationally, Nikki realized that Alisa was just as much a victim of this farce as he, perhaps more, because she was burdened with an unborn child. But judiciousness was not holding sway in his emotions lately and he quite unjustifiably and irrationally blamed Alisa for his predicament.

"Chin up, my dear," Nikki whispered sarcastically as he pulled Alisa's trembling body up with a tight grasp under her arm. "You wouldn't want to faint before all these pantingly inquisitive guests."

"I wouldn't feel like fainting now, if you could learn to keep your pants buttoned up," she hissed petulantly as Nikki quite single-handedly held her upright and guided her out into the hall.

"Remember the old proverb, my love. A dog doesn't worry an unwilling bitch," he retorted ignobly and Alisa blanched visibly at the bitterly insulting remark. If only he could have left his anger behind him on their wedding day.

Now she did look ready to faint. Quickly, Nikki slipped his arm under her knees, picked her up, walked rapidly to a curving staircase and ran up a flight of stairs. Once out of sight of the hundreds of guests he continued more slowly to Alisa's room, the long train and veil billowing behind them. She rested gratefully against Nikki's black silk lapels.

Discordant emotions raced through both their minds. Nikki wanted her and didn't want her, afraid of permanence, while Alisa wanted him at all costs

and deplored her submission and bondage. But she
was mostly aware of a desperate fatigue; she was
tired of parrying Nikki's acid remarks or frigid indifference and she was too weary to fence off any
more verbal ripostes. Her sensibilities were blud-
geoned, her nerves frayed. Nothing mattered any
more. She was beyond hostility, beyond apology,
beyond caring for pride. She was in his arms, com-
forted by his strong embrace. It was the only place
she longed to be.

Walking into her room, Nikki laid her on the bed,
strode into his chamber next door and returned
within seconds with a bottle of brandy and two
glasses. Quickly pouring Alisa a glass, he plumped
up the pillows behind her, arranged her unprotesting
form in a half reclining position and handed over
the glass.

Pulling up a chair near the bed, Nikki sat down
with the bottle and the other glass, poured himself
a full bumper, put his long legs up on the satin
counterpane and said mockingly in his casual drawl,
"Shall we both sheath our talons and attempt to
amiably muddle through this charade. It seems you
are mine now for the rest of our lives, and one must
survive, after all. To our future, dear. Do you think
we have one?" he jibed in a soft murmur, noting
the still pallid color of Alisa's complexion.

"You'd better drink yours quickly or you won't
last many minutes more, my dear. You look quite
pale," and lifting his glass in salute, Nikki drained
it in one swallow. Over the rim of the glass he held
her eyes for one long speculative moment, his glance
cool, measured, unreadable. Alisa found she could

not look away, transfixed by the depths of those golden eyes. Was it possible she had discerned an unease registered briefly? The expression closed abruptly, his eyelids fell, his hand reaching out to refill his empty glass. The moment was over.

"Come now," he insisted half-kindly in his natural lazy tone, "you must summon the necessary energy to withstand the lengthy receiving line of our well-wishers."

Obediently Alisa drank slowly; the liquor burned down her throat and coursed through her blood-stream soon reviving her failing senses.

Full of good spirits, Nikki entertained Alisa quite cheerfully for the next twenty minutes, single-hand-edly emptying a good two-thirds of the bottle while Alisa's color returned. Alisa glanced at Nikki com-fortably sprawled in his chair and smiled faintly. "You are appearing less irate about this marriage."

"Alisa, my sweet, I'm becoming more reconciled to the prospect by the moment, I assure you." The brandy and Alisa's serenity had improved his humor.

They were interrupted just as Nikki was about to kick off his shoes, thinking, to hell with the guests. Alisa looked so radiantly lovely, perhaps they should start the honeymoon immediately. His irritations could seldom withstand the dual pressures of plenti-ful liquor and a languorous female within reach in bed.

Princess Kaisa-leena opened the door and step-ping halfway through the threshold, inquired solici-tously, "Do you feel well enough to come down. The guests are quite impatient to toast the bride and groom."

Nikki smothered a curse in deference to his gentle mother and dropped his patent leather clad feet to the floor. He extended his hand to Alisa. "Shall we, my dear?" he inquired pleasantly.

Alisa and Nikki stood in the receiving line next to Prince Mikhail and Princess Kaisar-leena for over an hour, greeting the guests to the accompaniment of the mechanical phrases necessary to the occasion —Enchantée, So nice to meet you, Thank you so much.

Several grand dukes of both generations attended and after watching Alisa sink into a deep curtsey for a second grand duke, Nikki snidely muttered, "You won't be able to curtsey that low much longer, my blooming young wife; your belly will get in the way."

Alisa cast him a wrathful look of indignation and Nikki smothered a guffaw as he turned to greet yet another distinguished guest. Several moments later Major Cernov paused before them and taking Alisa's hand in his, raised it to his lips. He held it for a moment longer than necessary, while he murmured suggestively, "You are more lovely each time I see you, Madame."

"You honor me with the compliment, Monsieur," Alisa replied flirtatiously, paying Nikki back for his guffaw, while Nikki stood at her side wondering what would happen if he smashed Cernov square in the mouth. He restrained the urge, for that would be a ripe piece of gossip indeed. The bridegroom fighting a rival at his wedding.

Abruptly Nikki turned to his parents and said, "We are done with these civilities. If anyone else wants to congratulate us they can put it in writing. Come, my dear, you look fatigued," and he gripped Alisa's elbow, drawing her to him, re-establishing possession and whisked her away to a quiet alcove where he snapped his fingers for a footman carrying a tray of champagne glasses.

"Put the tray down," Nikki said and motioned at the table beside the sofa. Quite oblivious of his responsibilities to his guests, Nikolai Kuzan proceeded to empty the contents of the glasses while he grimly clasped Alisa's hand as she sat next to him on the green satin upholstery. He burned with jealousy at Cernov's remark and swore aloud several times between draining glasses while he dwelt on the gall of his old friend. Damn his impudence! Alisa enjoyed this indication of jealousy after having endured Nikki's bland indifference for so many days.

With his usual disregard for the courtesies of society, just as the dinner guests were filing into the supper room for the magnificent array of dishes produced by the Kuzan chef, Nikki pulled Alisa to her feet and pushed her ahead of him through the throng of well-wishers and up the stairs to the nuptial bed.

Quite foxed by this time, Nikki couldn't decide which bed to use for this momentous occasion— the termination of his bachelorhood and the beginning of his husbandly duties. Should he use the bed in his room or the one in Alisa's? Solving the dilemma by deciding to take turns in both, he hastily disrobed himself and pulled off Alisa's voluminous gown and eased off her petticoats as she giggled from the several glasses of champagne he had pressed on her during the course of his emptying the tray.

Nikki picked Alisa up and they collapsed on the bed, kissing and laughing, caressing each other. Then he kissed her long and carefully, fondling her ripe body until she trembled beneath him, threw her arms around his neck and eased herself beneath his throbbing stiffness, entering into the spirited love-play with abandon. It was no sense of husbandly duty or adherence to his father's admonitions that kept Nikki near his wife all night.

The following morning, Prince Mikhail and Princess Kaisa-leena took their leave for Le Repose amid kisses and hugs, exclamations of fondness and kind good wishes, with the exception of Nikki and his father, who stiffly and formally bade goodbye to each other, the strain in their relationship painfully clear.

Prince Mikhail was upset that his son still resisted his plan.

As his carriage passed through the dusty streets of the city, he relaxed his stern, forbidding expression, reached over and clasped the small hand of his wife sitting beside him and said wearily, "I hope I've done right by that young woman. Have I been too harsh to insist on their marriage?"

"No, Misha, our son resists the fact that he loves her; he'll come to accept it someday, and Alisa loves Nikki, of that I'm sure. It's important for the coming child to have both a mother and a father. Don't despair, all will be well," she said quietly and patted his large strong hand. Silently she whispered a Tzigane charm for the happiness of the union, for she knew how unyielding, independent and demanding Nikki could be. So much like his father.

"I will not interfere again," the Prince sighed unhappily. "Perhaps if left alone, they will build a life together for our future grandchild." Secretly he was not very hopeful, but at least the child would have a name, and the vast assets and resources of the Kuzan family as its patrimony. Money couldn't buy happiness but at least it offered luxury in one's despair, the old prince reflected cynically.

Before many weeks had passed in the pink marble palace on the Millionnaya, Nikki began to fall into his old habits. At first, he had grudgingly but dutifully run the rounds of parties, drums, balls, and picnics with Alisa, but always bored, indifferent, and obviously discontent as he either stood on the sidelines drinking and watching Alisa or else disappeared into the card room for hours. In less than a month he no longer made an attempt to hide the fact that he found these functions intolerable.

Aleksei had more and more taken his place as escort and lately almost exclusively squired Alisa to the festivities she chose to attend. Aleksei adored Alisa with the dogged infatuation of youth and was ever ready and eager to indulge her whims. Alisa appreciated Aleksei's youthful spirits and candor and thanked him with heartfelt sincerity for being a companion to her. His was a friendship she valued all the more as Nikki's interests drifted away to other pursuits.

Aleksei raged inwardly at the callous indifference and discourteous treatment Nikki gave his wife, but kept his indignant thoughts to himself. A verbal brawl with Nikki would accomplish nothing for Alisa's happiness and in the cool tenor of Nikki's current mood, he did not want to risk being forbidden the freedom of the house and Alisa's company. The young man fretted but held his tongue.

Soon Nikki began staying away from home nights, comfortably easing back into the habits of twenty years. Alisa sobbed in sorrow and rage the first time it happened. The pain Nikki saw in her face forced him to hurl back at her with a suppressed ferocity, "Damn you, stop whining! You knew what I was like when you married me! Did you not?" And then his voice dropped to a chilling murmur, "My whoring and drinking were well known to you, Madame, before you chose to become my mistress and then my wife. Surely it is not a shock to your delicate sensibilities. Do not, at this late date, become full of nonsense about honorable and virtuous conduct. You were hardly a model of propriety yourself."

"You need not insult me," Alisa whispered unhappily.

"By God, a femme facile can be insulted now," he said, wishing to hurt. "What next? Rockets to the moon, no doubt."

"But," his eyes narrowed dangerously, "do not consider flirtations, Madame, or that you have a freedom of—hum—shall we say—outside friendships. I have warned you in that respect. No man touches my wife. Whatever children are born of this marriage will be Kuzan by parentage as well as by name. And I would appreciate, Madame, in the future, if you would have the goodness to refrain from concerning yourself in my affairs."

Alisa cried in private at Nikki's casual freedom, but if she sometimes renewed that line of conversation he simply walked away, so as the weeks progressed she accepted his behavior because she had no other choice, but she refused to like it. She wanted to scream, Go away! Go away! If you don't care for me, Go away! Why should she be forced to suffer his reluctant forbearance as life companion. But the growing child, now kicking in her womb, the need for some security in a thoroughly male-dominated world required that she accept the grudgingly offered hand.

How can he be the same man? Previously he was capable of great kindness, so gentle yet so passionate when she was his mistress. Now he was cool, indifferent, an unresponsive man who happened to live in the same residence. She was paying a high price for her child's name. Once the seed is planted a man can ignore, or circumvent or disavow; paternity is an elusive state, but the receiver of his "gift" has no such option.

Alisa decided to make the best of this imperfect world. She would not retire from life, but chose instead to devote herself to Katelina and in the future, to the new child. Her child would have a name. Her husband, though it wrenched her heart to conceive of it, could resume his former life—apparently he already had. But she would not humiliate herself and beg for crumbs of affection.

And yet, she often broke into an uncontrollable torrent of unhappy tears. Her mind could not control her wounded heart.

Nikki never visited her bed anymore. She knew his need for women and her heart was consumed with pain at the thought. However, they were not the reason for his absence.

He spent his evenings gambling at the clubs, silent, taciturn, grim, quick to anger, while his friends remarked that marriage must not be agreeing with Nikolai Kuzan. He had even missed the annual war games at Tsarskoe late that summer, pleading an extended leave for reasons of health. The easy, masculine camaraderie of the officers would have been intolerable in his present humor.

He was drinking deep, and whispers warned to stay clear of Prince Kuzan; he was primed for trouble. When tired of brandy and gambling, Nikki could invariably be found in one of several Kirgiz night cafes on the Islands, drinking black coffee with lemon essence and opium, sweetened with sherbet, or smoking hashish. Both drugs soothed his frustrations, mellowed his irritations and assuaged his melancholy.

He would, with studied punctuality, arrive home before Katelina wakened and wait for her in the morning room where she would run down to chatter with Nikki while eating her breakfast. Dressed in his evening clothes, he would wait by the dying fire, feeling no sense of urgency or anything beyond a detached, dreamy interest in seeing his favorite moppet.

Nikki was considerate of Katelina in every way, bringing her home lavish quantities of toys and giving every attention to her childish dialogue. When it was time for Katelina's lessons in the morning, Nikki would retire to his bedchamber and sleep the day away, rising in time to join Alisa and Katelina for dinner in the enormous formal dining room. Dressed once more for an evening out, he would gossip cheerfully with Katelina while talking with a polite civility to Alisa. Once Katelina was tucked in bed he disappeared for the night without a word of explanation.

One evening at the dinner table, Alisa gathered her courage to ask Nikki if he would be available for a dancing party she was giving at the end of the week. He hesitated briefly, asked again what day it was to be held and then said with his customary cool voice, "I'll contrive to attend, Madame. Please remind my valet the morning of the occasion to wake me in time to dress."

Alisa was dressed and waiting in the drawing room the night of the party when Nikki sauntered into the room at ten o'clock, carrying a glass of brandy, already his fourth since putting Katelina to bed. He was attired with his usual negligent elegance in a superbly fitted brown velvet suit which showed his magnificent body off to advantage. An enormous turquoise and diamond pin fastened his carelessly tied cravat and sparkled in the brilliantly lit room. Alisa couldn't help herself as a press of confusing emotions smothered her. Nikki's presence still took her breath away and she was conscious of an unavoidable stirring of admiration.

Casting one desultory glance at the splendid, exotic floral arrangements which graced the room, he walked across the polished parquet, stopped halfway into the room and in a slow drawl remarked, "May I compliment you on your toilette, Madame? You are shown off to excellent advantage this evening."

A warm glow blazed through Alisa at these first

complimentary words she had heard from Nikki in weeks. Was he really proud of her good looks? In the fifth month of her pregnancy Alisa was wearing a slightly Empire gown of emerald green satin with ruching and ruffles of green velvet and embroidered Byzantine brocade decorating the flounces of green satin and outlining the low decolletage. Her beautiful breasts now further enlarged by pregnancy were swelling magnificently above the green satin bodice. Nikki's emeralds rested on the soft mounds of flesh while the enormous pendant hung suspended in a deep cleavage. A wreath of white violets and green velvet ribbon was woven into her fashionable upswept curls.

Alisa's warm glow was short-lived as Nikki tartly said, "However, may I caution you not to bend over too far or you may fall out of your gown." A slow anger rose in him at the sight of so much of Alisa's flesh exposed to the public eye, but he restrained his waxing jealousy and tossed off his brandy instead. Walking over to a side table he refilled his glass then perched on the edge of the table idly swinging one velvet-clad leg.

Receiving no answer save a narrowed glance from hot violet eyes, Nikki continued, "May I offer you a brandy, Princess. Personally, I find a need to fortify myself against the coming ordeal."

"If you please, Lord Prince," Alisa retorted formally. "I too feel the need of a drink."

They sat perhaps for twenty minutes drinking their liquor in a strained silence before the first guests arrived walking up the grand marble stairway flanked by twenty-four footmen wearing the Kuzan livery and were announced by two chasseurs at the doors to the ballroom.

Alisa, frustrated by Nikki's contemptuous stares, drank rather more than usual and was soon flirting outrageously with several of the young gentlemen who paid her court. She was constantly being complimented as the most beautiful woman in Petersburg and tonight she was in a dangerous mood to accept the flattery as she danced with the young officers and drank champagne with the ardent gentlemen surrounding her.

She even greeted Major Cernov cordially as he came over to pay his compliments and gaze down her low neckline. Alisa smiled at him sweetly, thinking how easily men could be diverted by a pink expanse of bosom.

Nikki stood apart with some of his friends from the Yacht Club pouring brandy down with great regularity and only occasionally listening to the conversation concerning the merits of the two new danseuses in the corps dramatique. His eyes followed Alisa around the room, and his temper rose as the evening progressed. He watched Alisa darting flirtatious glances at young gallants, thinking she was his wife, dammit, and he put away some more brandy as he considered the infamy of her actions.

When Cernov began bending rather too closely to Alisa's dainty ear while leering down her cleavage, Nikki took a drunken resolve.

Vile, little slut, teasing Cernov with your heaving bosom. He excused himself from his friends with a studied politeness and slowly sauntered across the room toward Alisa and Cernov, followed by several curious eyes in the group he had just quitted.

"Good evening, Gregor," Nikki said quietly, breathing brandy everywhere.

"We will not detain you, Cernov," he said in a cold murmur. "I'm sure you're anxious to join your friends," and with a short nod dismissed him. With the immeasurable arrogance instilled in one thousand years of Kuzan nobility, Nikki turned his head the merest fraction and a footman came scurrying out of the noisy crowd.

"Princess Kuzan is feeling indisposed and desires to retire to her apartments. Please escort her."

Alisa had no choice. If she refused, Nikki was entirely capable of provoking a scene in front of her three hundred guests. She went, her anger blazing high.

Experienced host that he was, Nikki signaled the musicians to begin again, abruptly breaking the still hush of expectancy that hung in the enormous ballroom. Nikki left immediately after, taking himself to the Kirgiz cafe while the guests continued to dance without either host or hostess, and only a delicious scandal to occupy them.

Early the next morning as the horizon lightened to a shimmering pink, feeling slightly, ever so slightly, apologetic for his drunken peremptory conduct the evening before, Nikki woke up a furrier on his way home and purchased some gifts for Alisa and Katelina. He had promised himself last spring he would dress Alisa in sables and the weather was coming on winter. Snow could be expected in a few weeks.

SEIZED BY LOVE 303

When Katelina and Alisa arrived in the morning
room for breakfast, Nikki occupied his usual comfortable chair by the fire, still dressed in brown velvet. Katelina scrambled onto his lap and began exclaiming over all the flowers still decorating the
palace and Chef's promise to serve party food for
breakfast.

"Come, Uncle Nikki." She paused. "I mean—
Isa," she remembered quickly. Nikki had insisted on
adopting her. Strong-arm methods, in addition to a
small fortune, had persuaded Forseus to sign the
consent papers. He had explained to Katelina in the
Finnish language Katelina preferred to speak that
she was to call him "father" now he had married her
mother. Katelina had gaily clapped her hands in delight and remembered on most occasions to make
the change from uncle to father.

"Come Daddy," she implored, "and eat some
party food with me."

"Look first at the presents I have for you and your
mother," Nikki insisted.

"You should eat some breakfast, Nikki," Alisa
suggested as she sat across the room noting his appearance. He looked pale, more fatigued than usual.

"Very wifely, I'm sure," he commented ironically
but ignored her suggestion. "Bring those to your
mother," and he handed two enormous boxes to
Katelina. She brought first one and then the other
to Alisa who was seated at the table watching Nikki
and Katelina. Why couldn't Nikki share some of that
kindness and love with me, she thought sadly. He
blames me for the marriage but if I had known how
miserable he was going to be married, I would have

refused. We were so happy those few weeks in the country. Now she was like some alien presence in his town palace; an albatross of duty around his neck, a wife.

Katelina was tearing off the silver wrapping and pulling out a gorgeous ermine cape with matching hat and muff trimmed with white velvet ribbons. Nikki helped her put on the new ermine finery and she whirled around the room jumping on a chair to gaze at her image in a mirror, then ran out of the room looking for Rakeli to show off her new finery.

Alisa slowly unwrapped the largest box and exclaimed in wonder at the splendid sable cape ensconced in silk tissue. Nikki lounged in his chair watching her.

"Try it on," he ordered quietly and Alisa's momentary happiness was shattered by his tone of command, however softly spoken. "I want my wife to be adequately dressed," he added.

That's all he cares about, she thought hotly remembering her unhappy departure last evening from her *own* party.

Well, she'd take his sable cape. Why not spend some of his fortune to remain "adequately" dressed? She tossed the cape around her shoulders and sullenly turned about, the superbly soft fur whispering as it twirled.

Nikki smiled faintly. He preferred her petulance to the moroseness she had affected lately. "Open the other one," he prompted.

Alisa ripped the wrapping violently aside and lifted out a short, snug-fitting, waist-length jacket of ermine trimmed with seed pearls.

"I can't wear it," she said with malicious delight at being able to refuse his gift. "It's too tight. It won't fit while I'm pregnant."

"Forgive me, a man's unpracticed eye, I'm afraid. Such a pity. Perhaps you can save it for Katelina when she grows older, for it won't fit you next winter either."

"It certainly will," Alisa replied waspishly. "I haven't gained that much weight. My figure will be quite returned by next winter."

"So sorry to disappoint you, Madame, but my father is so set on legitimate heirs, I intend to punctiliously demonstrate my filial piety and keep you pregnant. If he wants heirs, he shall have heirs."

"You aren't going to use me for a brood mare!" Alisa exploded angrily.

"I'll allow you a two-month rest after the birth of this child, but," he warned, "I shall plant my seed in you once again."

"The only part for which you are providentially qualified, no doubt," Alisa said scathingly.

"No doubt," Nikki agreed equably, "and a gratifying part, I might add, with your soft, squirming body as participant. Ah," he sighed lightly, a smile playing across his handsome face, "I quite look forward to my duties as stud for the Kuzan family and intend to pursue my function with great assiduity. If you do your part, Madame, little Kuzans should arrive with punctual regularity."

And so in this acrimonious, malevolent atmosphere of wedded bliss, the young Prince and his wife continued. As the weeks flew by Alisa became ungainly and awkward as the child grew. She relinquished most of her social activities and remained home with Katelina and occasionally Aleksei for company. Nikki persisted in his carefree bachelor life, solicitous to Katelina, but indifferent to his wife, now great with child.

Prince Mikhail with his usual host of reliable informants was kept apprised of the movements of his son and family. He was told that Nikki was living like there was no tomorrow, drunk or sleeping most of the hours of the day and night, while he and his wife had no more than a nodding acquaintance. Prince Mikhail wondered how long it had been since Nikki was sober. The old Prince viewed the situation with deepening and grievous concern. Not sure of his son's reception, he had Kaisa-leena write to inquire whether they would be welcome for Christmas and received from Nikki a polite but clear "no," explaining Alisa's delicate health made entertaining impossible as she approached the end of her term.

Prince Mikhail, now greatly distressed, decided to wait until after the birth of the child and if the marriage didn't improve and Alisa was genuinely unhappy, he would offer to help her in obtaining a divorce. The procedure was eminently simplified by his friendship with the Emperor. He simply could not have Alisa's wretched misery on his conscience. He had foolishly hoped for a reconciliation between his son and Alisa, but Nikki stubbornly refused to give up his licentious living. Very well, he would leave the choice to Alisa. Whatever she wanted, he would support her decision.

* * *

Nikki, Alisa and Katelina spent a quiet Christmas. Nikki indulged Alisa's request to celebrate the holiday in the Lutheran fashion since Katelina was familiar with those activities, so the festivities lasted many days, beginning with Christmas Eve on December 24 and continuing through the Russian Christmas on January 6. Katelina was deluged with enough gifts to fill a room and accepted the largesse with equanimity.

Nikki presented Alisa with a three-strand necklace of extremely rare black pearls. The black pearl, the jeweler had explained, was now the summit of every elegante's ambition and due to its rarity was the most expensive jewel to adorn a lady's jewel case.

A second gift of a large photo-portrait of Katelina had been contrived after many whispered conferences between father and daughter. Nikki had taken Katelina for two sittings at the fashionable "artistic photographer" at No. 4 Morskaija, until they were both satisfied with the portrait. A mischievous face framed in ermine peered seraphically from behind a frothy muff, and Katelina had signed the photo with her unsteady five-year-old hand.

An unpleasant stab of guilt struck Nikki as he accepted Alisa's gift to him; a watercolor sketch she had done at Mon Plaisir last summer. A wash of warm memories enveloped Nikki and a reminiscent smile softened the harsh-featured face for a brief moment.

Nikki actually stayed home several nights in a row to spend the holiday with his winsome daughter. He read her the Christmas stories and joined in the songs, surprising everyone by singing them from memory. He remembered his own early Christmases with a child's memory and tried to give some of that delight to Katelina. With a rueful pang, he had to admit that these evenings en famille offered a contentment and satisfaction that no liquor or opium could promote. How long had it been since he had sung Christmas songs?

Alisa was pleased to have Nikki sitting with her before the fire and her emotions leapt in happiness to have him near. She resolutely steeled herself to expect his disappearance soon, but she would bask unreservedly in the luxury of his kindness and company while she could.

Nikki watched Alisa as she read to Katelina or played the piano while they sang, and marveled anew at the beauty and charm of this woman who was his wife. He would find himself occasionally lapsing into recollections of their weeks at Mon Plaisir or in vague musings about the child she was carrying. Alisa was charming in cashmere dresses of a loose flowing style suitable for ladies "awaiting a blessed event," as "Madame Vevay so delicately put it.

For the first time in his life he thought about becoming a father. He even felt a kindly concern for Alisa's travail, soon to begin. She was small and fragile and the child was already extremely large. He must ask about her doctor, he considered absently, and then was coaxed into joining them in play and forgot the subject.

However, with Christmas over, Nikki embarked once again on his chronic, restless rounds of gambling and drinking, descending a little further into his own private hell. His melancholy deepened, his drinking increased, his boredom he could have cut with a knife.

XV
THE VOLTE-FACE

Returning home at his usual early hour one morning, Nikki found the palace already a bustle of activity. Maids were running up the stairs, footmen were scurrying on errands, even Sergei momentarily forgot to divest his master of his sable top-coat, gloves and walking stick, instead blurting out forthwith, "I'm so glad to see you Lord Prince, we were not able to locate you last night."

Nikki gripped Sergei's shoulder in alarm when he heard the nervous protestation.

"What's the matter, Sergei?"

"The Mistress, sir, she went into labor last evening and is having difficulty."

"Where's the damn doctor?" Nikki roared as he dug his fingers into Sergei and shook him. "The doctor is here, Lord Prince, but says he can do nothing. The baby is too large. It will not come."

Nikki released his hold on Sergei, tossed his gloves and stick aside and raced up the steps, bursting furiously into Alisa's bedroom. The drapes were drawn, the room was stifling, gas lights burned low in all the fixtures. Rushing to the bedside, Nikki looked fearfully at Alisa's still form. Her skin was translucently pale, her fists clung weakly to sheets tied to the bedposts above her head, small beads of sweat lined her upper lip and damp hair curled around her pallid face.

311

"Where's the damned doctor?" Nikki hissed to Maria hovering near. Alisa's eyelids did not even flutter at the sound of his voice. Holy Mother, was she dead already? He quickly bent to feel her pulse. It was extremely weak but not irregular.

"Where's the doctor?" he repeated in a louder whisper as he shrugged out of his fur coat, suffocating in this hot, close room. He twirled around and searched the darkened room.

"Here, Lord Prince." A little man moved forward. Nikki eyed him belligerently.

"What in hell's going on?" he growled in a repressed roar.

The poor doctor wrung his hands in panic. Prince Kuzan's temper was notorious. This Prince could send him to Siberia within the hour if he so chose. Dare he tell him the truth? Dare he tell him the child was too large and wouldn't be born? He could cut the woman open and probably save the child but not all women survived that surgery and she was very weak already. Without the surgery both mother and child would die.

"Well, doctor?" Nikki asked impatiently as he glared down at the hesitant, uncertain figure.

The little man decided on the truth. If worse came to worst, he could appeal to Prince Mikhail, who had a reputation for justice.

"Have you no tongue?" Nikki demanded furiously.

The doctor gravely told him the truth; at best, he might be able to save the child. He could do no more.

Nikki, in a blinding rage, picked the little man up bodily and flung him out the door, then he roared for Ivan and all the servants. Within seconds a crowd was assembled around him.

"I want every midwife in the city here within ten minutes!" he bellowed. "Ivan, check with that incompetent who calls himself a doctor and get names and addresses. Send out the troikas to pick them up. Immediately!" he stormed and swung back into the bedroom.

The stableboys set a new record that morning harnessing up the troikas and as the last buckle was wrenched into place, the drivers lashed the horses and sped off, the sleighs flying over the crisp white snow.

Within ten minutes the first midwife appeared and within twenty minutes nine women were standing in the hallway outside Alisa's room.

Nikki, who had been watching Alisa in an agony of despair and fear, returned to the hallway and scrutinized the assembled women. Four he dismissed on the spot as being too dirty and pushed the other five into the room to Alisa.

After examining her, four of the five women shook their heads and refused to touch her. They believed she was going to die anyway and if they assisted, they would be blamed when she died. None of them cared to incur the wrath of Prince Kuzan.

The fifth woman said very simply, "There is not much hope, Lord Prince, she is very weak, the baby is much too large, but I will try."

His world reeled madly. No hope? Alisa would die? All his wealth and power were helpless. Despair opened like a black chasm. He resolutely shook it off. Nikki released his breath which he had been unconsciously holding, dismissed the other women with a wave of his hand and in a voice deep with emotion said, "If you cannot save them both, sacrifice the child; take it out any way you have to; I don't care, but I will not lose my wife. Do you hear?" he whispered fiercely, "I will not lose my wife!"

The woman shuddered at the piercing eyes staring at her and could not answer such a statement. Was he mad?

Alisa lay in a deep, unconscious state from which she would frequently drift up and hear the muted words and quiet sobs of the servants; the whispers and the questioning voices. Time became disjointed, erratic; fragmented vignettes fluctuated madly, images of her and Nikki at Mon Plaisir, mindless longing for peaceful oblivion from the pain, visions of the pine forests and clover fields of her childhood. Take me away, take me back. There must be something more than this wrenching, brutal, unnatural pain—this unbearable agony of labor.

Why, she moaned, had she ever lain with Nikki in that spring meadow and wanted him to make love to her? She had forgotten how painful, how devastatingly wicked, how agonizing the contractions of labor were. The pain crept over her slowly and then sank in like fangs of a crazed animal, ripping and tearing her apart until she screamed in frenzy. She would cling to the sheets, pulling until her arms ached with the effort, twisting, turning, trying to elude the monstrous, ruthless, unceasing beast.

Now nothing hurt any more. She floated powerless in a sequence of dreams and blackness and whispered sobs. She's dying. The baby won't come. Dear God, was she dying? Was it she they were whispering about? She wanted to see Nikki and

Katelina. I have to explain to Katelina. She's so young. She won't understand. She wanted to see Nikki. Nikki! she screamed, Nikki! in her floating world and to those around the bed a pitiful faint whisper spoke—Nikki.

"I'm here, my love," he answered brokenly and she opened her eyes slowly and in a golden haze of light his swarthy face, those tawny eyes, looked lovingly into hers. Her hand fluttered up to touch him but she had not the strength to lift it.

"I love you," he whispered. She smiled faintly at those words she had not heard for many months. She tried to say I love you, too, but the sound would not come.

What were they doing to her body? Don't touch me, she wanted to say, leave me alone. The blackness enveloped her golden haze and she thought, how remarkable that a dead woman can still hurt so.

The midwife was instructing Nikki quietly. "Press down on her stomach, she has no more strength for contractions. I will work my fingers in and try to force the baby's cranial plates together. If we can just inch the head through we can pull the baby free."

She ruthlessly cut the opening wider. Her sensitive fingers edged into Alisa, probing and pressing, feeling for the bony plates that would compress and ease the size of the skull. For perhaps three minutes she worked, sweat dripping from her brow. Nikki did what he was told, exerting pressure on Alisa's swollen abdomen when commanded, repeating to himself in a hopeless inaudible monotone, Help her. Help her, God. Sweet Jesus and all the Saints, help her.

At last the fullness of the baby's head slid through and a great sigh passed round the room. Nikki's bitter dispair lifted and he dared to hope. Very slowly, the midwife guided out first one small shoulder, then the second, the long torso emerged and finally the chubby legs. The baby was a boy; fat, healthy and now vigorously bawling in a nurse's arms.

Nikki scarcely glanced at the child whose birth might have come at too high a price. Alisa's hands had released their limp grip on the sheets. He looked up at the midwife.

"Will she live now?" he asked with a look of anguish, desperately afraid of the answer.

"She is young, Lord Prince, and if no hemorrhaging begins, she has a chance."

"Thank you." he said quietly. "For your work today, you shall live in comfort the rest of your life. And if my wife lives, all the generations of your family will never want. I cannot lose her." Nikki moaned and the great dark head bowed over the bed as he wept unashamedly.

He kept a vigil through the night, not daring to sleep for fear the faint breathing would stop; offering a thousand penances to God if he would let her live; invoking every charm and superstition and childhood prayer to succor the frail, battered body of his wife.

In the awful hell of guilt and shame tearing at his brain, one thought reeled over and over, I love her and she cannot die. And now he knew he had loved her from the first, even while he suppressed and denied the human passion within himself. He had never intended to love her, had sworn never to love any woman again, did not intend for her to fall in love with him. It just began as sport, a game to idle the time away, and now he couldn't help himself. Was it too late now, too late to try and make her happy, to give her the love she deserved?

He dropped his head into his hands and cried, "Oh God, I've been a damn fool!"

Hours later, in the lightening dawn, Alisa's eyelids fluttered open and Nikki jumped from his chair. Her eyes moved to the figure bending over her and she saw Nikki through a golden haze.

"Is the baby born?" she whispered weakly.

"Yes, love, a boy." He reached for her limp, wet hand.

Her eyes sparkled in triumph. "You have your heir," she smiled faintly.

At too high a price, Nikki agonized, but smiled in return and simply said softly, "Thank you, love, for a fine son. Is there anything at all you want? Anything in the whole world?"

Alisa smiled again and whispered faintly, "Will you stay home some nights now?"

"Every night," he promised and thought, just live so I can stay home with you every night. Just live!

"It was worth it then. . . ." and her words trailed off as she gave a contented smile and sank back into a deep untroubled sleep.

Nikki stayed by her bedside night and day for three days. Her pulse was weak but never failed. He talked briefly to Katelina each morning and then immediately returned to his vigil. He was unkempt and haggard, gaunt, exhausted, but now on the third day, hopeful. Alisa had not hemorrhaged and he had been able to feed her some light broth yesterday. Yes, he could almost dare be optimistic. She would live!

Nikki had sent for his parents immediately after the birth of his son and his mother had competently taken charge in the nursery. At first seeing his father, Nikki had begun to apologize but Prince Mikhail brushed aside his attempts indulgently. "Apologies aren't necessary, my son. I too was young and fiercely independent once. I only hope you can find as much happiness with Alisa as I have found with your mother. All the hashish in the world cannot replace the comfort of a woman who loves you," said the old Prince with a wink. "I think you will not be frequenting the Kirgiz night cafes so often, now, eh, my boy?"

"No father, most assuredly not." Nikki laughed softly.

Several days later Alisa, feeling quite strong again, was sitting up in the gilded bed holding her large, healthy son and cooing into the pale blue eyes already full of golden highlights. Nikki came into the room and marveled at the beauty of the scene— Alisa, her rosy complexion restored, playing with his fine, lusty son. His child; immortality in his image; his mark left on the world.

Motioning for the maid to take the baby away, Nikki walked over to Alisa and seated himself on the bed. "Don't you want to hold your son?" Alisa asked.

"My dear, I've done all the holding of babies I intend to this day. Katelina insisted we take Sasha on our silver platter rides down the stairs, so early this morning we spent most of an hour exhibiting this delightful occupation to the youngest member of our family. I held Sasha in one arm, Katelina sat between my legs and we sailed down the marble stairs amid squeals of excitement from that hellion of a daughter we have."

"Good Lord!" Alisa's eyes opened in alarm. "Sasha's too young!"

"Indeed, Madame, I must agree," Nikki rejoined, eyes twinkling, "for after the third ride, he promptly fell asleep in my arms and missed the next four trips." His eyes softened. "You look very lovely this morning, my dove."

"Thank you, and thank you for staying at my bed-side for so many days. Rakeli informed me that you were very solicitous," Alisa said teasingly, feeling quite giddy and tremulously joyful.

"Well, I hope, Madame, I know my duty," Nikki replied in mock dismay. "I'd like to talk to you." he said seriously.

Alisa's heart sank. Now that she was out of danger, perhaps he would no longer feel any concern for her. She lay back against her pillows prepared for the worst. "Yes, Nikki," she said fearfully.

"As soon as you are recovered sufficiently, I'll have you taken out into the country. I have a great desire for my children to be reared away from the dirt and bustle of the city."

So that's how he's going to manage, Alisa thought bitterly. She remembered his promise to stay home every night with her. He wouldn't have to break his promise this way. She would be out of the way and he could come and go as he pleased.

"I shan't do it! I won't stay in the country!" Alisa replied defiantly. Already her mind was racing to find alternatives. Prince Mikhail and Kaisa-leena would understand. Perhaps divorce, freedom for both of them, was the only answer. But now, she felt too tired to care. Her defiance slowly died.

"Perhaps you could be persuaded to stay if I were to accompany you. You see, quite unaccountably, I have developed an overwhelming penchant for country air."

Alisa's tired glance lifted swiftly, glimpsing Nikki's merry eyes and smile and suddenly she felt blissfully happy.

Nikki clasped both her hands in his and holding them in his sure, strong grip said, gently, as he looked into dark violet eyes, "And in addition, I am unfashionably besotted with the woman I married." Alisa put up her arms in an open, childish gesture of need. Nikki enfolded her in his arms.

"We will be happy, you and I. I will see to that."

"Yes," Alisa murmured softly as Nikki bent to kiss those tempting lips, "you have always been able to see to that."

As Nikki lifted his lips from hers, Alisa softly queried, "Nikki, could I ask something of you?"

"Of course, love." he whispered huskily, nibbling at her ear.

"Would you consider giving up such mistresses as Sophie who are constantly in company with us? I never know what to say to them and feel so foolish and awkward." It was half statement, half question.

He paused for a moment, contemplating a lie, but he could not dissemble after all, and having lived a life renowned for the uniqueness of his depravities, he did not want to be forced into a posture he could in no way carry off.

"I will forswear one day at a time, I promise you that."

With a mischievous glance Alisa murmured, "And I, my Prince, can go my own road too, then? It's the sophisticated fashion. We will both discreetly look away on occasion."

Nikki threw back his head and laughed.

"You damned impertinent minx. You still don't know your place. Will you never learn submission and duty? Remember, I know how to guard my own. Egad, woman," he grinned, "I suppose we shall bicker and scrap incessantly and be at each other's throats from morning to night."

"I suppose so, my Prince," Alisa replied, flashing a teasing look up through heavy lashes, "but it *does* keep your melancholy at bay and I *do so* enjoy the making up."

EPILOGUE

An elegant chapel was constructed at Mon Plaisir and when Alisa questioned the enterprise, Nikki sheepishly explained that he had promised to erect the church if God spared her life during Sasha's birth.

"Good Lord, who will use it except the servants?" she asked incredulously, but a tiny glow of pleasure was lit somewhere within her heart at the sentiment.

True. It would not be used often except by the servants. But occasionally, he knew, he would enter the holy sanctuary alone, and alone give thanks that the woman he adored was still with him—in marriage and in love.

The Prince did indeed fill his nursery; not by force as he had once threatened, but rather with the full acquiescence of his affectionate wife who assured him that all births were not as difficult as Sasha's. A nursery wing was added by necessity after their third child was born and Prince Kuzan was often known to remark that he quite heartily approved of the concept of filial piety, and was doing his damnedest to satisfy his father's desire for heirs.

Nikki also admired the old Persian saying: Three things are most pleasing in the eyes of God: to conceive a child, to plant a tree and to write a book.

Some day, he said, he would consider moving on to subjects two and three.

Nikki appeared in town infrequently and on those sporadic occasions, he was usually accompanied by his family. During these visits he proudly displayed his beautiful and growing children, and the pink marble palace resounded with their noise and activities. His clubs would see him rarely and to other women he was to all practical purposes lost forever. They would repine and cast soft sighs after the tall, handsome Prince but he very happily ignored them and found his satisfaction and contentment in the company of his beautiful wife and enchanting children.

As their first-born son Sasha grew to manhood, the boy showed a marked affinity to embrace the same dissipated life once enjoyed by his father.

"Sometimes I think you positively encourage Sasha's debauchery, condoning any hellish scheme he concocts, overlooking the most blatant escapades," Alisa would occasionally remark testily to the Prince.

"Now, dear, let the boy have his head."

"Yes, that was always your maxim, you lecher, and look what happens. You know," she said darkly, "when I discovered the younger children's governess in bed with Sasha, he was scarce fourteen."

"I know dear," Nikki soothed placatingly, "but that didn't happen again. Sasha, no doubt, took your motherly advice to heart."

After that indiscretion, Nikki had taken his reckless son aside and warned him about too blatantly offending his mama. "I'll spare you my advice which I conceive you will in no part accept at this youthful stage, and only recommend, for the sake of my domestic tranquility, my boy, that perhaps the summer house on the point by the lake would be more discreet."

And so the boy went on, but that's another story.

NOTES

1. The remark concerning the Elector of Saxony was, needless to say, not meant literally, for Prince N. Kuzan had some way to go on that score. Augustus the Strong, Elector of Saxony, was aptly named, since he had the distinction of siring 354 illegitimate children. (page 24)

2. The art of tracking wild animals by their footprints was brought to perfection in Russia by a certain tracker known by the name of Lukash—Big Luke—whose methods were quickly adopted by others, so that presently all professional trackers came to be known as Lukash, plural Lukashee. The original Lukash was in the employment of Polovtseff. (page 51)

3. Owing to the frequent severe attacks of asthma to which Alexander II was subject, he rather dreaded going to bed at all, and when he was suffering from this chronic complaint, he would remain at work at his desk all night, keeping himself stimulated, although this is denied by the people in his immediate entourage, by occasional sips of champagne; Clicquot being his favorite brand. A shower-bath in the morning would suffice to freshen him up. (page 60)

4. Alexander II became enamored of Princess Catherine Dolgorouky and made her leave the Smolny Institute (a fashionable finishing school for patrician young ladies) at the age of sixteen, before she had completed her studies. She went to live with her eldest brother, Prince Michael Dolgorouky, to whom Alexander II presented a very beautiful house on the Quai des Anglais. The ground floor was occupied by Princess Catherine, who had her own domestics and carriages. (page 88)

5. The Amber Room is encrusted with exceptionally fine amber. Originally the room was arranged by the architect

Schlueter for the Prussian King Frederick I. Peter the Great admired the room on one of his journeys and Frederick agreed to exchange it for fifty Russian soldiers over 6'7" for a special guard troop. (page 150)

6. Prince Mikhail Kuzan fell in love with the young gypsy. The traditions of the tribe are strict. If a girl has a love affair, even if it be with a Prince, she must set up an establishment. The ceremony of marriage is not complicated. There is no need of priest or registrar. Any man who takes a Tzigane must obtain the consent of the chief of the tribe and declare that he intends to live with her maritally; further he must pay a ransom to the chorus, for he deprives it of an artist bringing in a good profit. Prince Mikhail, after a whirlwind courtship of five days, submitted to all the demands of the Tzigane regulations and paid the high ransom, for every rate is doubled for Princes, especially love ransoms. (page 168)

7. Cora Pearl, the daughter of a humble London music master, in spite of her coarse features and vulgar tongue, and due to her lovely body, rose to the rarefied heights of the highest paid courtesans in the Empire of Napoleon III. (Sums such as 5,000 francs, which was equivalent to 200 English pounds or about 1,000 American dollars, were not unheard of for twelve hours of her company.) Prince Gortchakoff described Cora Pearl as "the acme of sensual delights." A journalist of the day wrote of her "almost superhuman knowledge of the art of love" while M. Kracauer, in his biography of Offenbach, says, "she was able to keep in the front rank, because of her inordinate talent for voluptuous eccentricities." (page 183)

8. Sterlet was the famous luxury brought to Petersburg from the Volga, the Black and Caspian Sea. Even in winter they were transported alive and shown swimming to the guests as they passed through the hall at a dinner party; and when they are ready for the fish (the third course in Russia) they are cooked. In winter they cost from 10-15 dollars apiece (c. 1850), which makes a dinner an expensive affair, as every guest has a fish. (page 230)

9. This is not an original thought as you can see but I find this charming sentiment appealing for its universality, both encompassing and traversing the ages. The original quote from Harriette Wilson's Memoirs follows: (Harriette Wilson, by the way, was one of the high-class courtesans of early Regency England)—Lord Ebrington to H. Wilson c. 1810:

Nothing can be so gratifying and delightful to my feelings, as the idea of having inspired a fine woman with a strong irresistible desire to make me her lover, whenever the desire is not a general one. I remember having once made the acquaintance of a woman who was greatly to my taste, and who, as I almost fancied, was disposed to favour me in return. After much difficulty I obtained her consent to indulge me with a private meeting and she agreed to come into my chariot, in which I took her up at the end of a retired lane at the back of her father's house. She was a young widow. We were scarcely seated, when her very natural frank and flattering exclamation of "Oh how very happy I am, to find myself at last here alone with you," produced such a pleasant effect on me that I have never forgotten it. (page 243)

10. Although it was not difficult to obtain a divorce in Russia, witnesses were needed to attest on oath and in the presence of the priest that either husband or wife was unfaithful. This was very easy as far as gentlemen were concerned for all of them were unfaithful but it was different in regard to ladies.

An example of the Emperor's favors:

Prince Bariatinsky did not succeed in obtaining his divorce because his wife, Lydia, had been prudent enough to remain faithful. But for highly placed nobles, in moments of insuperable difficulty, there was always recourse to the Emperor.

On the cover of the file case presented to him, the Emperor, without examining or caring what the documents contained, wrote as a favor to the Prince, the words "Please accelerate."

Two days later a gentleman asked Lydia Bariatinsky

whether she had noticed her husband with his wife at the theater.

"What wife?" the Princess asked.

"The wife your ex-husband Prince Bariatinsky has married," he answered.

"How can that be since I won't give him a divorce?" The next morning Lydia Bariatinsky learned that her husband had obtained his divorce in 48 hours thanks to the Emperor's words: Please accelerate, and that the Prince was already married again. (page 275)

11. When Alexander II sent for his son Vladimir and informed him that a Princess of Mecklenburg-Schwerin had fallen in love with him and that he, the Emperor, wished his son to marry and settle down, the handsomest of Alexander II's sons is reported to have remarked, "Poor girl!" Upon which the Emperor indignantly inquired what he meant by that exclamation and received this reply, "What sort of a husband shall I make, Sire? I am drunk every night, and cure the headache of the next morning by getting drunk again." (page 285)

OTHER FICTION
FROM
PLAYBOY PRESS

MAIDEN CASTLE $1.50
SHEILA HOLLAND
Sabine's Cinderella marriage to Roger Amherst was the
talk of the town, for Roger was the wealthy owner of
Maiden Castle, and Sabine, a lowly lady's maid. But
none of the gossips knew that Sabine was already pregnant and that her handsome husband was not the
father. A Georgian romance.

LOVE'S BRIGHT FLAME $1.95
SHEILA HOLLAND
Eleanor of Aquitaine was the richest heiress in medieval Europe. A woman of charm, intellect and explosive passion, she married Louis, King of France, in a
political match that was to prove a personal disaster.
Desired by many, her power blazed a fiery path across
the Continent, leaving no man unmoved. But it was to
Henry, King of England, that she gave herself completely, and forever.

SWEET JAEL $1.50
SARAH FARRANT
A beautiful penniless orphan, Jael was hired as social
secretary and companion to the mistress of Pengrail
Park. Soon she fell desperately in love with Ralph, the
lord of the manor, and quickly resolved to have him at
any price. Step-by-devious-step she plotted and planned,
using all her charm, youth and "innocence" in a
scheme to diabolically murder Ralph's wife and son,
and thus to become the sole mistress of Pengrail Park.
A Victorian thriller.

THE DRAGON AND THE ROSE $1.95
ROBERTA GELLIS

Henry had been hunted, betrayed and attacked by his
political enemies since the day he was born. He had
conquered his fear of the constant danger surrounding
him, but could he conquer the woman he had agreed to
wed—the woman who represented all he had learned to
despise, the one who would profit most from his death?
Beautiful, passionate and clever, Elizabeth had been
born of royal blood and possessed the arrogance and
self-control of a queen. Forced by her mother to marry
a man she abhorred, she went to her marriage bed with
head held high and a heart filled with fear.

ROSELYNDE $1.95
ROBERTA GELLIS

In an era made for men, Alinor is at no man's mercy.
Beautiful, proud and strong-willed, she is mistress of
Roselynde and her own heart as well—until she meets
Simon, the battle-scarred knight appointed to be her
warden, a man whose passion and wit match her own.
Their struggle to be united against all obstacles sweeps
them from the pageantry of the Royal Court to a dar-
ing Crusade through exotic Byzantium and into the
Holy Land. The first book of the magnificent medieval
romantic saga, THE ROSELYNDE CHRONICLES.

ALINOR $2.25
ROBERTA GELLIS

A woman alone . . . trapped in a deadly maze of
treacherous power plays and volatile liaisons, Alinor
Lemagne is irresistibly swept into an intoxicating,
breathless passion for the darkly sensual man whose
forbidden love promises only pain and peril. Swirling
from the bloody battlegrounds of France and England
to the rich pageantry of the king's court, her passionate
adventures weave a breathtaking tale of danger and
desire—and a beautiful woman's desperate quest for
love.

LOVE'S GENTLE FUGITIVE $1.95
ANDREA LAYTON

A runaway to the New World, ravishingly beautiful
Elizabeth Bartlett tries to escape her secret past—only
to learn that shame and degradation are the price for
her freedom. Frightened and vulnerable, she is rescued
from brutal slavery by the one man who could return
her to England and disaster. On a brave journey
through the wilderness, she succumbs to irresistible
temptation and falls deeply in love with the handsome,
bold protector who has aroused her most turbulent yet
tender emotions. As their surging desires find release in
rapturous ecstasy, Elizabeth surrenders her heart—and
her destiny—to the passionate stranger who could
choose to love her . . . or betray her.

THE SCANDALOUS LADY $1.50
MAGGIE GLADSTONE

As one of the dazzling Lacebridge belles, Sara was
expected to marry a man of wealth and position. Instead she scandalized all polite society by running away
to pursue her dream of stardom on the London stage.
There she set out to prove her worth, never dreaming
that she would capture the heart of Covent Garden's
most handsome and sought-after leading man. The first
in a series of four delightful regency romances.

THE SWORD AND THE SWAN $1.95
ROBERTA GELLIS

Rannulf was known throughout the land as a bold
warrior. Face-to-face with an oncoming army, he could
decide matters of life and death. But now, face-to-face
with one gentle woman, he was hopelessly confused
and uncertain. Startled by Catherine's pale beauty when
he first saw her, he was dumbfounded by her passionate
radiance now, and he felt a desire far different from his
usual impersonal need for a woman.

WILD IS THE HEART $1.95
DIANA SUMMERS

Born into wealth and privilege, Aurelia was sheltered from the gathering storm of revolution. But with the fall of the Bastille, her golden world was shattered forever. Swept into the dark currents of political intrigue, she must use her dazzling beauty to survive as she becomes wife, mistress and courtesan to the most powerful men in France.

MOMENT OF DESIRE $1.95
RACHEL COSGROVE PAYES

In London's seamy underside, where the teeming masses knew only of deprivation and hunger, Mellie's survival depended on her expertise at an exclusive brothel. In all those nights of love, not one man kindled a fire in her except one: a mysterious nobleman whose mission was shrouded in secrecy. Their one night of passion ignited a raging fire of forbidden love, hate and revenge.

DANCE OF DESIRE $1.95
BARBARA BONHAM

In a country seething with the terror of the Inquisition, young Micaela rose from poverty to become one of the most famous flamenco dancers Spain has ever known. Devastatingly beautiful, she was sought after by men of power, wealth and position. But her heart belonged to the one man she could not have—the dashing Javier, escort to the powerful Duchess de Vallabriga.

PASSION'S PRICE $1.95
BARBARA BONHAM

In a heartrending story set against the harshness and isolation of the vast prairies of 19th Century America, a lovely young widow and a lusty family man struggle in vain against a forbidden but powerful attraction for each other.